The Hounds of Ardagh

The Hounds of Ardagh

Laura J. Underwood

Five Star • Waterville, Maine

First Edition
First Printing: September 2006

Published in 2006 in conjunction with Tekno Books and Ed Gorman.

Set in 11 pt. Plantin by Carleen Stearns.

Printed in the United States on permanent paper.

Library of Congress Cataloging-in-Publication Data

Underwood, Laura J.
    The hounds of Ardagh / by Laura J. Underwood.—1st ed.
        p. cm.
    ISBN 1-59414-376-5 (hc : alk. paper)
    I. Title.
PS3621.N385H68 2006
    813'.6—dc22   2006016572

Heather Ale Jig
By Laura J. Underwood

(As sung on some nights by Manus MacGreeley when his
spirit is out and about and he has nothing better to do than
torment poor Ginny.)

Once I was flesh
And once I was bone,
But now I am spirit
And oh, so alone.

I wander the moors
When the moon's bright and big,
And sing to the tune of
The Heather Ale Jig.

Come join me in dance.
Come feast on the ale.
Come wander the moors
And I'll tell you my tale.

'Twas under a full moon
I met my cruel fate
On the blade of a rogue
Whose friends numbered eight.

Though mageborn I was,
My power was pale
For my senses were soft
With the sweet heather ale.

One blade took my heart

And two in the back,
And though I had courage,
'Twas power I lacked.

My plaidie was crimson.
My blood stained the moors.
My vision was fading.
The rogues left me poor.

I died on the moors
With the moon bright and big,
And cursed to the tune of
The Heather Ale Jig.

So come ye fair lads
And remember my tale
Ne'er give your fool heart
To the sweet heather ale,

Or ye'll wander the moors
When the moon's bright and big
And die to the tune of
The Heather Ale Jig.

Chapter One

The throaty growls of the moor terrier alerted Ginny Ni Cooley to the mischief on the moors that night. Admittedly, mageborn hearing was much sharper than that of normal folk, but Ginny had come to accept that little Thistle still had a greater advantage.

"Wheesht," she said, and she set aside her mending to cross the room and stand by the door of the small cottage she called home. With her eyes closed, she stretched her mage senses to test the magical currents that ebbed and flowed through Tamhasg Wood. Here and there she touched the vague essence of some little bogie or another. The frid that hid under the lea stone, hoping for a passing morsel spared by superstitious travelers. The shy wood wight who dwelled within the bottom oak near the stream. The mischievous hob that had made off with a half-dozen of Ginny's eggs just last week. Minor creatures, in her opinion, and all needing little more than iron nails and warding spells—and the occasional tongue-lashing—to keep them civil and in the woods where they belonged.

Tonight, however, things felt different. Though the frid and the wood wight rarely traveled about, the hob wandered quite a lot. Only now the little thief had gone to ground in an old badger's den, and Ginny sensed that he trembled in fear. What could be wrong? Did it have anything to do with the faint cry of power wavering just out of the reach of her mage senses?

"Manus?" she said. Surely not, for it wasn't like the

spirit of her old mentor to stay so far off even in mischief. Granted, he was probably out on the moonlit moors looking for his murderers, for it was there he had lost his life to a bandit's blade. Mageborn flesh was as mortal as any, and Manus was no more able to cast spells than a tree when he had drowned his sorrow in heather ale, a habit that had cost him his life. That did not stop him from being a bane to her existence.

Ginny pushed aside the thoughts with a shake of her head. Whatever was out there this night was on the move and coming her way.

She sighed and drew back her senses. Thinking about Manus sometimes threw her concentration out of sort. Granted, she owed him much, for he'd given her home and hearth when she fled her own as a lass, and had taught her about the burgeoning power she carried, never so much as asking for anything in return. Yet there were times he would vex her sore to the point that she wanted to scream. More so these days, for Manus' spirit came and went as he pleased, and he had little else to occupy his time other than haunt his old cottage and the vast moor around Tamhasg Wood.

Thistle growled again, and this time he approached the door as though the threat were right outside. Ginny shook her head and threw the bolt. She felt nothing immediate enough to warrant staying inside for the moment. Quietly, she opened the door and stepped out into the yard. She heard the faint chuckle of stoats on the hunt and the lone whimper of an owl somewhere out in Tamhasg Wood. The Blood Moon was three nights past full, lighting the path and giving her an ample view of bony branches of trees and the moors beyond. A faint mist rose from the warm ground, sending tendrils dancing about the cool night air. A bogie night to be certain, though she could not sense any about, and that aroused her curiosity all the more.

"Manus?" she called again, and wondered if he could hear such a quiet call.

"Oh, I could hear it if you whispered, lass," his voice boomed around her.

"Horns!" she hissed, nearly jumping out of her skin as she whipped about in search of his presence. "Why must you always do that?"

Mist rose into the shape of a man who wore his plaid kilted in the old style, bereft of trews. Tumbles of auburn hair and merry blue eyes became visible as the spirit of Manus MacGreeley manifested before her.

"Because you always squeak in such a feisty fashion, lass," he replied, wagging his eyebrows in the comical manner that always irritated her. "What's got you outside so late?"

Thistle darted about them, marking his territory in true moor terrier fashion. Normally, he was gleeful to see his old master, but the small terrier seemed more attracted to something off in the wood. The hackles of his shaggy brindle coat were spiked high as he continued his throaty growl.

"Wheesht, Thistle," Manus said sharply. "What's got him so . . ."

Ginny waved her hand to silence him. A new sound joined the normal chorus of the night. Hounds. A whole pack of them, from the noise, and they were on the trail of something.

"Odd time to be hunting," Manus said curtly as he frowned. "I'll go see what the curs are about."

"Please do," she said and watched him become part of the mist once more, whisking away towards the source of the commotion. The ruckus grew louder, and by instinct, she decided that it might be time to put Thistle inside and herself for good measure, when she heard the cry of a human voice raised in terror.

"Horns!" she said. "Manus, what's happening?"

His spirit surged into view. "There's a lad heading this way with an *unseelie* pack of hounds on his heels. I don't like the look of it, Ginny."

"Why?"

"You'll see."

Within moments, a boy of no more than eleven came charging into the clearing. His clothes and cloak were tattered and torn, and streaks of tears tracked through the mud, dirt and scratches that covered his face. He came straight at her, crying for help, when she saw the reason for his distress. A black beast in the shape of a Keltoran staghound thundered out of Tamhasg Wood on the lad's heels. Its eyes blazed like fire as it led a pack of red-gold hounds in its wake. And Ginny needed no more than a glance to know the staghound was not what it seemed. She raised her hand as the lad stumbled and fell onto the path that led to her cottage. The black beast leapt for the lad when Ginny called, *"Gath siaghead buail!"* and sent a magebolt flying across the short distance.

The black hound yelped when the bolt struck its chest, and Ginny smelled the acrid scent of singed hair and sulfur. That moment was all the lad needed to gain his footing once more and charge towards Ginny.

"Inside!" she shouted as he passed, and he apparently needed little encouragement to obey. Ginny cast him a furtive glance before concentrating on the task at hand. She reached out with mage senses and jerked elemental essence from the fire in the cottage hearth to feed her spell, then stretched her hands towards the oncoming black monster. At that moment little Thistle chose to assert his territorial rights and charged the staghound with a savage snarl. Ginny had no choice but to hold back her spell.

"Thistle! Wheesht!" Manus cried, for all the good it served. The moor terrier was not about to let any canine, mortal or otherworldly, enter his realm uninvited, and typical of his tenacious breed, it did not matter that his opponent was nearly twenty times his size. Ginny had seen him go after large stray dogs that wandered into the Tamhasg Wood from neighboring holdings, and was always amazed to watch them flee when Thistle expressed his displeasure for their company.

The staghound roared and snapped huge jaws at the moor terrier, and only by the grace of speed and agility did Thistle avoid a bite that would have taken off his head. He charged on under the beast and latched onto a hind leg. The black beast howled and turned in a circle, trying to rid itself of the small creature firmly attached to its hamstring. Thistle clung to his quarry, no longer able to touch the ground. The rest of the pack closed in, eager to tear the flying terrier from the staghound's leg. Clearly, courageous or not, Thistle would have no chance against such odds.

"Ginny, do something!" Manus called.

"I am!" she retorted, and concentrated on gathering the essence to feed her spell again. No white fire could be cast now without doing Thistle harm as well, but there was something else she knew this dark creature with its coal bright eyes would find just as unsavory. *"Solus geal!"* she cried.

A huge ball of white light exploded in the midst of the pack. Not knowing what they faced, the red-gold hounds scattered with frightened yelps and fled for the moors beyond the forest. The black beast gave a howl that was not canine in any form. It whipped about fiercely enough to dislodge Thistle and sent the moor terrier flying across the path towards Ginny. He landed at her feet with a yelp. She wasted no time seizing Thistle up, and though he struggled and raged at his unseelie adversary, she popped him into the cottage, closed the door in his wake, then turned once more to face the black staghound.

The creature had lost some of its hound-like shape, reverting to a more demonic form as it was burned by the white mage light. Unearthly howls filled the air as it fought to escape the light's power.

"Curse you, mageborn!" the black demon snarled in a voice that sounded like many and sent shivers down her spine. *"I will return, woman! You will not keep me from him!"*

Throwing Ginny one last hard glower, the creature fled into the shadows of Tamhasg Wood. She sent the light rolling after it for a distance until her control waned. The darkness fell, and quiet filled the night, save for the astonished whistle of the spirit mage at her side and the faint whimpers and growls escalating within her own cottage. Apparently, Thistle had found something else to disturb him.

"What now?" Ginny snarled, displeased with the whole matter of having her night disrupted in this manner. She should have known better. Any time Manus was about, trouble was likely to invade her peaceful life and make her privately curse the day she had found his holding. She pushed open the cottage door and stormed inside, only to pause.

Thistle stood over at the hearth, crouched low and snarling in a territorial manner. The lad sat in Ginny's chair, hunkered sideways as he stared wide-eyed at the ferocious little dog.

"Horns," Manus murmured from the doorway as Ginny stopped and stared. "Will ye look at that!"

For what had their attention was the thick pelt of red-gold fur that ran down the lad's bare back, and the long whip of a hound's tail tucked fearfully between his legs.

Chapter Two

The lad was in shock, and Ginny realized this a moment or two of after shedding her own surprise at the sight of him. She closed and bolted the cottage door, then confined Thistle to the far end of the room with a barrier of hardened air. Alas, the spell did little to prevent the moor terrier from vocalizing his belief that another canine had entered his territory, though under the circumstances, Ginny understood how he could be so mistaken.

Still, she could not let such matters deter her. Even with Thistle at a safe distance, the lad cowered, wild-eyed as a frightened hare. Cautiously, she approached him, trying to assess what manner of care he needed.

"Here now," she said softly. "No one's going to harm you, lad. Let's have a look at you."

"Careful, Ginny," Manus said. "He might bite."

She threw the mageborn specter a sharp look of reproach before she drew a stool from the hearth and sank onto it. The lad continued to cower, and now she could see he was panting rapidly in the manner of a dog. With determination, she reached out and touched the ragged tatters of shaggy red-gold hair where it fell into the lad's face. He stiffened at first, then blinked and relaxed, as though seeing her for the first time. His lower lip trembled.

"There now," she said, knowing full well she had never been one for practicing maternal tenderness. Her own siblings had declared she was as hard as stone just because she was more interested in her uncle's old books than their silly games and problems. They never seemed to understand that she had problems of her own, especially when the mage sign manifested and forced her to flee her father's desire to marry her off to a man thrice her age, no matter what the laws of Keltora said about mageborn rights. *And all for naught but more fat Highland cattle to increase his herds.* But where did she run? Straight to the door of a strange man who lived alone on the edge of Tamhasg Wood and was thrice her own father's age. Not that one could tell this at a glance. One legacy of mageborn blood was that it kept a mage looking young.

Still, some inner sense told her to go there, and Manus was only a little startled by her sudden arrival in the midst of a storm. He agreed to take her in, and she had only intended to stay for the night. Fate seemed to have other plans. When Manus discovered her essence bore the taint of a mageborn, he convinced her to stay and learn about her ancient power. At first, she assumed he had less honorable intentions in mind, for she was nearly eighteen and still a maid, but he never made any such demands of her. Only that she learn to use the magic essence in her flesh and blood.

Ginny shook her head. *I suppose a smile would not hurt just now,* she thought, and she faintly stretched one for the lad's benefit. "What's your name, lad?"

Luminous eyes of green met her gaze. "Fafne," he whispered. "Fafne MacArdagh . . ."

It was Ginny's turn to blink in surprise. "Of Dun Ardagh?" she asked, and he nodded. Briefly she glanced at Manus, who rubbed his chin in thought.

"Dun Ardagh's near ten leagues from here!" Manus said. "Three days across the moors as the crow flies. How could ye have run all that way, lad?"

15

Fafne's gaze rose and widened at the sight of Manus' translucent visage. "Cernnunos, protect me!" the lad cried and started to scramble. " 'Tis a spirit!"

Ginny quickly seized the lad's shoulders. They felt bony and oddly shaped under her hands, as though some unnatural transformation had slightly deformed them. They were strung over with the sinewy muscles of a youth who quickly proved too exhausted to fight her.

"You needn't worry about Manus, lad," she insisted. "He's naught but air these days."

Fafne's struggles ceased. "You're not afraid of him?"

She shook her head. "He's perfectly harmless. A nuisance, but harmless otherwise."

"Thank you for that vote of confidence," Manus muttered.

"But . . ." Fafne began.

"Don't fret yourself," Ginny insisted, rising to head for the corner where her own wooden tub was stored. "Now, you look a frightful sight, so why don't we get you cleaned up and into some warm, dry things and feed you, and then we can worry about what brought you to my doorstep."

"But I want to know now," Manus said with a pout.

"I would think the dead would have more patience than that," she said as she flitted by, passing through his shoulder with her own. It had taken her time to get used to doing so without a shudder. Still, Manus jumped aside with a little gasp.

"I wish you wouldn't do that," he said. "It gives me a chill."

Ginny rolled her eyes and pulled the tub towards the hearth. She was tempted to drag it through Manus, but there was water to haul and heat, and old clothes to find to replace those rags, and she wondered how she was going to work them around that tail.

She set about swiftly with her preparations. While raising water from the well, she cast about with mage senses, but felt nothing of the strange hounds and their demonic mistress. Thistle gave up his assault on the invisible barrier, and settled into a terrier sulk, gnawing the corner of the table leg, and no amount of fussing from Manus would make him stop.

Ginny ignored them, concentrating on getting Fafne out of his rags and into the tub once the water was warm. The lad proved as reluctant as a hound at first, but gave in to her wishes when she promised food and drink after. What surprised her was to note that Fafne seemed less concerned with propriety than with getting wet, which sparked the memory of something she read long ago in one of Manus' books. Something about how prolonged transformations from human to animal form could result in certain behavioral changes. And those thoughts were closer to confirmation when Fafne shook himself like a dog as he rose from the tub at the end of his scrubbing. Ginny held her tongue about the mess and threw a drying blanket over the lad, getting him over before the fire. There in the light, she used what little knowledge she had of wounds and their care, treating his bruises and cuts with witch hazel and comfrey. *Strange,* she thought as he sat steaming before the fire. Fafne smelled a bit more like a wet dog now.

Fixing him some herb tea to calm him, she brought forth a platter of goat's cheese and bread. He practically dove on them in his hunger, and she was forced to take the platter away to keep him from eating it all, noting the wary eye with which he fixed her.

Once fed, though, he started to look sleepy too, and Ginny realized he was too exhausted to give her much useful information. *This can wait until morning,* she decided, and getting Fafne into one of Manus' old shirts, she settled the lad in the old loft pallet. He curled into a puppy-like coil and fell asleep immediately, and she took the light, leaving him there.

"I thought you were going to ask him what brought him here," Manus snarled as she came out of the loft.

"He's too tired to give a straight answer," Ginny said. "We'll ask him tomorrow."

"That demon creature might come back tonight," Manus said. " 'Twas no ordinary beast, you ken."

"Yes," Ginny said and poked around the cottage for a few of the older volumes Manus had collected, finding one with bands of brass and dark brown leather covers. "Even I recognized the Nidubh."

"Daughter of Darkness," Manus muttered and seated himself on the stool by the fire. The bright flames made his essence grow dim. "Hound of Arawn. Mother of the Wild Kin."

Ginny flicked a hand towards Thistle and muttered, *"Rach air falbh balla,"* but the moor terrier showed no inclination to accept the gift of his freedom just then. Thistle cast her a surly, sidelong glance from under shags of coarse hair before renewing his assault on the table leg. She set the book on the table and carefully drew open the brittle pages scented with herbs and must. Intricate drawings greeted her, and she passed over them until she found the one she sought, a sketch of a giant black hound with snarling fangs and eyes of fire, carefully inked in red so that they seemed to glow on the very page.

"Mother of the Wild Kin," she repeated. "I heard the Wild Kin once, you know, when I was very young. My mother said they crossed the moors under the black moon, and that you could hear their cry on the wind, so I used to sneak out of bed and open my window facing west . . ."

Manus looked at the fire and muttered,

Shut the window North and South,
And close it to the West.
Good comes only from the East,
And Evil from the rest.

Ginny smiled. "My father used to recite that," she said.

" 'Tis older than the Great Cataclysm," Manus said. "Just like the Mother of the Wild Kin. What happened when you saw them?"

"It was dark, and there was no moon on the fields. In the shadows, I only thought I saw faint forms undulating across the heather, but what I heard was a song that was filled with death and promise. It mesmerized me, and I started to climb out of the window and follow that promise."

"And?"

"My older sister awoke and bitterly complained that I was letting all the heat out of the room, and practically dragged me back to bed. She couldn't hear their song, and sometimes I wish I hadn't, for every night thereafter until mage sign manifested fully in me, I heard it calling me in my dreams."

"I don't like the scent of any of this, Ginny. Once that creature sets its sight on a man, he can only dig his grave. Whatever that lad's done to warrant such evil is beyond reason."

She nodded, studying the sketch again. It was little more than an example, and very little text, other than a few notations about using white fire to burn the creature. "It does seem strange, especially with all those other hounds on the creature's heels. I thought only the Wild Kin hunted in pack, and that the Nidubh ran alone."

"So did I," Manus said, and rose from the stool. "I think I'll go out looking about for a bit. You keep the place barred and warded, lass."

"As if I did not," she said stiffly. "Are you thinking of going north to Dun Ardagh?"

"Would I do that?" he asked.

"In a heartbeat," she said and smiled, crossing her arms over her chest. His answering grin was just as cocky. "Just be careful and let me know what you find."

"Now, since when does a spirit have to worry about danger?" he retorted.

"You're dead, Manus, but your essence is not immortal. Or have you already forgotten your encounter with that Black Hunter last year?"

"Thank you for the reminder," Manus said and his form became as the mist, slipping into the chimney and rising with the smoke. "I'll keep my nose clean . . ." His voice echoed around her, then faded to a whisper and was gone.

Ginny shook her head and set about strengthening the wards that kept the cottage safe from the denizens of Tamhasg Wood, and hoped they would do as well to keep the Mother of the Wild Kin at bay.

Chapter Three

The quiet that filled the cottage after Manus' departure was a welcome sound to Ginny. She settled herself before the fire and concentrated on the wards, testing each one with mage senses. They felt strong and pure, and that pleased her. One would never have thought a mageborn who learned the art as late in life as Ginny had would have possessed such fine control. She supposed she should be grateful to Manus for that, though it seemed to her that once he departed and she was on her own, her ability to learn increased tenfold in the silence.

There was a time, she recalled as she took the kettle and started a cup of soothing tea, when Manus' sudden departure some nights filled her with anxiety. She had never understood why in those days. Having fled her father's house at eighteen, and sworn no man would ever move her heart, she often found it disquieting to think she missed Manus on those nights when he went wandering the moors alone. He would never tell her where or why, but she knew he returned late, for she slept in the loft and heard his rattling and stumbling about as he worked the magelock he'd set to respond only to her touch and his own, and fumbled about in the lower chamber. Most mornings, she would come down and find him sprawled unceremoniously on the cot, an aleskin limp and reeking on the floor. That he drank too much bothered her only at those moments, for sober, he could be quite a charming and intelligent man.

Yet he never took advantage of her. Never pressed any

sort of affection. At first, she thought he might be a man who preferred the company of his own gender. Indeed, it was not until after his death that she even learned he'd had a wife, and that all his wandering and drinking were because that woman had died and left him alone.

That addiction had been his undoing and nearly hers as well, for it had been Ginny's misfortune to go seeking him when he did not return at his usual hour, and to find him dead among the heather, his plaidie soaked in his blood from the knife wound in his heart. Manus had no kin of whom Ginny was aware. With no one to turn to, she had buried him there on the moor under a cairn of stones and quietly mourned his untimely passing.

But that was not to be the end of it, she quickly learned. A mageborn's essence had the power to hold itself to this world, and in his inebriated state, Manus had not been so willing to accept that he was actually dead at first. Only when he tried his hand at spell casting and failed was he forced to resign himself to his fate. Mageborn needed flesh to cast magic, for the power they possessed was as much a part of that flesh as the essence it held. If they could find a willing body to share their spirit, they could cast spells again, but only if that other was also mageborn. So poor Manus was limited to being able to shift and change his shape from normal to hideous or solid to mist on a whim, an ability with which he seemed to delight in causing all manner of grief. In spite of the fact that he could have left for Tir-Nan-Og whenever he liked, he was not so eager to pass on to the Summerlands as mortal souls were wont to do. Instead, he chose to stay on the moors and enact what vengeance he could on his murderers, should he be so fortunate as to catch them.

Ginny recalled the first night he came back to her after

he died. She was tending the fire when Thistle began to whine as he always did when Manus returned, and at first she assumed the little moor terrier was grieving for his master. However, he kept insisting on going out and, when Ginny opened the door to let him run, she found Manus—or rather a pale configuration of his likeness—standing before her, looking more than a little confused.

"Ginny," he said. "I canna open the door or feel my hands . . ."

She had often felt proud of the fact that she did not faint, as she knew a number of her fair gender who would have under such stressful circumstances. But she was mageborn herself, and made of sterner stuff. The idea that he would come back to torment her in that fashion only fed her natural ire. She had planted her hands on her hips and fixed him with a stern glower and said, "That's because you're dead, Manus MacGreeley."

"I canna be dead," he muttered. "I mean, how can I be? I don't feel dead!"

"That's because you were probably too drunk to feel anything when you died!"

Ginny had not known then whether to feel hurt or relieved. Anger came often enough over the matter before he passed away. Sometimes, she thought she had wasted her life coming here to live with a man whose love of his precious heather ale outweighed his common sense. She reminded herself that she could have ended up worse off than she was, and Manus was teaching her the magic she had been denied in her father's house. Mageborn were solitary by nature. Mortalborn had little enough trust for magical things. Granted, Keltorans were more tolerant because they felt closer to magical things than the rest of Ard-Taebh, and folk in the latter kingdoms of that great realm tended to look on Keltorans with a jaundiced eye. Keltora even had laws decreed by their king to protect those born of a magical legacy. A woman who was mageborn could not be forced into marriage—at least that was what the law stated.

Ginny was twelve when mage sign manifested in her. A ripe and proper age, according to Manus. But where other folk in Keltora would send their mageborn children either to the Council of Mageborn's fortress of Dun Gealach in Caer Keltora or to a local mage for proper training, Ginny had remained at home. Her father was one Fergus MacCooley, chief herdsmaster to the Laird of Wildfen, and responsible for maintaining the cattle of Wildfen's young Laird, Robin MacFarley, amidst his own. Always eager to be thought a man of means, Fergus forbid any mention of his middle daughter's "affliction," as he intended to find her a suitable husband instead. Ginny was denied the much-needed training her blood legacy craved, all to satisfy her father's greed.

As a result, she knew little of that heritage before Manus came into her life. By then, she had possessed the untrained power for six years, and knew nothing of disciplines or strictures. It was not uncommon before that meeting for fires in the MacCooley household to flare at Ginny's approach, or for objects to leap from tables and shelves when she was filled with anger. Still, her father was a man with an iron hand, and always quelled the whispers that his middle child was cursed.

Naturally, these strange occurrences did not go unnoticed by the suitors her father pressed upon Ginny, once her elder sister Katharine was wed to a high-ranking officer in the Laird's personal guard. Ginny had no control over the magic that manifested around her, but she did notice that events became worse when she fell into unbridled fits

24

of temper. And usually that temper flared when the suitors presented their causes, telling her that she was a most natural beauty and declaring their undying love for her.

This love, she was quick to note, generally headed for the nearest door in haste when crockery started to fly, for Ginny was not above telling these suitors what she thought of their declarations of affection and poetic descriptions of her person. She knew that the beauty she saw looking back at her from her elder sisters' mirrors, though not unpleasant, was best described as sparrow drab. Where her sisters had fair hair, Ginny's was a dark auburn, and while they fluttered golden lashes over blue eyes like their father's, Ginny's eyes were hazel flecked with gold. *Eldritch as a wood nymph,* she had heard others whisper. *As fey and earthy as a Seelie queen.* Hardly a face filled with the radiance the suitors extolled, and so it was that she vowed their flattery would never move her to accept a single one of their offers.

But there came a day when the herdsmaster of a neighboring croft declared that he wanted a new wife to replace the one the gods had gathered away. He offered ten head of his own fine, fat, shaggy Keltoran Highland cattle in trade for MacCooley's second daughter. Ginny had hoped that she would reach adulthood and gain the right to leave as she pleased, but the arrival of Ben MacWaddle's proposal sent that hope fluttering away. Father accepted the offer without even asking for her consent. That night, she caused the hearth fire to lap the mantel, and sent cups and saucers scattering about the chamber. MacWaddle startled her by taking it all in stride. He declared that he had already worn down six temperamental wives, and he looked forward to taming the seventh.

But Ginny was not about to allow herself to be put to

such a task. Had Ginny's mother been alive, she no doubt would have been party to her middle child's reckless decision. That night, after Fergus declared the matter of wedlock to kith and kin, Ginny took what little she dared to call her own—two books left her by her late mother and the clothes on her back—and fled. She crossed many leagues over the course of a sen'night, fearing to stop for she felt certain her father would likely set the dogs on her to bring her back.

She had no earthly idea what drew her to Tamhasg Wood, but the call was akin to some inner song that rang in her blood from time to time. The Wood itself revealed all manner of strange and wondrous things to her mageborn eyes. The hob, the frid and the wood wight among others. Wisps of beings she had only heard about in the tales her mother's folk would share at ceileidhs.

Then a storm rose fierce, whipping rain and wind to saturate her clothes, and Ginny sought shelter amid the bony trees of the ghostly forest. But they provided little protection, and so she pushed on until she saw a glimmer of light off beyond the trees. The ramshackle cottage of stone and wood with a thatched roof overhead exuded a hint of the song in her soul. She pounded on its door, begging mercy and shelter, and praying for a good farm wife to let her in.

Instead, the wood parted to reveal a tall, handsome man with his plaidie and fiery hair somewhat askew. Behind him a dog barked noisily, a small moor terrier with the ferocity of a grey highland wolf. The man fixed her with a squinty stare, and she could not help noticing the odor of heather ale lacing his breath when he muttered, "Well, Thistle, look what the wind has blown in. A drab, wet little bogie hen."

Those unkind words spoken in such a light and rude

manner almost convinced Ginny to turn on her heel and head elsewhere.

"I guess that wasn't terribly funny," he said in a less teasing tone. "Come on in by the fire, lass, before you catch yer death. But first, might I know your name?"

"Ginny Ni Cooley," she said, pushing drenched hair from her eyes and shivering from the cold rivulets of rain managing to slither inside her clothes.

"Then enter my house and be welcome, Ginny Ni Cooley," he said, and stepped back to give her the door.

She practically fell into a realm of cluttered warmth that revealed a serious lack of a woman's hand. He bundled Ginny over by the fire, stating his name, then ordered her out of her wet things while producing dry clothes from a chest which he had to clear off before it would even open. When she refused to undress in his company, he laughed and assured her that her virtue was safe. Still, he obliged her indignity by going up into the loft until she announced that she was done. The dress he gave her was only slightly larger than her own, and in her outrage, it never occurred to her to ask how he came by such a garment.

He then offered her a portion of stew and hot tea, and asked where she was from and what brought her so far. In spite of her distrust of his gender and person, she found herself spilling her tale. At the end he told her to hold out her hand and to speak a word that rolled more comfortably off her tongue than she would have thought possible.

"*Solus,*" she had said.

A faint hint of blue-green light swelled about her hand, dancing across the palm. The bright sparkling tickled her skin and touched something deep inside her. With a gasp, she shook the little lights away, then looked up to see an indulgent grin. Manus whispered, "*Solus,*" and a golden ball

27

of light swelled in his own palm. He offered it to her like a precious flower. Hesitant, she took it in hand, where it tickled as before, but this time she held it and did not let it die. In fact, it grew brighter in her grasp.

"I do believe there's still hope for ye, lass," he said, and offered then to teach her what she longed to know about the magic in her soul . . .

Something brushed one of Ginny's wards, jerking her out of her rambling thoughts. A hint of ancient power pressed the mark she had laid on a cornerstone out in the yard, then withdrew and moved counterclockwise to try another. Ginny sat as still as the stones that bore her protective spells as each ward was assaulted in turn until the creature returned to the first.

Once more, the creature lunged at her magical barrier of protection. She flinched as she felt white fire lash out to burn the beast that so wanted inside now. Its dreadful howl of pain broke, filling the air, and was answered by a chorus that seemed to span the moors around her for leagues. Thistle sprang upright from his repose by the hearth and added his high-pitched voice to the baleful choir. And up above, on the pallet in the loft, she heard a frightened cry.

Ginny bolted from her chair and scrambled into the loft to find Fafne battling blankets and scrambling towards the eaves. She caught him before he could wedge himself into one of the narrow spaces. At first, he fought her grasp, but she refused to relinquish her hold. She reached out with mage senses and jerked power from every source of essence within the cottage and cried, *"Ladh sinn samhchair,"* building a wall with her will. Silence fell over them like a blanket, cutting off the hideous noises. Even Thistle's bay could not be heard from below. Only Fafne's hoarse whimpers and her own quick breath.

"She's coming back," he muttered. "She's coming back. Cernunnos, save us, she's coming back . . ."

"Who's coming back?" Ginny asked.

"The woman with the moon on her hair," he murmured. "The woman with glacier eyes. She told us they would never know what became of us . . . she . . . told . . . us . . ."

The whimpers faded as exhaustion once more swept the lad into slumber. Ginny was half tempted to shake the lad back into awareness, but he needed his sleep. She gently drew the blankets around and over him, and left him coiled in his fetal knot, wrapped in the silencing spell, and went back down to the room below.

Thistle greeted her at the foot of the ladder, wagging his tail and panting proudly, as though he had done his part to rid the world of evil.

Ginny merely sighed. Of the cries, she heard nothing, but the sense that the creature had not wholly given up still ached at the pit of her stomach.

She might not get much sleep this night.

And she hoped Manus would be all right.

Chapter Four

Torches whipped in the wind as the Blood Moon's baleful light flooded the stonework of Dun Ardagh. Manus had not seen this mighty rath with its block-square keep since a year or so before his own death. Too many bad memories were housed inside these thick walls for him. His beloved wife Mary had been born in this hold.

Daughter of a guardsman and a kitchen wench, Mary had served in this place until the day Manus came to call and set his eyes on her from across the hall. On that day, he was smitten by the sight of her raven black tresses and clear blue eyes, and thought the gods had blessed him when she agreed to be his wife. He had warned her, of course, what it meant to wed a mage, but apparently she was just as smitten by him. The life they had shared as man and wife was like a dream until eighteen years ago, when she had walked into the Summerland to receive the reward of a long mortal existence. She had left Manus to bury her frail remains in a cairn on the moors, and to mourn her loss and his solitude. There were times he regretted that they'd had no children, but what was the use of siring sons and grandsons he was destined to outlive? The heather ale became his solace instead. A poor companion, as Ginny would say, and perhaps the lass was right. Look at what the ale had done for him.

Manus solidified his form just outside the walls. It would be better that he did not appear so suddenly before prying eyes. Folks in Keltora were a suspicious lot. A spirit in old days was believed to herald doom or misdeed in some households. Nor did it matter that the spirit was not one of their own bloodkin. Of course, mortalborn could not choose to stay and haunt a place as Manus did, unless they died in some tragic manner or possessed a strong will for revenge. Mageborn spirits were tied to the mortal world by the magic that coursed their blood and existed in everything around them, and they could stay in this realm as they pleased, so long as their spirit had not been sundered. Manus counted himself fortunate in that respect. He had died a fairly ordinary if not untimely death, stabbed through the heart by men who wanted nothing more than his coin.

He stood on the road and studied the walls with a serious frown. Where were the gate guards? The oaken outer doors of the gatehouse hung open, and silence drifted out of them like a fog. *Curious,* Manus thought and made for the gap, cautiously entering the shadows. Too bad he couldn't touch or smell anything in this afterlife. Just see and hear. No casting spells either, and that sometimes infuriated him. Then again, in this existence, walls and doors were no problem whatsoever, unless magic had been used to ward them against spirits and bogies alike.

The gatehouse tunnel disgorged him into a large courtyard with buildings pressed into every available cranny around the massive structure of the keep. He spied the smithy and the stables, and the central well, but little more. Other than the outbuildings, the yard was empty. No hens, cattle or goats. Not even a crow or an owl disturbed the tomb-like peace that reigned among a clutter of baskets, boxes, scattered clothes and weapons.

Where is everyone? No guards walking along the walls. No servants scuttling about doing the evening chores. To the best of Manus' recollection, this keep always teemed with life day and night. The MacArdaghs were a well-known clan, favored by King Brendan MacMorroch. If Manus remembered well enough, Fafne was but the youngest of three lads with a fair number of sisters besides. There should have been near seventy folk living and working in this hillfort: family, servants and all.

So where were they?

And how was it the torches were still lit?

He approached the nearest torch, stretching out his hand. Though he could not touch it, he could still sense mage matters and as he slipped ethereal fingers into the flame, they dissolved, but not before he found the magic at work within the blaze. *Bloodmagic*, he thought as he shook his hand and manifested the missing fingers once more.

A sense of unnamed dread filtered into his essence. Manus made for the main doors, gliding through closed wood like a mist. Inside, he found an emptiness devoid of life. The stables had long ago been moved to the outer yard, and this vast space now held stores for times of harsh winter and long siege, and cots for the small contingency of guards under MacArdagh's command. But silence and chaos filled that space now. Bedclothes thrown off in haste. Armor, weapons and clothing scattered about with the reeds on the floor.

Manus strode purposefully towards the stairs, climbing them to the hall above. Here he found the clutter and chaos amplified. A table overturned. Food scattered among more richly adorned clothes, fine armor and weapons. As though every member of the household, from master down to lowly potboy, had stripped themselves of every stitch they wore and left the keep.

But to go where?

Manus frowned at the difficulty of his position. He could touch nothing solid to see if it held mortal warmth or living essence or hint of violence. He could smell nothing to tell him how old or how long it had been since whatever occurred here. Ginny would be able to do these things, so he would have to coax her here, but he was helpless to decipher any of these events on his own.

All he knew for certain was that the Keep of Dun Ardagh was as quiet as a barrow grave and as empty as air.

Or was until his essence sensed an ancient flare of power. Startled, Manus shifted himself into invisibility and drifted over to one of the narrow windows. There, he peered out at a sloped roof leading down into the courtyard at the slender figure of a woman who stopped at the edge of the gatehouse shadows. She motioned with her hands, but before the torchlight fled, he saw that she was fair as alabaster and had moon white hair. A marriage plaid draped off one of her shoulders, almost wanton in its manner. Alas, from where he was, he could not see the pattern of the tartan she wore.

Being spirit had not taken his mage sight or senses, and what he could see was the black figure of the giant Keltoran staghound that sidled up to the woman, eyes glowing like twin coals. *The Nidubh!* The very beast that had come close to devouring little Thistle! Though invisible and never one to call himself a coward, Manus ducked back from the opening to hide when those red orbs briefly swept in his direction.

"Just what makes you think the boy will come back here?" the woman said in an impatient voice.

"*Where else would he bring them?*" the hound replied. "*They will want to know if whatever he tells them is true, and we must make certain they tell no one else.*"

33

"And you are certain the woman who helped him was mageborn?"

"White fire is not a gift of the mortalborn," the hound said. *"And the cottage is surrounded by strong wards and spells. I tried to go back, but I was unable to pass them without pain."*

"And what of her companion? Was he really a mageborn spirit?"

"Aye, I sensed that he was otherworld and blessed with power."

"He'll have to be sundered, of course," the woman said with a scowl.

"Of course," the hound agreed, *"and if you will permit it, I shall take his essence."*

She merely nodded. "What of the others? Where are they now?"

"Scattered," the hound said, *"but I will soon bring the pack to heel again. No one will know who they are anyway."*

The woman nodded, looking impatient under the moon. "I cannot stay here and wait with you, Nidubh," she said. Her glacial eyes scanned the dark recesses of the keep as though she sensed something. Manus stayed still and invisible. He remembered all too well that mageborn eyes saw what mortal eyes could not, and that included spirit essence. "Rory MacElwyn is not to be trusted alone in his present state of mind. I cannot leave him for long."

"Then go," the hound said *"I will wait for the last seed of MacArdagh to return in the company of his new friends, and I will let you know when they arrive. And this time, the white fire of the little hedge sorceress will not stop me from rending every one of them . . ."*

"Be careful what you plot, beast!" the woman said. "No hint of death must be found here, or I will make certain that Arawn knows who to blame."

"It shall be done as you wish, mistress."

The woman turned and blended into the shadows while the hound trotted closer to the keep. Manus waited only until he could see neither before he drifted his essence through the narrow window. There he paused to get his bearings, and spied a bit of cloth caught in the stone with a number of red-gold hairs. Had he the ability to fetch them along, he would have, but he had no form. Better he leave this place as swiftly as possible and make for Tamhasg Wood.

Ginny would need to be told of this place. And warned that whatever had happened here in Dun Ardagh could easily spell doom for both them and the lad with a bloodmage involved.

Rory MacElwyn.

Where had Manus heard that name before?

Chapter Five

Long hours after midnight, Ginny felt safe enough to fall asleep. She had hoped to spend the rest of the night in relative peace, but Manus saw to it her wish was spoiled when he awoke her before the break of dawn could dim his company.

"Ginny!" he cried with his ethereal shout, the one that wailed about the cottage like a storm wind. She sat up on her cot, angry and confused as she tried to orient herself to time and direction. Mainly, she wanted to make sure the magebolt she was tempted to conjure didn't strike little Thistle.

"Ginny, wake up!" Manus howled.

"I'm awake!" she groaned, pushing hair from her face and drawing the covers about her shoulders when she felt the chill of morning air left where the fire had gone down. She really needed to find a ward to keep Manus out before the sun was high. Ever since she had welcomed him across the threshold to save him from the Black Hunter who wanted his soul, Manus had come and gone from the cottage as he pleased.

"You'll never believe what I've discovered, my lass!" he went on, materializing at the foot of the cot and towering like a brigand about to ravage a maid. And in some ways, she wished he would, for it would give her an excuse to scream in outrage and obliterate him with white fire. Mentor or not, she had little patience with anyone who woke her before sunrise. "The keep of Dun Ardagh is as silent as a tomb!"

"As was this place before you came in," Ginny muttered.

"No, really. The whole place is deserted."

"Deserted?" she said, trying to rationalize the word through the morning fog smothering her brain.

"Aye, and that's not all," he said, and she wished his enthusiasm would wane. "While I was there, the Nidubh arrived in the company of a bloodmage."

Bloodmage was the word to sharpen Ginny's senses. What would a bloodmage be doing with the Nidubh at her side? As a rule, such demons only served Arawn. "Which bloodmage?" Ginny asked.

"We weren't exactly trading introductions, so I can't say as I caught her name, though she did say something about someone named Rory MacElwyn not being trustworthy to leave alone," Manus said, seating himself lightly on the foot of Ginny's cot. "Anyway, I was busy trying not to let her know I was there. Bloodmages have a bad habit of stealing mageborn essence as well as mortalborn lives."

"But what were they doing there?" Ginny asked.

"Talking about us . . . and the lad," Manus said. "They're determined to capture him and they think he'll return to the keep. Oh, and the Nidubh was quite anxious to silence you and me, but the bloodmage let the creature know she didn't want death found in Dun Ardagh. She's up to no good, that one is, Ginny."

Ginny frowned. "Well, that's rather obvious, if she's got the Nidubh at her side. But why would Arawn give her such a beast for a servant, unless . . ."

"Unless she made some bargain with him," Manus said. "It's not unusual for the Dark Lord of Annwn to promise power in trade for souls to fill his Cauldron of Doom, ye ken. Why I remember my auld Uncle saying as much when I was a lad. He said that so long as a soul was regularly provided, the one making the sacrifice could keep their own."

"All this sounds like a matter for the Council of Mage-born," Ginny said. "But how to alert them to this creature . . ."

"Simple enough," Manus said. "Ye gate yourself to Caer Keltora and Dun Gealach . . ."

"Not that simple," she said. "I don't know the gate spell, remember?"

"Why not, lass?"

"You never got around to teaching it to me," she said. "Every time you were supposed to, you would go wandering the moors to meet with your precious Tamhasg maiden . . ."

"Jealous, were ye?"

"You wish," Ginny retorted with a glower, unwilling to admit that at the time she was. "At any rate, I never learned that spell, and it's the one spell a mage cannot learn from a tome."

"Well, that's of little matter," Manus said. "Ye can let me borrow yer flesh and . . ."

"No!" Ginny said, and hopped off the edge of the cot to pace over to face the fire. "I will not allow you to use me that way, Manus MacGreeley!"

"I have no flesh to cast the spell, Ginny," he reminded her pointedly as he floated up off the cot and suspended himself in midair. "And you lack the knowledge and skill . . ."

"It's not for lack of skill!" she said. "You denied me the spell because you were afraid I would use it to go else-where and leave you alone with your dog and your heather ale."

"Now, that's not true!" he said sourly, coming back down and landing at her side. "I would never have stopped ye, if ye wanted to go elsewhere to learn your craft!"

Ginny crossed her arms and turned away. That was as bitter a slap as any. *So it wouldn't have mattered to you if I'd stayed or left.* She glared at the fire and whispered, *"Loisg,"* to make the flames rise and crackle.

"Look, we're getting nowhere," he said. "You're right to believe we should let the Council of Mageborn know about this woman and her beastie, as well as the fact that Dun Ardagh is as empty as a cracked bucket. But surely ye canna be proposing that we walk all the way to Caer Keltora! Mind you, it would matter little to me in my present state, but think of poor Thistle. His legs are short enough without wearing them off by walking all the way to Caer Keltora, and I canna believe ye would be so cruel as to leave him here alone with no one for company."

"No, we'll only have to walk as far as Auntie Maeve's cottage at Ghloelea."

"Now, what do ye want to go bothering that old harridan for?" Manus groused.

"She's not an old harridan," Ginny said. "She's a delightful old woman who just happens to enjoy telling tales on you, Manus MacGreeley . . ."

"She's as mad as a bogie hen."

"Mad or nor, I'm sure she'll be more than happy to gate us to Caer Keltora."

"If she remembers where it is," Manus muttered. " 'Twould be simpler if ye'd let me share yer body, Ginny."

"Not to me, it wouldn't," she said and stooped to fetch her kettle and start the morning tea to sift the rest of the fog from her mind. Never in a million lifetimes would she consent to sharing her flesh with Manus' soul.

"Why not?" he insisted. "Are ye afraid I won't give you back yer flesh?"

"I don't want to talk about it," she said, dipping water

39

from the barrel by the door and putting the kettle on the ring over the fire.

"You are afraid," he said. "I ne'er thought I'd see the day Ginny Ni Cooley was lacking courage. 'Tis not like I'd want to keep yer body, lass. In case ye haven't noticed, ye lack certain key matters that I consider important to a man."

"You are impossible!" she snapped.

"And you don't have a good excuse for refusing to let me assist you," he said. "After all, that bloodmage and her bogie hound want my essence too. It would be best for all of us if you'd forget yer inhibitions and let me in for a while."

"I said no, and that should be answer enough, Manus!" she retorted. "Now, I am going to have my morning tea, then I am going to wake up that poor lad and learn exactly what happened at Dun Ardagh. And once that is done, we will go to Auntie Maeve and let her open a gate to Caer Keltora for us, and if you don't like that, you can stay behind!"

He glowered, though the expression looked more like a rude pout. Then the cock began to crow to herald the arrival of dawn. Manus would have to leave for a short time now. Since he had died at night, the hours from dusk to dawn were his time to prowl the moors. Come dawn, his spirit had to return to its cairn for a brief repose, even though it could rise and pester her in daylight, as he had on numerous occasions.

"Auntie Maeve," Manus muttered as he began to fade. "The woman can barely find her way out of her own garden, and you think she'd going to be able to gate us all the way to Caer Keltora without losing us in some black void . . ."

Ginny ignored him and went looking for the tea jar. She

found it as the water began to boil, sprinkling bits of dried leaves into the water to brew. She used that time to wash herself from the ewer, then pulled on her overtunic, divided skirt and boots. The tea tasted delicious, filling her with warmth and settling her unease.

Time to awaken the lad. With a sigh, she clambered up the ladder.

Shadows normally filled the loft, for it had only a small window shuttered against cold and light, and that was usually closed. But as Ginny crested the edge of the loft, she viewed light spreading across the boards. Morning revealed the rumpled bedclothes left scattered about, abandoned along with the nightshirt she had given the lad. The small shutters hung open, letting a breeze chill the air.

But of Fafne MacArdagh, there was no sign.

Chapter Six

Manus once taught Ginny that the bogie residents of Tamhasg Wood did have their uses from time to time, and over the years she had learned which ones could be bribed or mildly terrorized to assist her. With her plaid shawl about her shoulders, she snatched up her wooden staff with the bits of feather and stag horn dangling on little leather strips wrapped about the neck of the hart carved into its head. Thistle bounced enthusiastically at her heels as she headed straight into the woods and made for the badger den. The moor terrier was more than willing to do his part, diving into that dark recess with a fearsome bay while Ginny marked a circle of runes in the dirt near the mouth of the hole.

Within moments, the hob came scrambling out of the den. It was a spindly-limbed creature with a long nose and luminous eyes, and every inch of it was covered with a clay-colored pelt, and even stretched out, it stood only slightly higher than a man's knee. At the sight of Ginny, it squawked and ducked from the swipe of her staff. She had no intention of hitting it, but the hob didn't know that and leaped into the circle of runes just as Thistle burst out of the hole.

"*Cearcall duin!*" she said, then seized the moor terrier by the rope collar she had taken time to put on him before leaving her cottage, and knelt so she could meet the hob's startled gaze as the circle around it began to glow white. "Wheesht, Thistle."

"No fair!" the hob complained in a peevish manner as it hopped from one foot to the other.

"You wouldn't know fair if it bit you on the nose," Ginny said. "You stole eggs from my hens three nights back."

"Hungry," the hob said.

"So I've noticed," she said, and, with her staff leaning against her shoulder, she drew forth a pair of eggs from the pouch on her belt. She set them on the ground just outside the glowing circle. "These are for you, but there's a price."

"What?" the hob said and eagerly reached for the eggs, only to be driven back by the magic in the circle. With a sulky sigh, the creature crouched on its haunches and glowered at the eggs, licking its lips.

"Last night, did you see anyone leaving my cottage?"

"Saw boy with tail, naked as new mouse, bolting about the forest after a hare. Couldn't catch it so he sat doon and cried like bairnie, then go."

"Go where?" she asked.

The hob shrugged, gesturing towards Tamhasg Stream and the moors beyond. "Go that way," it said. "No food, so hob no go after."

"Was there anyone else about the wood?"

"Too many hounds," the hob said and bared rows of teeth at Thistle, who snapped and lunged at the small creature, and would have had it for breakfast had Ginny not twisted her fingers around the rope collar.

"Tease him again, hob, and I'll let him go," she warned.

The hob made a face at her instead. "No fair. No do nothing to you last night."

"See to it that you continue to do nothing," she said. "Anything else?"

The hob shook its head, wagging the long nose. "Let go and keep dog out of hole now," it said.

Ginny nodded. She drew a length of rope from her pouch, looping it through Thistle's collar so she could rise and keep the moor terrier back. Then she whispered, *"Cealcall fosgail,"* and broke the edge of the circle with the end of her staff. The glow winked out, and just as fast, the hob snatched up the two eggs and bolted for the badger hole. Thistle strained on the leash, and Ginny was forced to lean back to keep him in hand. With a swish of clay-colored fur, the hob disappeared into the dark recess.

This news is not good, she thought as she dragged Thistle away. Fafne's partial transformation was starting to have an effect on him if he was chasing hares in the dark. She set out for the stream, crossing it at the narrow point. The moor terrier was now trying to lead the way, so she unknotted the leash and let him run on ahead. Better than ending up in the water.

Not far from the stream was a simple cairn that lay at the base of a hill topped by a circle of seven monoliths known as the Maiden's Lament. The latter was a place of ancient ritual concerning young girls and womanhood that had fallen into disuse long before the Unification of the Fourteen Kingdoms of Ard-Taebh. According to local legend, a young lass took her life among those stones. She used a dagger stolen from her unfaithful lover after she caught him dallying at the local inn with another. Now, it was thought to be haunted, and Ginny knew this rumor was not entirely without good cause. But the spirit in this place was no maiden scorned. Instead, it was the mageborn spirit of a man whose bones had been placed under the cairn of stones by Ginny's own hands.

She placed herself at the foot of the cairn and tapped them with her staff. "Manus?" she said. "Are ye able to rise?"

A thick fog slithered out from between the cracks in the

stones and hovered over the cairn.

"This high enough?" Manus replied as the mist slowly manifested into his pale form. Sunlight made him nearly as thin as the air.

"Fafne is gone," she said. "We've got to find him."

"Gone?" he said and followed as she started to climb the Maiden's Lament. "And just how did he get out of the cottage, lass?"

"Through the little window in the loft," she said, frowning when she heard the excited cry of the moor terrier as he flushed a hare and bolted after it. Ginny shook her head and continued to climb. With luck the hare would go to ground before Thistle caught it.

She had reached the top now, giving her a view of the rolling green and brown of the moors, splotched here and there by patches of purple-headed thistles and variegated heather blooms. *How far could one lad in the throes of exhaustion go?* she wondered.

"Without you or Thistle hearing a sound?" Manus insisted, floating up beside her.

"I put a spell of silence on the loft," she said, catching his incredulous stare. "And unfortunately, the spell keeps you from hearing sound made inside its range as well as keeping out sounds beyond its barrier."

"And just why, in the name of Cernunnos, would you go and put a spell of silence on the loft?"

"The Nidubh came back last night, and with all the noise it and those other hounds were making, Fafne was frightened."

"Why didn't you tell me the beastie came back? For all we know, it has him now."

"I doubt that," Ginny said. "The hob saw Fafne chasing hares on the moors."

45

"That's not good," Manus said. "Means the lad's regressing into the half-life this spell has on him. Really, ye should have come and told me this, Ginny."

"And just why should I tell you everything that happens in the night, Manus?" she said. "You're in no position to do anything about that creature, and anyway, you never bothered to give me any such courtesy when you were alive!"

His expression folded into a mask of male confusion, the sort of expression that told her he didn't really want to contemplate what she had just said. "Well, it looks like I was right," Manus said with an ethereal sigh.

"Right about what?" she said, giving him a hard glance.

"You should have questioned him about what happened at Dun Ardagh before you sent him up to the loft to sleep."

"He was too tired to give me an answer," she said.

"But not so tired as to keep him from heading out to prowl the moors and answer the call of the Wild Kin in his blood after dark," Manus said.

She knew, of course, it would be useless to strike him with her staff, so she thumped it into the dirt instead and whistled for Thistle. There was obviously no sign of Fafne from up here. Part of her feared that the lad might have gone straight into the jaws of the Nidubh and its deadly pack of red-gold hounds after the hob saw him, though she would never let Manus know that, as she would hear no end of it from him.

"Let's go down to the village and see if we can pick up any gossip there," she said, starting across the circle of stone to climb down the overgrown path on the northern side.

Not far from the mound, she came to the western moor road and, following it east to the crossroads, she made her way north into Conorscroft. Manus faded to invisibility to accompany her. He had wandered into the village in spirit form only once, and sent several of the locals into fright. Ever after, Ginny had to pretend to assure them that she had exorcised his spirit into the other realm so they would stop talk of hiring a more experienced mage to come sunder him. In life, she had known there were folk in Conorscroft who didn't like Manus too well, and it had nothing to do with him being mageborn. They were quite grateful to have Ginny's mageborn help.

Unfortunately, Manus' flippant nature often caused him to step on enough toes to make him socially unpopular in these parts. After his death, Ginny could not count the number of times a villager would come to her in the market and commend her for having the patience to put up with "that man." She had never told them that she was still doing so.

The market of Conorscroft was already active, as merchants and farmers and tinkers gathered to hawk and sell their wares. She wandered among them, hardly noticed except for a few "good mornings," politely spoken by folk for whom she had done one favor or another. Manus said it didn't hurt for a mageborn to keep in the good graces of the locals by finding lost objects or predicting good and foul weather now and again. And there were those who came to her from time to time asking for amulets of protection. She drew the line when they asked for love philters, for she didn't like the idea of some lad or lass seeking to gain what they could not have by natural means and good fortune.

She was passing the smith's stall when she heard a tinker lamenting that his cart horse had lost its shoe when it panicked on the road past Dun Ardagh.

"What spooked it?" the smith asked.

"Hounds!" the tinker replied with a glower. "A whole pack of them running down sheep in the fields. All of Dun

47

Ardagh is overrun by hounds these days."

"Whose hounds are they?"

"No one knows. The crofters all say the hounds came out of nowhere, and that they be savaging farm beasts for leagues, but no man knows from whence they came, except to think it may be a curse."

"For what?"

The tinker shrugged massive shoulders under his common plaidie. "Who knows? 'Tis a plague of hounds on Dun Ardagh, and some folk think the bad luck come on the MacArdaghs for naming a traitor to the crown."

A traitor to the crown? Ginny thought. She would have gladly broken into the conversation at that time to ask more, but she was interrupted when a commotion rose from across the square. A farmwife from one of the small crofts scattered about the northern edge of Conorscroft charged into the square, waving her two ells of marriage plaid like a pair of bat wings behind her.

"There's a bogie in my barn!" she cried at the top of her lungs, "savaging one of my hens!"

Folk began to gather fast.

"Call MacBorlyn and have him fetch his hounds!" one said.

"Get the rowan arrows!" another wailed.

"I don't like the sound of that," Manus whispered.

"It's a horrible bogie!" the woman shrieked at those who gathered. "Half-boy and half-hound, all covered with blood from devouring all my hens!"

Ginny didn't need to hear any more. She snatched up Thistle and headed in the direction from which the farmwife had come.

And hoped she could find the barn before the growing rabble stormed it.

Chapter Seven

Locating the barn in question proved easier than Ginny hoped as she raced north from the village square towards the crofters' farms. It was a simple matter of following the wild chatter of hens who had seen what they imagined to be a fierce predator. As Ginny bolted into the farmyard, she found a mass of chickens scurrying in all directions, refuting the farmwife's claim of her terrible loss.

Like many of the smaller farms, the barn was an outbuilding attached to the side of the house. As Ginny approached, she spied Manus hovering over the thatched roof.

"Ginny, Fafne's in here," he called to her.

She wasted no time entering the barn, where more hens ran up and down the straight aisle, proving again that in the state of panic the farmwife had not bothered to count her fowl. The standing stalls lining each side were empty. Like as not, any large livestock were out in the fields working or grazing. There was certainly no sign of Fafne in any of them. Ginny quickly closed the doors.

Thistle struggled wildly in her grasp, forcing her to let him down. He ran straight to the loft ladder and put his forepaws on the bottom-most rung, barking furiously at something overhead. Oh, for a tatter of linen to muzzle the little beast, for she felt certain his incessant barking would just make matters worse.

"Wheesht," she said, and pushed the moor terrier aside so she could climb the ladder. She reached the loft just as Manus glided through the thatch. Ignoring him, she scanned the loose straw and stored sacks of grain until she spied a shivering form crouched in one corner.

"Fafne?" she said gently.

He was caked with mud from head to tail, though Ginny could see no sign of the "blood" the farm wife had howled about. Nor did she see evidence of any hens being savaged. Just a small, frightened lad, quivering like a newborn pup. He blinked at her, eyes feral with unease at first. Then recognition filtered through the fear, and tears began to stream down his cheeks in rivers.

"It's all right, Fafne," Ginny said. "I won't hurt you, but we must get you out of here now."

"What's happening to me?" he lamented in a pitiful voice. "Why am I here? I don't remember . . ."

"It doesn't matter just now, lad," Ginny said, easing over to where he sat hunched in a pose not unlike a dog that feared his master's wrath. "We've got to get you out of here now."

"But why is this happening?" he repeated.

"We can't know that until you tell us what happened to you at Dun Ardagh," Manus said.

Fafne blinked at the spectral mage. "But . . . I don't know. It all happened so fast . . ."

"Now is not the time," Ginny said. "We're about to be visited by a mob of angry villagers, and I really don't want to try and reason this out with them."

She took Fafne's arms and drew him from the corner as she spoke, throwing her own shawl around his shivering form for warmth. There was no resistance as she led him towards the loft ladder and guided him down the rungs.

Thistle could be heard below, running about and barking in such a frenzied manner. Thistle and stone, Ginny wished again that she'd brought a means to muzzle the moor terrier, as well as the rope.

"Now there's a good use for your silence spell," Manus quipped as he floated down to the floor. "Thistle, wheesht! You'll tell the whole village we're here . . ."

"I think they already know," Ginny said, pausing halfway down the ladder as the faint rumble of voices raised in anger filtered through to her mageborn hearing over the natter of hens and Thistle's sharp voice.

Fafne panicked, and probably would have bolted back up into the loft had Ginny not clutched the shawl together around his shoulders. She might not have been large, but the lad was thin from his ordeal and lacked the strength to fight free. She hauled him protesting down the ladder and into the aisle of the barn, looking frantically about. There were small side windows, but they would be seen exiting one of those. Only the one doorway faced her.

"We've got to find a way out of here," she said. There was no telling how the locals would react to find their mageborn consorting with a bogie beast and the spirit of the man they thought she had exorcised. She had heard tales of mageborn being attacked and hanged for lesser crimes.

"There's no time to flee," Manus said. "Put your silence on Thistle and hide yerselves in the first stall." He gestured to one side. "And leave the rest to me."

"And just what do you think you're going to do?" she asked as she herded Fafne into the stall, then scrambled after the moor terrier. He struggled as she snagged his collar and ran the length of rope lead through it. Then she touched him and said, *"Samhchair thu iadh,"* and though his little body bounced frantically from the rhythmic snap of his animated jaws, Thistle made no sound. Briefly, she wondered if she could use the same spell on Manus, but since she could not touch him . . .

"Hurry," Manus said.

51

"And just what do you think you can do to stop them?" she asked again. "After all, you have no power and, as far as they are concerned, I sent you on to the Summerland."

"Wheesht, lass," Manus said. "I'll not destroy their faith in ye. Just watch and learn. You might just be a spirit one day, ye ken?"

"Watch and learn," she fumed as she scampered into the first stall and crouched before Fafne, clutching Thistle's rope to keep him from spoiling the game. Just what did Manus think he was going to do without the ability to cast spells?

But she quickly realized there was reason not to underestimate his cleverness. Manus took a deep breath and leaned forward. His essence shimmered and shifted, gliding from man to beast. The plaidie and shirt faded and left a thick pelt of red-gold fur down his back as he became a creature not unlike Fafne in appearance. Only Manus, true to nature, could not resist altering the form a little. He was larger by far, and grew talons from his hands and feet. And his face was more lupine with huge fangs protruding from the mouth. Had Ginny not known it was him . . .

The barn door burst open, and the rabble of voices rose in a startled chorus. Manus threw back his head and howled fearsomely enough to send chills washing down Ginny's back. Then waving those talons, he snarled and charged at the crowd that had grown still in its tracks.

Her first inclination would have been to scream for his foolishness, had she not recalled that mortal weapons were useless against the mageborn dead. Besides, the villagers reacted with frightened howls and screams of their own. They scrambled out of the barn in mass, fighting to be first through the door, looking like a flood of terrified rats and scattering like the hens that were being trampled under the mad rush.

Then someone shouted for rowan and fire, and Ginny heard a rally of cries to support the battle plan. She peered around the end of the stall in time to see Manus stop out in the yard. Though the sunlight dimmed his essence a bit, the effect was still extraordinary. He arched his back and snarled as the crowd turned, then changed course and began fleeing north, whooping and yipping like a demented hound.

More than enough of an invitation to encourage the locals to charge after him waving pitchforks and cudgels. Ginny stayed where she was until the last villager left her line of sight before she grabbed Fafne and dragged him and Thistle out of the barn. Quickly, she headed south, taking a wide berth around the village and making for the western moor road. Fafne panted from the exertion, but she would not slow down for a moment. She dared not even look back, praying to all the gods that no one noticed their flight.

At length they came to the brook, and only then did she slow her pace. Thistle was calm enough to be released, and she even removed her silence spell from him so he could start whining and yipping as they made their way through Tamhasg Wood. Fafne was silent in an uneasy manner. She let him keep his peace, maintaining her grasp on the shawl firmly looped around him to preserve his modesty.

They reached the cottage in due course. Ginny worked the magelocked door, leading the boy inside where she got him over to the lowering fire. He hunkered there, whining like a pup that wanted its mother. She quickly fixed him tea and bread with honey, and he devoured both as though he hadn't had a meal in days, even snarling a warning when Thistle ventured close and begged for a taste. The reaction so startled the moor terrier, he backed under Ginny's chair and growled back.

"None of that, you two," Ginny said. She dragged out one of Manus' old shirts and pulled it over the lad's head, then helped him kilt a bit of what must have been Manus' boyhood plaid about his thin waist. The tail drooped between his legs. Too bad it wasn't flexible enough to coil around under the kilt. She even found him a pair of stockings and shoes that were too large for his feet.

"Now," she said. "Why did you run off last night?"

"I . . . I couldn't help it," Fafne said quietly. "I . . . I heard the Wild Kin calling, and I had to answer."

"How could you have heard them through the silence spell I put on the loft?" she insisted.

"I . . . I wanted air. I opened the window, and as I leaned out I heard them. It wasn't like before. They were calling me to join them. I . . . I had to go . . ."

Ginny heaved a sigh. She remembered that eerie song in the night, the summoning that went to her soul.

But why would the Wild Kin call one who was not mageborn?

Thistle alerted her to Manus' sudden return. The moor terrier raced over to the door just as Manus' form materialized through the wood. Fortunately, he'd had the good sense to abandon the hideous shape she last saw him wearing for his own.

"Lost them up by the loch," he said, grinning with wry mischief. "You should have seen their faces when I ran straight into stone and just disappeared. No doubt, ye'll be hearing from them soon enough to exorcise the frightful beast." He grinned as he said that.

"I should be so fortunate," she said with a weary smile.

"So now, do we get to hear this lad's tale?" Manus asked. "And I'm not referring to the furry one he's got tucked betwixt his legs."

Ginny pulled a stool over to sit on it and face the boy. "Yes," she agreed. "I think now would be a good time to find out just what we may be up against before you lose all sense of your true self, lad."

"What?" Fafne looked up at her with a frightened stare.

"Start at the beginning," Ginny insisted firmly. "What happened at Dun Ardagh, and just how did you become half a dog?"

Fafne sighed, and slowly began his tale.

Chapter Eight

"What I seem to remember best that night was the moon as it rose," Fafne began carefully, the firelight washing him pale, "for it cast a bloody hue upon the fields around my father's dun. Blood Moon, my Gran once called it, when she was alive to tell us tales of the ancient days and the Old Ones. She said it was never wise to let the light of it touch you before it rose high and white, as it always brought bad luck. So maybe I am to blame for that dreadful night, for while my family feasted, I stood on the tower and let that light wash over me. Then my sisters came and said my mother had called for me. She wanted me to play the harp for the feast.

"We were celebrating my father's latest honor. He's a great man, ye ken, a favorite chieftain who has pledged his loyalty and sword to King Brendan." Fafne's eyes shone with a hint of pride. "My father fears no man, and would stand alone if he must against any who would wish MacMorroch's fall from the throne of Keltora. We were celebrating because Father had uncovered a plot to rally followers against the King who were willing to go to war to bring back the dreaded MacPhearsons. It was Father who learned that Tomis, son of Rory MacElwyn, was revealed to be the instigator of a plot to commit treason and assassinate the King. Tomis was taken prisoner less than a sen'night back and, last I heard, he was being taken to Caer Keltora to answer the accusations against him and answer to the King's reckoning. In addition, my father received a letter of commendation and was granted a parcel of land between Dun Ardagh and Dun Elwyn that had often been in dispute. And was asked to come to Caer Keltora within a moon to stand witness against the traitor's plot."

"Rory MacElwyn," Manus muttered. "She said that name . . ."

Ginny hissed for his silence and touched Fafne's hand. "Go on," she insisted.

"Father felt quite pleased with his accomplishment," Fafne said. "He boasted to every man, woman and child in Dun Ardagh how he had learned about the plot, how he had heard Tomis MacElwyn speaking to a retainer about when the King's life must be taken, and how he had a way now that would assure that death. He says that Tomis did not say just how, but there was a hint that magic would be involved.

"Anyway, Father ordered a great feast to celebrate the settlement of the dispute and the fall of the traitor. He called every man, woman and child in Dun Ardagh to join the affair, and it was quite a merry time until she came.

"At first, no one took notice of the noise in the courtyards. After all, when folk are dancing and shouting and laughing, who's to know? But the merry voices gave way to shouts of terror, then hideous howls like a hundred hounds had entered the rath. Before we could question what was happening, the doors to our hall fell open, and in came the woman and her hideous fire-eyed hound."

"Did you know her?" Ginny asked. She'd been hard pressed to keep silent before now.

Fafne shrugged. "I cannot say that I did, though my Father looked startled to see her, so I think he must have known her. She gave us no time to speak. Hounds of every color began to pour into the room, snapping and snarling after us like we were sheep to be herded into the fold. My father, my elder brothers and the men-at-arms took up their weapons to try and drive the hounds away, but the black beast with the fire in its eyes led the charge, knocking them down as though they were children. Their weapons proved useless against that fiend, even though I had heard that a bogie fears steel, for its heart is cold iron.

"One by one, the beast deprived them of their weapons and forced them back, while the rest of the hounds drove us into a small knot over by the windows that overlooked the yard. I was pressed into a corner near one of the narrow windows, and I could see the courtyard was filled with hounds, a whole plague of them, it would seem.

"The woman approached us, standing in the midst of the hounds, and fixed us with a cold eye. 'Witnesses need voices to speak against a traitor,' she said. 'Know this. Not one man, woman or child among you will die, but there shall be none to know or tell of your fate . . .' Then she raised her hands and began to speak words I did not understand. A golden ball of fire burst to life in our midst. Father ordered everyone back and Mother tried to throw herself over my younger sisters to protect them as the ball of fire grew. It touched Father first, and the sound he made was so terrible, I could not bear to watch. I turned away like a coward, when it occurred to me I was small enough to fit through the window and run for help.

"I dove into that narrow slit, only to become wedged in my panic. Behind me, I could hear the screams and howls, and the cries were so terrifying to me, I fought harder to slip through the gap. I could feel my skin and clothes tear on the rough stones . . .

"That was when I felt the pain, and thought the ball of fire must have spread enough to burn my back. I shrieked and struggled harder, and it was as though I felt myself growing smaller. Whatever it was, I could move forward again, and with a push I fell out of the window, slid down the roof and tumbled into a hay cart. My back ached as though my spine were being pulled apart, and at first I feared it was broken in the fall, but then I realized I could still move.

"I practically fell out of the cart and landed in the yard, where I saw nothing but hounds running madly about the rath. In terror, I rose and bolted through the gates, believing that was where the others had fled, but as I reached the outer gate, I saw no one. Just more dogs.

"It was then that I heard the hideous howling and the snarls of the hounds, and I looked back towards the keep in time to see the black beast gliding through that narrow window like a spirit thing. Behind it came a flood of red-gold hounds, and I could hear the woman shrieking in anger that they had better not let me escape.

"Fear took my heart to hear those words, and gave me the speed of the wind. I started to run, down the road at first, then cut into the forest and crossed many fields, hoping to escape them. I must have run all night when dawn found me too exhausted to go on. I fell and slept where I was, only to awaken when I heard the terrible baying that came with the gloaming. There was naught I could do but rise and run again.

"I lost track of the passing of time. I seemed to run forever, sleeping only when the morning came. And then I was here, and you helped me, and it was only then for the first time that I realized I had grown a tail. I swear to you, I never had one before . . ."

His story ended with a little sob as he hid his face in his hands. Ginny reached out and touched his head to reassure him, and traded glances with Manus.

"I don't know what became of my family," he said weakly. "I don't know why I feel as I do, but I'm frightened."

"There now," Ginny said. "Your ordeal will end once we reach Caer Keltora."

She rose and stepped away from the lad, looking hard at Manus now.

"The Nidubh must not be a true bogie if it cannot be harmed by steel," she said.

"Demon," Manus agreed, "and that's worse than any bogie."

"We must let the Council of Mageborn know this. If a bloodmage has cast a spell of transformation on all the MacArdaghs, she must be more powerful than you or I alone can manage."

"Aye, well, I'm with ye there," he agreed. "But being as I am unable to cast magic without flesh . . ." He gave her a knowing look, and Ginny started to give him a piece of her mind when a fist thumped the cottage door, sending Thistle into a barking frenzy and startling everyone else in the room.

"Mistress Ni Cooley!" a voice cried. " 'Tis Master Warren."

Ginny frowned, gesturing for the others to be silent. She crept over to the door and opened it just wide enough to allow her to look out at the hulk of the village smith. He was not alone. Several men of the village backed him, and most of them were easily recognized as men she saw at the barn. Pushing Thistle back with her heel, she stepped outside and closed the door, praying that Manus would keep his tongue and that of the lad.

"Is something the matter, Master Warren?" she said.

"Aye, we've need of your good skills, lass," he said.

"That bogie what you must have heard Mistress MacAlden carrying on about this morning, it ran straight into the stand of rocks on the northern side of the loch. There's women fearing for their bairns now, lass. Ye must come and do yer magic to get rid of the bogie beast, if ye can."

Ginny resisted the urge to roll her eyes and tell them they had been deceived, for it would certainly not do her reputation any good. "Well, I shall come and do what I can directly."

"If ye could do something now, folk would sleep better this night," he said, and the murmurs of his followers indicated that they all agreed.

"Very well," she said carefully. "I need to gather a few items to assist me, and then I'll be right along. You and your men go back and make certain the beast does not leave the rock before I get there."

Grunts and nods went the round. Clearly, this sounded like a good plan to them. The small crowd quickly dispersed down the path towards the road and the village.

With a sigh, Ginny thrust herself back into the cottage and fixed Manus with a dark stare.

"This is all your fault," she said.

"I had to do something," he said.

"So what are we to do now? The villagers will expect me to rid them of a bogie that does not exist!"

"Oh, lass, don't be fretting yourself so," Manus said with a cheerful grin. "I have a most wondrous idea."

"I was afraid you would," Ginny said with a sigh.

Apparently, it was going to be one of *those* days.

Chapter Nine

"Once we get to the loch," Ginny said, "I don't want you to draw matters out unnecessarily. We'll just do this and get it over with. No wild chases across the moors, agreed?"

"Fine," she heard Manus mutter as he wandered invisibly at her side. "But if we're too quick, the locals may be difficult to convince that you know what you're doing. Simple folk expect magic to be complex. A single *begone* and a wee bit of fire will do very little to impress them."

Ginny sighed. She might as well have expressed those words of warning to the ground at her feet. Manus had once told her that the only reason he tormented and teased her as he did was because he thought this afterlife owed some amusement to a mageborn spirit. "Elsewise, I might be bored to death . . ."

She had, at least, done him the courtesy of taking his advice and putting her magelock on the door and the windows as well, leaving Fafne and Thistle firmly locked inside the protection of the cottage. "With luck, they won't chew each other to bits," Manus had said, "though I'd be willing to bet little Thistle would have the advantage."

Thankfully, Manus remained silent for the rest of the walk. Ginny followed the road through the village of Conorscroft and northward towards Loch Conor. There, on the farthest slope, she could see a single stone, all that remained of a circle from ancient times that had been treated with far less respect than others around the area. Many of the original stones from this collection had been carted off to add to field walls and broken down to cobble the market square. Ginny frowned when she saw the locals were standing around the stone bearing staffs of rowan and sacks of salt. Indeed, a few were actually sprinkling a circle of salt around the stone itself, as though that would keep the bogie imprisoned.

Master Warren was directing the work, and he looked relieved to see Ginny arrive. She sensed Manus going over to slip into the stone to do his part as she approached the brawny, handsome smith of Conorscroft.

"Mistress," Master Warren said. "The beast has not come out as near as any can tell, though some swear they have heard it howling and others wonder if there's a kinship between this bogie and the hounds we hear are cursing Dun Ardagh."

"One never knows," she said and nodded. "You and the others should stand back as far as possible while I set the circle and try to trap the creature, in case the circle doesn't hold it."

Master Warren gestured to those around him, and they managed to clear the locals back far enough to suit her. All eyes were focused on Ginny as though she were a prize heifer on the block. *Might as well get on with this insanity.* She turned to face the circle and held forth her staff, giving it a shake that rattled the bones.

"Arise, foul creature of the dark realms!" she said in a loud voice. "By salt and wind and fire and water, I summon you forth! Obey me!"

Not exactly an original bit of spell casting, she had to admit, and hardly the words one would use to summon a real bogie out of such a stone. On the other hand, she couldn't risk raising something that neither she nor the villagers would want hanging around Conorscroft. Elsewise she would be forced to come back and do this again.

A howl sounded from within the stone, ringing across the placid waters of the loch. Villagers muttered and hitched themselves back a few more steps in awe and fear. The howl was repeated, long and mournful.

"Come forth, fiend!" she shouted again. "I command you!"

Manus practically burst out of the stone this time, and as before, he wore the monstrous form of the bogie beast the villagers feared. He lurched over to the edge of the circle of salt, then threw himself back as though repelled by the crystalline white matter mixed into the heather. There he stood and snarled, flexing his muscular build and raking the air in Ginny's direction with those talons. She was aware of women hiding their faces or peeping out from behind trembling hands while men glowered at the naked beast so openly displaying its exaggerated manhood to their wives. Ginny merely eyed the false form with cool indifference, and thumping her staff on the ground, she shouted, *"Loisg!"*

Fire flared to life at the edge of the salt circle, and Manus twisted and howled and raged as though fearing those flames would really consume him. Ginny began to mutter under her breath. *"Fribble antwar mowry agora,"* she said and watched the gleam of amusement that filled Manus' eyes. The words she chose were mere child's babble and meant nothing, but the villagers looked impressed to hear what they assumed were words of the mage tongue. She walked the fiery circle in a clockwise motion, thumping the heel of her staff on the ground at each cardinal point, then came back to where she had started. Reaching into her pouch, she pulled forth a handful of leaves and straw and tossed these high into the air where the gentle wind sent them fluttering across the flames. Where they touched fire, there was a hiss and a pop, and they would ignite and spiral to the ground.

"Begone and never more come to this place, foul fiend, begone!" she shouted.

Manus' long howl ripped the air and had several of the locals cringing as he made himself vanish.

Cheers went up all around her. With a sigh, Ginny called to the water in the loch and conjured the essence of that element to dowse the flames before the heather could catch and endanger the crofts and grazing grounds around the loch. And she sensed the shift of magic essence as Manus slipped quietly away while she listened to the villagers carry on in gratitude. They offered her brass sgillins to pay for her wondrous services, but these she refused, asking instead for bread and cheese, and a small supply of candles. The folk of Conorscroft seemed relieved that their mageborn wanted little more than practical things. Once the items were produced, Ginny was able to get on her way and return to her cottage. She could imagine the tales of her victory that would be repeated in the tavern tonight. And wondered what manner of tales they would tell if they knew the truth.

She found Manus seated on the rim of the well as she strolled up the path. He looked quite pleased with himself.

"Did ye see their faces?" he said. "All that tittle-tattle ye nattered for a spell was pretty convincing to them, lass. I dare say they'll be talking about this for generations to come, and bringing all manner of problems your way for a time, now that you've proven your worth by vanquishing the dreadful bogie."

"You were obviously enjoying yourself," she said as she released the magelock on the cottage door and stepped inside.

" 'Twas my pleasure to be able to assist you," he replied, following her through the opening.

She sighed and glanced over by the hearth. Fafne and Thistle were curled together on the floor asleep like a contented pair of well-fed pups. A faint smile stretched her lips as she put her rewards away. Part of her felt just a little guilty for taking these wares in trade for doing nothing. On the other hand, if she considered them compensation for disturbing her precious peace, she felt a little better.

"Now, we just need to take the lad to Caer Keltora . . ." Manus began.

"It's past noon," Ginny said wearily. "A little late to be starting out for Auntie Maeve's. We wouldn't get there until dark, and I don't relish the thought of facing the Nidubh and her pack in the gloaming."

"We wouldn't have to worry about that if you'd just let me use your body for a bit, lass," Manus said.

"No!" she retorted, narrowing her eyes to let him know she would brook no further argument on the matter.

"But every night we delay getting this lad to the Mage Council of Caer Keltora, 'twill make matters all the worse for him," Manus insisted. "You know as well as I that the spell of transformation, even half done as it is, has already started to affect the lad. Look at him. Chasing rabbits under the moon and frightening the hens. Delay matters longer, and 'twill be harder even for those great mageborn to separate the dog from the lad."

"I know the danger," she said, "but I will not consent to having you use my body to open a gate, and you've no right to demand such of me. Now do me the courtesy of respecting my wishes in this matter, or I swear, Manus, I'll lock your spirit in that cairn and never let you out again!"

Fire filled his expression for a moment, and she wondered if he was going to burst into a conflagration before her eyes. Instead, however, he threw up his hands, wearing a look of disgust and started back for the door at a brisk march.

"You're a hard creature, lass," he growled. "Small wonder I found the heather ale better company even after ye came."

With those words, he whisked his essence through the wood of the door and vanished, leaving her alone with the lad, the dog and her own dark distress.

Chapter Ten

Thistle and stone, why does she always have to be so stubborn! Manus thought as his essence surged southwest through the lower end of Tamhasg Wood and towards the brook. *Lock me into my cairn, indeed!* It wasn't like he was planning to use her to spell cast for the rest of her natural life. As much as life restored would have pleased him, he had grown rather fond of this existence. No responsibilities. No pain of loss.

Still, it galled him at times to think he'd given her shelter and knowledge, and for all his kindness and patience with her, she had hidden her feelings behind a mask of indifference. The lass was too solemn for her own good. Granted, he understood why she loved her solitude. He had loved his own before Mary captured his eye and gave him reason to believe the mortalborn were more than a lackwit bunch of bogie-shy fools determined to waste his precious time with their petty problems. *Hout Awa, the things they used to come asking my assistance for!*

He stopped his restless flight through the boles of trees and hummocks of moss to come to rest at the edge of the brook near the wood wight's bottom oak. He sensed the shy bogie within her tree. Her essence grew still, as though she feared he had come to summon her for some task. Manus sighed and floated himself to the ground amid the gnarled roots to stare at the water washing its way across stones smoothed by time and flow.

The folk of Conorscroft used to come asking him for

love philters and good crops and to find lost objects, and though he did these things and received reward for them, he always felt that he was wasting his power on trivial matters. Three or four generations of giggling lasses and lumbering lads had started to wear on him after a time. If only they would set real challenges for him to master. But it was no use. Conorscroft was nowhere near any of the major ley lines, that grid of power that crossed the world. It boasted no demons. No clan wars. Not even another mageborn. In all the years Manus had lived here, the only mageborn he had met were those who traveled, stopping in occasionally. In fact, the only other mageborn he knew that had ever lived anywhere around Conorscroft was the old Uncle, who Manus came here to learn his craft from as a lad. The mage blood didn't flow in the veins of the locals, he learned long ago. Even his own Uncle was an outsider.

There were times he swore he was the only mageborn around the height and breadth of Keltora before Ginny showed up that miserable night. Even then, the fey touch of her mage essence had excited him. But the lass herself was another matter. Pretty she was, in a shy, birdlike way, but her sharp and willful manner gave the beauty a cold edge, like a sparrow hawk ready to defend its nest from any interloper. Too young to be so old and untrained. Still, when she came, he thought briefly that the gods had cared enough to send him mageborn company this time.

Not true, he realized as the months wore away. Ginny might have been as winsome and quiet as a mouse on the outside, but she hid the heart and temper of a badger underneath the stoic fey countenance. She kept to herself, never wanting to be close to anyone, and woe betide any man foolish enough to believe he could reach into the den where she hid her heart and draw back all his fingers.

Sometimes, Manus cursed the men who made her feel this way towards those of his gender. Most particular among them, he cursed her father, for the man had dared to come after her once he found out where she had hidden herself. He arrived one evening before Manus went wandering, banging on the cottage door and calling for Ginny to come out or face the consequences. Manus had been tempted to let Thistle tear the man's ankles to shreds. Fergus MacCooley was a man who would not take telling, a man who would have wound his kilt the wrong way for the sheer contrary nature of it.

By then, Ginny had learned enough control of her untrained power to keep the hearth fire normal. She showed no fear as her father ranted how she had no right to run off because she wasn't yet of age. He threatened to drag her home by her hair if she didn't come with him willingly.

Manus was not about to allow that to occur. He could have easily slammed this man to the ground, even without the aid of his magic, but he knew it was not a wise mageborn who uses his strength and attacks an unarmed man in any fashion. Mageborn might be protected by their birthright in Keltora, but they were subject to the same laws as mortalborn where assault was concerned. So instead, Manus took a more political route and brought up the matter of the King's laws concerning mageborn. He let MacCooley know that if he so much as tried to force Ginny to leave this place or to wed a man against her wishes, the man would find himself in chains before the Mage Council in Caer Keltora. Any man who broke the King's laws and denied a mage child their freedom and training would forfeit all he owned to the Council and the King, and spend the rest of his life in a dungeon, provided he was allowed to keep his head.

MacCooley backed down to hear this, muttering all manner of unkindness against every creature born to be a mage. Ginny was left alone by her family after that, and she told Manus she was grateful, but it never went beyond that.

How long Manus sat brooding, he could not say. Time was irrelevant to one who walked the path of the soul. But he did realize that the world was shifting from bright to gloomy as the sun sank behind the western moors, and an eerie stillness filled the air.

Across the brook, mage eyes detected a movement that mortal eyes would never have seen until it was too late. Forms were undulating across the heather, a gentle flow of red-gold beasts. There was no moon up yet, but he did not need it to see the pack. Twenty of them in all, the color of fire and sunset, crossing the moor to the far side of the water.

Manus slowly rose to stand as a translucent figure on the far edge. Folk believed that spirits and bogies could not cross running water, but he knew this to be false. Besides, these hounds were not unseelie, in spite of the hint of magic that surrounded them. They were flesh and blood under a wicked enchantment. Living beasts that were once women and men.

Cautiously, they hovered at the edge of the brook and drank deep of the cool water, tongues lapping the flow as their sorrowful eyes scanned the bank beyond. That they could see him, he had no doubt, for it was believed that dogs possessed the second sight. Thistle had certainly proven that to be true, for he saw Manus every time he visited the cottage.

Manus moved forward, standing over the water. Some of the hounds shied back at the sight of him. Others moved around, always wary, eyes fixed on him. He studied each hound in turn until one in particular caught his eyes. A handsome beast with a masculine gaze, the hound did not turn aside as the others did. In fact, there was a strong hint of recognition in the stare, and Manus felt that he knew that look. He came on across the brook and crouched before the hound.

"Gabhan?" Manus said. "Gabhan MacArdagh?"

The hound growled low, backing off a step.

"You've nothing to fear from me, Gabhan," Manus went on. "I want to help you, and your son. You remember Fafne, don't ye?"

The hound stopped growling. The eyes fixed Manus with a plea.

"The lad's safe enough for now, and as soon as we get him to Caer Keltora, the Mage Council will be told of your tragedy. They'll stop her, Gabhan, and they'll find a way to free you from this curse."

Another snarl broke the night, not the earthly sound of hounds, but the ethereal wail of a beast not of this world. The red-gold hound shied away suddenly, leaving a straight path to Manus, who looked up in time to see the black form surging towards him with eyes of fire blazing.

The Nidubh.

Manus generally prided himself on not being a man easily deterred by matters of grave and immediate concern, but the sight of that hideous creature lunging towards him across the heather was enough to send his heart—had he still possessed one—thundering. A crude epithet escaped his lips, along with a sound that was a cross between a rooster's squawk and Thistle's yelp, as he scrambled to get back across the brook. Then again, he reflected as he floundered in a clumsy manner that belied his spectral state, demons had no fear of running water either. The Nidubh came charging at him, jaws snapping as he flitted backwards towards the southern depths of Tamhasg Wood.

He sprinted his essence through a huge tree just as the Nidubh threw herself at him. The beast apparently forgot to shift forms, because she slammed into the solid oak, knocking herself back. That delay was what Manus had hoped for. He spun himself invisible and rose towards the tops of the trees. The Nidubh circled around under him, barking in frustration. Then she shifted her own form and sprouted wings, and Manus felt his soul lurch in dismay. Horns, he'd forgotten that Greater Demons could shift shape with ease. And in spite of his invisible state, the Nidubh could see him. Not good.

He willed his essence to streak towards the cottage. If he could get inside the boundary stones marked with Ginny's wards before the Nidubh caught him, he would be safe enough.

He hoped.

Chapter Eleven

The afternoon waxed quietly for Ginny once Manus departed in a huff. She refused to allow herself to dwell on the lump his words left in the pit of her stomach. *Found the heather ale better company, indeed!* Just like a man to consider his ale better solace than a woman. *As if we existed solely to satisfy their whims and bear their bairns! As if we could not feel!*

She pushed the anger away and busied herself with preparing for tomorrow's trip to Auntie Maeve's cottage over in Ghloelea. Naturally, the wards of her own cottage would need doubling to keep bogie folk and bandits at bay. And as much as it irked her to have to bargain with the creature, she was sure she could convince the hob to look after the hens in exchange for their eggs. Of course, she would have to make certain the little bogie understood that the free meals stopped as soon as Ginny returned. She would have asked one of the villagers, but they were always uneasy about coming into Tamhasg Wood without their local mageborn there to protect them. They believed it was haunted, no matter how hard Ginny tried to convince them otherwise.

She packed a few items of clothing and food into an old leather shoulder sack Manus had kept for such occasions when he was alive. Then she worked on putting the cottage in proper order, physically and magically. The former involved old-fashioned straightening, while the latter took more time and required concentration as she sat in the center of the cottage and sent mage senses out around her to test and strengthen her boundary stone wards.

Thistle aroused in the middle of the afternoon, and whined to go outside, so she let him. The departure of his warmth awoke Fafne as well. She set the lad down with the task of peeling tatties so they could have a warm stew in their bellies that night. Fafne proved awkward with the knife, gouging as much potato as skin until he was down to lumpy knobs for the pot. A waste, Ginny thought, but did not say so, and wondered just why she felt less impelled to scold him.

Because he's not to blame for the misfortune that has fallen upon him. A feeling she knew all too well from her own childhood. She had not asked to be mageborn, but the gift of magic, Manus explained, had nothing to do with choice. It was in the bloodline, passing dormant through some and active in others, and even mageborn were hard pressed to know just which member of the family would be blessed with the talent until the signs manifested. There were families throughout Ard-Taebh in which the mage blood was so strong, several mageborn appeared in a single generation, while others might have to search several generations back in their ancestry to know the reason. Ginny, at least, knew she had a great uncle on her mother's side who had been a formidable mageborn by his reputation. But alas, mage flesh was still mortal, and Ginny was given to understand that his death was as ignoble as a bit of bad beef and spoiled gravy devoured late one night after a rigorous bit of conjuring.

The meal was ready by sunset. As the gloaming fell, Ginny called Fafne to the table, ending the game of tug-o-war he and Thistle championed with a bit of rope. Apparently, the pair of them had reached that point of canine tolerance which dogs generally shared, though she wasn't sure at the moment which one had claimed the alpha role. Probably Thistle, since he had already firmly planted himself in that position after Manus died, leaving Ginny to resign herself to knowing that she could sometimes order the moor terrier about until she was blue with rage. He was quick to obey only when it truly suited him to do so, though food seemed to be the key to Ginny's moderate success. Like most dogs, Thistle was a glutton.

She was serving the tattie stew when the distant baying of hounds caught her ears. Both Fafne and Thistle perked up at the sound, and the moor terrier quickly abandoned his place under the table where he had been waiting for scraps, bolting over to stand in the southwest corner, hair bristling as he growled and scruffed the floor with his hind feet.

Oh, dear, Ginny thought and closed her eyes, stretching mage senses towards the commotion. She felt Manus' essence first, and behind it came the black surge of demon essence that could only be the Nidubh.

"Stay inside," she said to Fafne and, snatching up her staff, she headed for the door.

She closed it behind her, taking a moment to set the magelock by tracing a glyph and whispering, *"Fuirich duinte."* Then she bolted around to the southwest corner of the cottage. Mage senses urged her to look up, and she did, her chin nearly falling to her knees in astonishment. Manus was streaking through the treetops in an erratic pattern, and flitting behind him like a giant bat after a moth came the Nidubh. In a mad game of tag, they wove and dodged around the bone-bare branches of the wood. Occasionally, Manus would go through a tree, but the Nidubh would manage to whip sideways to avoid a collision and be after him again.

"Manus!" Ginny cried.

"No time to chat, lass!" he called down and dove groundward. She saw his essence vanish into the soil before the Nidubh landed and started to dig with unbridled fury.

Unwilling to watch the mad spectacle go on any longer, Ginny planted the heel of her staff on the ground before her and tightened her hands about the wood. She closed her eyes and shifted her concentration into the staff, using it to anchor her mage essence to the earth as her senses reached for the boundary stones. Long ago, under Manus' teaching, she had fused elemental power into each one, and as Ginny touched that well of power, she drew its force to her and opened her eyes. The ground around the cottage began to glow, and the sudden swell of that magic distracted the Nidubh. A demonic parody of a hound's face swung around to glare at Ginny. She snapped one hand towards the Nidubh and shouted, *"Gath saighead buail!"*

A bolt of bright power sprang from her hand and raced at the Nidubh. With a howl, the demon hound flung itself away, but it could not avoid the strike. When the arrow bolt hit, fire exploded white around the creature. The Nidubh shrieked and fled towards the moors, engulfed in white flames, and in its cry of pain, Ginny heard the echoing howls of the red-gold hounds. Their song filled the wood like an omen of doom. Ginny found she could not bear the hideous chorus. It would drive her mad if she did not draw the spell of silence around herself.

Which she did with great effort, finding stray essence still wafting through the ground to feed the casting. She drew the glyphs and whispered the spell. Silence fell around her like a cloak, leaving the deafening echo on her ears like one felt from being near a waterfall too long.

Manus suddenly appeared before her, rising from the

77

ground like a mist. He gestured, but she could not hear him, only saw the frantic mask of his features as he yelled at her. In desperation, he reached for her, intangible hands gliding coldly into her flesh. She would have jerked away, but the spell to stop the Nidubh had been too draining on her. So she stood there, feeling the chill on her flesh where his hands were and wondering what he was about to do to her, when his voice vibrated inside her.

"Horns, Ginny!" his voice echoed in her head as though it were a hollow cavern. "The hounds are at the door!"

Ginny blinked and turned towards the cottage, then bolted back around to the front where she found the pack of red-gold hounds pawing and scratching at the stout wooden door. She quickly threw off the silence spell. Inside the cottage, Thistle's mad barking snapped a sharp contrast to the deeper throaty snarls of the hounds. She could also hear Fafne's terrified cries.

She stretched out a hand and started to cry, *"Solus,"* when she felt the sudden well of dark power, and heard Manus' warning shout. Turning, she saw the Nidubh had returned, looking mottled and scorched, and even angrier than before. Snarling, the demon lunged at her, and all Ginny could do was throw herself aside to try and avoid the attack.

"Hey, ye foosty auld besom!" Manus shouted, and Ginny felt his essence whisk past her, drawing the Nidubh's attention. "Your mother was a bogie hen, and your father was a frid, and ye couldn't catch yourself if you tried!"

The Nidubh turned, snapping its jaws at Manus, who barely slipped his essence out of reach in time. Still growling, the demon lunged again, but Ginny had taken the moment of distraction to charge to her feet, and seizing on the essence of fire from her hearth, she shouted, *"Loisg!"*

78

Fire encompassed the Nidubh, and this time it fled rather than be consumed. Ginny then turned to the hounds at the door and shouted, *"Solus!"* rolling light into their midst. Like the Nidubh, they fled. She quickly snatched up her staff and raced for the cottage, touching the magelock and whispering the spell to open it before throwing herself inside. This time, the bar was slammed into place, and she leaned against the door to catch her breath as Manus slid through the wall at her side. She ignored him, for her knees felt too soft to support her any longer, and her heart was anvil strokes hammering inside her chest, making her light-headed. Too much power drawn too fast without sufficient stricturing could leave a mageborn weak.

"You look as though you'd seen a ghost," Manus said with a mischievous wink.

Ginny merely sank to the floor, resting her head on her knees. When she finally stopped trembling and looked up to survey the cottage, she found Fafne crouched in the corner behind the tub. Thistle was merrily helping himself to a portion of stew that the lad had spilled in his frantic flight.

First light, she thought. *We will leave at first light, and please, Arianrhod, protect us!*

There'd be more than one magelock put on the door to-night.

Chapter Twelve

A restless night passed like treacle, and by the time dawn broke and Manus returned to his cairn, Ginny was exhausted. All through the dark hour, she felt the Nidubh's anger. The creature prowled the edges of the reinforced wards in a restless manner, determined to find a weak point, but if Ginny was anything, she was thorough. Still, her skill did not stop the Nidubh from calling on other sources of torment. Out on the moors and through Tamhasg Wood, the red-gold hounds bayed until Ginny wondered how their lungs could not ache. She was forced to restore the spell of silence around her cottage to keep Fafne and Thistle quiet. At least, they managed to fall asleep.

Manus remained with Ginny through the night, puzzling as to how the Nidubh had been able to pass the boundary stones uninvited. No demon could cross such wards without assistance from some source. The bloodmage was Ginny's first offering, but Manus declined to agree. Bloodmagic possessed too obvious a taint to go unnoticed except where it was carefully disguised, and he was more inclined to think the bloodmage in question had more pressing matters to attend.

"Elsewise she would have been here long before now," he said. "She seemed far more concerned that her intended sacrifice might do himself harm. No, I think it was the other hounds who let the creature in. They're mere flesh and blood, and your boundary stones are not set against mortal beings. They came to the door, and since the Nidubh is in command of them, they could have easily opened the way for her demon essence to follow."

He went on to speculate that if the hounds had managed to get into the cottage, there would have been little Ginny could do to keep the Nidubh from crossing the threshold as well. Such a suggestion left Ginny cold to the bone. To fight the Nidubh out in the open was one matter. To fight such a creature within one's sanctuary against the world was no advantage at all.

Ginny struggled from her bed when morning light finally crept through the cracks in the shutters. Wrapping her plaid shawl about her shoulders, she stepped over Fafne and Thistle coiled together before the hearth so she could start water for tea. She could have boiled the water more quickly with magic, as some mageborn were wont to do, but the ever-practical side of her believed magic was not the solution to everything. Coaxing the fire to burn, however, was another matter. Ginny couldn't begin to recall the number of arguments she'd had with Manus over the matter of practical use of the power they both possessed. Like many male mageborn, Manus was too much in love with making a grand display of the most trivial spells, and saw nothing wrong with a flamboyant display of power.

Once the tea brewed and slid its warmth down her throat and through her limbs, Ginny felt alive enough to cloak herself for travel and rouse the lad. Fafne muttered protests for the early hour, but they had a long way to go that day. Auntie Maeve's cottage in Ghloelea was more than half a day's walk, and Ginny wanted to get there well before dark.

She hurried the lad through preparations, then collected two eggs to make her bargain with the hob. The small creature was more than agreeable on the matter of the hens, swearing to look after them as though they were its own, and she halfway wondered if that meant a few of the birds would be missing when she returned. With Thistle on his rope leash towing Fafne, they set out through the wood and over the moor. She stopped at Manus' cairn, calling him forth as she collected one of the smaller stones from the pile and placed it in her belt pouch. Manus could roam freely as far as Dun Ardagh, and even a little ways beyond, but Caer Keltora was too far outside his incorporeal range. He would need the company of one of his cairn stones to provide a means of extending the limit and, since he could not carry the stone himself, Ginny had to oblige him.

They crossed the moor for quite a ways before making for the western road. The last thing Ginny wanted was for the villagers of Conorscroft to see her walking along with the two creatures she was supposed to have banished from their midst. They followed the road with their backs to the rising sun. At Manus' suggestion, Ginny laid a spell to cloak the trail her own mage essence might leave, and though she would not be able to maintain it over the two leagues they would be walking, for a short ways, it would help create a gap that would slow any who might try to follow her by magical means.

Midmorning, they stopped to rest on the roadside. What little traffic they had seen consisted of a tinker's wagon going east. Ginny stopped the man to ask about the road.

"Dogs everywhere," was his reply. "They're making short work of lambs and calves for a good league around Dun Ardagh."

"Have you been to Dun Ardagh?" she asked.

"Naught much there to see. The place is deserted these days. No one wants to go up there because of the dogs."

Ginny mulled this news as they continued on their way.

The hounds that were once Ardagh's household were obviously staying close to home, which was good in a sense. But their behavior indicated that they were straying farther and farther from their human nature, if not their home. And if locals, unaware of who the hounds truly were, started taking matters into their own hands, it could turn into a massacre.

At length, they came to a path off the road that led through a patch of pines. Ginny started into the thin shade with a smile, following a trail that few other than mageborn could discern among the trees. They emerged on a misty moor from which Ghloelea took its name. Even now, in the warm spring afternoon, patches of fog drifted over the ground like spirits wandering from their graves. The land here was damp and boggy, and ancient willows were fond of planting themselves about its sodden expanse. As a child, Ginny had witnessed that very old willows did indeed still walk from time to time, so she did not blame them for congregating in a place that suited them best.

Auntie Maeve's cottage was stone and sod, so at first glance, it always reminded the visitor of a barrow mound. But barrows didn't billow smoke through chimney holes, leaving Ginny to wonder if the mist on the moor had another purpose. It was not unlike a mageborn to set such spells about to disguise their dwellings.

As they came closer, Ginny could see a dozen or more hens ranging about in search of grubs and worms. They scattered, however, when Thistle bolted merrily barking into their midst. The moor terrier stopped short when the cottage door opened to spill forth a striped ball of feline attitude as wide as it was tall. With a yelp, Thistle dove for the safety of Ginny's divided skirt. Apparently, his last encounter with this porcine furball was still a fresh memory.

The cat waddled forward and issued a nasal growl of warning as it seated itself among the hens and glowered at the dog invading its territory. As if understanding that they were safe, the hens lined themselves behind the cat to continue their foraging.

"Even her cat's as mad as a bogie hen," Manus whispered in Ginny's ear. "I heard a tale once that the beast raised the chicks like kittens."

"Now, now, Orcla," a woman said from the depths of the doorway. "That's no way to greet our guests."

As Auntie Maeve emerged from the shadows, it was hard not to notice that she bore a very strong resemblance to her cat in that she was round and short. She had piles of frothy white hair on her head, a long portion of which fell down her back in a single arm-thick braid. Her clothing appeared to have been conjured from an assortment of tartan scraps, all carefully sewn to create a lovely pattern that shifted like an aurora with each movement, and made it difficult to tell where the plaids ended and Auntie Maeve began.

There were those who declared the old woman was more seelie than human, but since all mageborn were descended from the Old Ones who mixed their blood with that of mortalborn after the Great Cataclysm, it was easy to understand why. According to Manus, Auntie Maeve was older than the Unification of the Fourteen Kingdoms of Ard-Taebh, and might have been nearly as old as the Great Cataclysm itself, but since she had long ago forgotten her own age, no one could be sure.

"Ginny, my child," Auntie Maeve cried, her face lighting with delight as she strolled forward with far more grace than one would have expected for her age. "It's so kind of you to stop by for a visit with me. How are you, my child?"

Soft hands like warm dough reached out to take Ginny's

face and plant a motherly kiss on her forehead.

"I'm doing as well as to expected under the circumstances," Ginny said.

"Well, it's good to see you anyway," Auntie Maeve said. "And you too, Manus, my lad."

She released Ginny and reached for Manus' hand. He stood there with a mask of amusement on his face to see her do so. Auntie Maeve didn't seem the least disturbed when her fingers passed through his ethereal form. Besides, her attention had already drifted to the shy figure now standing back of Ginny, tail tucked between his legs in uncertainty.

"And who is this fine-looking lad?" Auntie Maeve said in a gentle voice that must have put the lad at ease, for slowly the tail slipped free and began to wag.

"If he rolls over and shows her his stomach, I'll laugh," Manus said quietly.

Auntie Maeve cast Manus a warning glance, and he hitched back as though expecting some retribution. Ginny sighed and stepped towards Fafne, reaching out to take his arm and lead him closer to the old woman.

"This is Fafne MacArdagh," Ginny said, "and he is the reason we've come to seek your help."

"MacArdagh?" Auntie Maeve said with a puzzled look. "Oh, dear."

"What?" Ginny said.

"So this is the reason for all the disturbances I've felt these last few days." Auntie Maeve walked around Fafne with a critical eye. She studied the tail and gently stroked fingers through the patch of pelt jutting from the neck of his shirt. "Partial transformation," she muttered more to herself. "This is most fascinating. I don't ever recall seeing its like before."

"Can you help him?" Ginny asked. "Can you change him back?"

"Well, I'm not exactly sure," Auntie Maeve said. "As I said, I don't recall *seeing* such a spell before, though I have *heard* of it happening under certain conditions. Tell me, lad, who put this curse on you?"

"I . . . I do not know her name," Fafne said.

"But she's wife to Rory MacElwyn," Manus was quick to supply. "I do recall she said that name."

"MacElwyn?" Auntie Maeve looked even more intrigued. "Are you certain, Manus?"

"I heard her say so myself," he said, looking a little put out to have to repeat the information.

"Oh, Blessed Lady of the Silver Wheel, that is interesting," she said.

"Why?" Ginny asked.

"You mean you haven't heard?" Auntie Maeve said.

"Heard what?" Ginny insisted.

Auntie Maeve sighed and looked around. "Perhaps we'd best all go inside," she said. "Such matters are not wisely spoken of outside proper protection, you know."

She turned and started for the cottage, shooing Orcla ahead of her. Ginny picked up Thistle to follow. The last thing she wanted was for the moor terrier to get his courage back and start a fight with Orcla. There were still scars visible just under his chin from their last disagreement.

"Well, come along," Auntie Maeve said. "You too, Manus, enter and be welcome."

"Fixed the wards on the door, did ye?" he asked as he bowed and paused at the threshold.

"No, but you reek of a hint of demon essence that tells me you've had a recent encounter with such a fiend, and that alone would bar you from my door if I didn't know you, lad," Auntie Maeve said blithely as she led them all into the comfortable dark of her cottage. "Hmph. Thinks I don't notice such things, just because I'm getting old. Would anyone care for a bit of cinnamon tea?"

Not one objection to the offer could be heard. And Ginny couldn't resist a smile. She could not recall ever seeing a spirit flush with embarrassment.

Chapter Thirteen

Though Auntie Maeve's cottage was dark and shadowy at the mouth, Ginny saw well enough to make her way into the earthy depths. They passed through a short tunnel that opened out into a bright, cheerful chamber where the walls had been carefully planked to keep out the cold and support shelves full of books and trinkets. The deep-seated windows were full of plants and herbs in troughs and hanging pots of every kind, and had colored glass pieced together to form pictures of mythical beasts behind the ornately worked wooden shutters. The polished oak of the furnishings around the stone hearth looked oddly opulent. The craftsmen who so carefully worked the wood had been quite skilled. As Ginny leaned closer, she could see woven knotwork carved to form both beasts and men.

Manus once hinted that Maeve was of noble blood, and that her kin, the MacAldens, had died out in Keltora long before the Unification, though a fair number of them still resided in the kingdoms of Loughan and Gwyrn. Such news left Ginny to wonder just how old the curtained bed with its lovely scroll carvings really was. Orcla waddled over to the bed, and used a set of carefully placed wooden steps to clamber up onto the quilt and make herself at home with true feline pomposity, watching Thistle through narrowed eyes as she settled into a single wad.

A little pot of tea was already brewing on the table. Auntie Maeve encouraged everyone but Manus into chairs, leaving him to deal with his ethereal self as he pleased. He made a face at her back and hovered in the air as though it were his favorite place, but if the feat impressed Auntie Maeve, she didn't show it. Instead, she made certain Fafne took one of the stools, claiming one with a tail would find it a more comfortable seat to occupy.

"Well, now," she said, serving tea to those who could drink it. "So have ye not heard that the traitor MacElwyn was taken to Caer Keltora to face the King's justice for plotting against the crown?"

"Yes, we've heard all about that from Fafne," Ginny said, glancing at the lad, who was trying to balance his wooden mug and pet Thistle at the same time. "It seems that was the event being celebrated at Dun Ardagh when the bloodmage came and put this curse on his family."

"And which bloodmage was that?"

"The woman who mentioned Rory MacElwyn could not be trusted to be left alone," Manus said.

"Oh, you saw her, did you?" Auntie Maeve asked.

"Aye, and the beast that answers to her."

"The Nidubh, you mean?" Auntie Maeve said.

"You know of the Nidubh?" Ginny asked.

"Oh, yes, I am well aware of that creature," Auntie Maeve said, taking a chair for herself and looking into her cup. "And as for the bloodmage, MacElwyn is her husband and she is none other than the Lady Edain. She wed Rory MacElwyn seven years ago, just past Summer Solstice."

Summer Solstice, Ginny thought. That was less than a sen'night from today. "Does MacElwyn know his wife is a bloodmage?" she asked.

"I rather doubt that," Auntie Maeve said. "Bad enough to have your son a traitor to the crown. And considering that'twas a bloodmage who killed the King's kin and forced the war that gave MacMorroch the crown, I doubt Rory

89

MacElwyn would be so foolish. Besides, I can't say that I've ever noticed any ill magic about Dun Elwyn before recently."

"Then where did she come from that MacElwyn would not know she was a bloodmage?" Ginny asked.

"That's the mystery of it all," Auntie Maeve said with a sigh. "She arrived in Dun Elwyn not more than a sen'night after Summer Solstice, and within a fortnight she was MacElwyn's second bride."

"What became of the first?" Manus interjected.

"No one is quite sure," Auntie Maeve said. "She was found dead, alone in her chambers, wearing a grimace of fright and pain. The healers thought her heart might have given out, since it was never very strong. Rory and his son Tomis were disputing borders with the neighbors at the time, so the lady was alone with her servants."

"Magic, then," Ginny suggested.

"None was found by the mageborn MacElwyn hired to look into the matter," Auntie Maeve said, looking surly for a brief moment. "But then, I was not asked to look."

Ginny saw Manus roll his eyes.

"And anyway, MacElwyns always had a dark and tragic history," Auntie Maeve continued. "The death of kin is rather commonplace in their walls, and very few of those have crossed to the Summerland by natural means."

"Not exactly a popular crowd," Manus said.

"Certainly not with the crown. Their ancestors supported the bloody MacPhearsons when the Black Cat of Dun Creag Dhubh was given the throne by that fool Ard-Ri who initiated the Unification."

" 'Tis said he didn't know what they were like," Manus suggested.

"He should have asked," she retorted sharply.

"So MacElwyn has never been popular," Ginny said, not willing to let the two of them start a tiff. She'd witnessed such senseless battles before, and knew they would go on for hours in this fashion if not stopped.

"Not at all," Auntie Maeve said. "But not a man foolish enough to wed a bloodmage willingly. In fact, auld Rory was a rather peaceful man. The only reason he still spat with MacArdagh over the borders was because it gave him a purpose that would keep others from saying he did not live up to his plaidie or his name."

"Then why would Edain want to turn every man, woman and child in Dun Ardagh into hounds?" Ginny asked.

"To stop them from standing witness, perhaps," Manus said. "After all, that night I saw her with the Nidubh, she and the beast were discussing how they had to find Fafne and us before we could spoil all her plans."

"What plans?" Auntie Maeve asked, giving him a hard look.

"To make sacrifice at the next Solstice. Apparently, she has made a bargain with Arawn to trade a soul for her own each seven years."

"But whose soul was she planning to trade?"

"Rory's, I'm willing to wager," he said. "She seemed eager to keep him from doing the deed to himself in his grief."

"Then that would explain what I heard," Auntie Maeve said.

"Which was?" Ginny said.

"Since Tomis was taken as traitor, Rory MacElwyn has been sick with grief. The first night after the young man's capture, he tried to throw himself from the walls of his own dun, but it seems his Lady was there and coaxed him otherwise. Since that day, I have heard that he is despondent and

91

will not eat, and that the Lady has ordered that all his weapons be locked from him until he recovers. That she keeps him locked within his own bedchamber, constantly attended, to prevent him doing himself harm."

"Where did you hear this?" Manus asked.

"From Orcla, of course."

"From Orcla?" Manus repeated and cast Ginny a look that said, *I told you so . . .*

"That's what I said," Aunt Maeve retorted stiffly, her lower lip jutting in determination. "Orcla's always been a valuable ear to the wind for me. She travels much farther than I am able, and she talks to all manner of creatures along the way. I do believe it was the crow that nests in the tower of Dun Elwyn what told her."

"And just how does Orcla impart this information to you, woman?" Manus said, crossing his arms and narrowing his eyes.

"She speaks to me," Auntie Maeve said.

"Speaks to you?" Manus said, feigning astonishment.

"Manus," Ginny hissed. She could see by the glint in his eyes that he was trying to start a row.

"No, I'm fascinated," he said. "I've ne'er heard a word from Thistle in ten years of his company. I'm curious as to what language the cat uses to speak to her, that's all."

"Manus MacGreeley," Auntie Maeve said in a dark manner. "You young mageborn have no idea how much the mageborn of my generation could do before the Unification. Those of us who were firstborn from the union of the Old Ones and mortalkind learned many spells and had many capabilities that you could not begin to comprehend. And one of those abilities was to understand the language of animals, which I would hardly expect you to be capable of, since it's impossible for you to shut up and listen to your betters even to draw a breath! Now, if you wish to continue the privilege of entering my household, I would suggest you learn better manners than to mock an old woman who has seen ten times the lifespan you enjoyed before you got yourself topped by a mere bandit! And if you don't wish to behave, I shall have to give serious consideration to putting your essence into a bottle just to keep you quiet."

Manus sulled up, crossing arms and legs as he floated aloft, and glowered at Auntie Maeve.

"Can you really put him in a bottle?" Ginny asked.

"Oh, yes, and he knows it, since I did it to him once before when he made me cross," Auntie Maeve stated proudly.

"Now, that is a spell I would love to learn," Ginny said, smiling up at Manus' essence.

"Then I shall teach it to you," Auntie Maeve said.

Manus looked like he wanted to chew the stones of the cottage into slivers.

"However, there are other matters I need to consider for now," Ginny said. "Foremost on the list being getting this poor lad to Caer Keltora to see if the mageborn there can find a way to free him and his family of this curse."

"It's a long way to Caer Keltora," Auntie Maeve said with an uneasy shrug.

"But surely you can gate me there," Ginny said.

Auntie Maeve slowly shook her head. Her face was a map of the passing of time she had seen, and suddenly she looked very ancient. "My dear, the gate spell is quite a drain on an old creature like myself. I doubt I could find enough power to hold open a gate all the way to Caer Keltora and Dun Gealach. I'm not as young as I used to be."

"I told you," Manus said pointedly, and Ginny started

thinking more seriously about that bottle spell.

"But there has to be some way we can get word to the Mage Council about what has happened here," Ginny insisted.

"Well, there might be one way," Auntie Maeve agreed, "but I fear it means you'll have to go to Alansglen."

Ginny made a face. Alansglen was at least three days south of Auntie Maeve's on foot, if one cut straight across the moors. "Why Alansglen?" she asked.

"There are several mageborn there who would gladly help you. I just wish I could, my child, but an old mageborn knows her limits."

"Then, I guess we'll be back on the road in the morning," Ginny said with a sigh. Not a prospect she looked forward to, but what other choice did she have?

"Oh, you might not have to take the road, dear," Auntie Maeve said. "That much I can try to do for you."

"You can gate me to Alansglen, then?"

"Oh, no. Even that would be too far for me. But if I can find my scrying mirror, I might be able to contact one of the mageborn living there and see if they are willing to open the gate for you."

"Ginny?" Manus said. "There's always my way."

"No," she said and frowned at him for daring to make such a suggestion again.

"You'll stay the night, of course," Auntie Maeve insisted with a weak smile.

"Of course," Ginny said.

Three days to Alansglen.

By the Lady of the Silver Wheel, I hope we can make it there some way.

Chapter Fourteen

It was said that a spirit must sleep when the cock crows and sunrise sets the land afire, and that it could not walk again until the gloaming laid shadows upon its place of rest. Not entirely true, Manus knew all too well. Granted, he had to return to his cairn, or at least some portion of it, when the cock gave cry at dawn, but it was his experience that the dead did not sleep. That they waited inside their graves, counting the hours that no longer mattered until they could not abide the boredom. But dusk and dawn had nothing to do with the affair. Granted, Manus was more at home in the night; he felt more alive under the swell of the moon and the strength of the shadows. And he had died in the dark he so loved.

Tonight, he felt the old restlessness seeping into his essence. The women had long ago given over to slumber, as had the lad. Thistle and Fafne were curled together by the fire. Mother Maeve claimed her own bed, and Ginny was wrapped in blankets on a pallet drawn out for her comfort. She looked so vulnerable just now. So innocent and precious, tempting him to stretch forth a hand and rake fingers gently through the dark auburn tumble of tresses, only to watch them pass through the strands with no more disturbance than a faint breath. Alas, this spirit had no flesh with which to touch and feel. At least not in the physical sense.

Heart was another matter.

A little late for regrets, ye fool, Manus thought and turned away. No chance of ever changing what had been now. He had made his choice long ago, and for that matter, so had she. To wish for what was not meant to be was a waste of good time and energy. Too late to want what he could never have now.

He made a face, glancing at the table where Ginny had settled his cairn stone for his convenience. Quiet pervaded the whole cottage under the veil of the dark hour. Uneasy silence that burned him to action. The stillness was too much for a restless soul like his own. He needed his moors and his moon.

He stepped away from Ginny's sleeping form and became no more than mist, slipping through the cracks in the window frame and through the decorative gaps in the wooden shutters.

Outside, under the waning moon, the world was blue-white. Manus let his essence rise into that light, soaked it in like the warmth of the sun as he stretched spirit awareness around him to touch the wind that nudged clouds across the sky. He let his essence drift with it, like a swimmer on a stream, let it pull him along like a leaf caught in an autumn gale. The land flew beneath him, lochs and glens and moors and forest all becoming a rapid blur of indigo with flashes of milky white.

He found himself over a small farmstead north and west of Auntie Maeve's barrow-like abode. A flicker of amber candlelight attracted him, so he glided his essence down towards a shuttered window and once more slipped in through the cracks.

A woman's heavy moan shook him. There were several women about a bedchamber, and a young man, kilted in a plaidie, standing off to one side, holding the hand of a frail, damp lass who sat in a birthing chair. His whispered words of love and encouragement could barely be heard under her agonized cries, but Manus listened all the same, listened to the ease with which they fell from the young man's lips. *He truly loves her,* Manus thought, and briefly felt a twinge of envy that he had not been able to share such a moment with his Mary. He could not smell the coppery tang of blood, nor feel the closeness of the warm room. He could only watch as new life surged from between her slick thighs. Its fresh tingle was something he could sense, and it flickered with the hint of mage essence like a glim in the dark.

How easy it would have been to snuff that glim. To seize it at its moment of birth and become flesh again. The temptation was overwhelming, and Manus forced himself to withdraw from the house, to speed through the air and make for the home that was once his. To glide into the cold of his old cottage where dark shadows ruled in Ginny's absence. There, he seated himself before the hearth, running fingers through his hair, fighting the ache within. How could he even consider taking another life to restore his own! What would Ginny have thought of him for such a deed, for desiring to be flesh again so he could have another chance . . .

And why should he care what Ginny thought? Mary was the one whose love had sustained him in life and given him much to live for, and she was most likely laughing at him even now from the Summerland for being such a mutton-headed fool. *Mary, what have I done?* If she were here now, she would likely have scolded him for his faithless desires . . .

"Why should I scold you for wanting what is natural?" a voice frail with age seemed to whisper out of time. *"I will be dead and gone, and you are still a man . . ."*

"Mary?" he said, raising his head to stare at the shadows above. She did not answer, so he pushed himself up, passing through the wooden beams and board to enter the loft where the old trunk now sat gathering dust. "Mary?"

He put hands to the wood and leather, but they only passed through, groping uselessly at the dresses and shawls and womanly trinkets she had worn and adorned herself with in life. Nothing could he touch. Nothing could he feel, and it spurred remorse in his soul so that he sat there, hands in the depths of her trunk and wept as a child would. Wept for the loss and the pain that never seemed to go away, no matter how long it had been. No wonder he had made a mess of his life, drowning her memories in heather ale. How could he blame Ginny for being unable to see what was in his heart when he had buried it under a cairn of stones with his beloved Mary's bones.

The ale had been his undoing. It had made Ginny hate him, and he could not blame her.

"Mary, I was so stupid," he whimpered. "I thought she could become what you were to me. I thought she could make me whole again. Instead, I drove her to despair."

Had he life and flesh to scourge now, he would have made himself pay for his stupidity.

He jerked himself away from the trunk, threw himself into the air, passing through the thatching of the roof and sprinting out into the night. Anguish was still in him, making him careless as he flitted about the sky, filling Tamhasg Wood with a beansidhe's wail. What did he care that the windows of Conorscroft would rattle from his cry? That the folk who lived there would believe they were being haunted by yet another bogie, and be back to beg Ginny's aid against the frightful beast. Wasn't that the whole reason to have a mageborn in the village? So they could solve all your problems with the whisper of a word and the flick of a hand?

When Manus suddenly felt the raw power of some dreadful unseelie darkness surging at him, he realized almost too late that there was a price to be paid for losing one's head in such a feverish manner. Still, he did his best to wrench his common sense back in place and flee from the evil essence of the Nidubh as the demon lunged for him. He barely twisted out of the way, barely escaped the snapping jaws eager to ensnare him. He shifted his essence into an intangible form, and sought refuge in the higher clouds.

However, the Nidubh did not bother to pursue him. Instead, the wretched demon hovered and laughed.

"We wondered where you were," she said in her fractured voice that sent shivers through his essence. *"We did not think you would have strayed so far from the little hedge witch's company, but it has been to our advantage that you did."*

"What?" Manus slipped out of the cloud and floated down to face the creature whose fiery eyes burned him over a fang-filled grin.

"You should never have left them unprotected, you know," the Nidubh said. *"My mistress has what she wants, and I will soon have what I desire."*

"What do you mean, ye wretched excuse for a bogie!" Manus demanded, lunging at the creature, only to pass through its cold form.

"You will find out when the cock calls," the Nidubh said, looking back over its shoulder at him. *"If you desire to wait so long, that is."*

With that, the Nidubh rolled into a ball and gated out of sight, leaving nothing more than a puff of black smoke to indicate it had even been there.

For a moment, Manus just hovered in the air, glowering at the empty space. What in the name of Cernunnos did the creature mean? *My mistress has what she wants . . .*

Fafne? Ginny!

"Horns!" Manus snarled and like the wind, he sprinted across the land, making for Auntie Maeve's cottage as fast as he was able. And once there, he hovered over the stone and sod structure, his entire essence tightening with horror. In the distance, he could hear the familiar high-pitched bay of a moor terrier on the rampage.

One end of the cottage now bore a gaping hole. Manus charged through the opening and found himself in the midst of chaos. Furnishings smashed and overturned. Boot prints and paw prints side by side amid smears of blood.

"Ginny!" he cried, wishing he had the power to throw the rubble askew. But all he could do was reach under broken wood and stone and hope to sense some semblance of mageborn life.

Which he did find back behind the overturned table. But it wasn't Ginny who lay unconscious on the floor. It was Auntie Maeve.

"Maeve!" he shouted. "Maeve, can ye hear me?"

She must have, for she moved, groaning and trying to push herself over with great effort.

"Maeve!" he shouted.

"I hear you, Manus," she muttered, slowly opening her eyes and looking up at him. "No need to shout, lad."

"What happened?"

"I don't know how they got past my wards," she said, wearily shaking her head as she cautiously pulled herself into a sitting position with great effort. "I never felt them coming. I wouldn't have known they were here at all had that wretched dog of yours not started yapping."

"What happened?" he repeated, wishing he could seize her and give her a hearty shake.

"I don't know. Your dog started barking, and then there was rock flying, and men and dogs pouring into the place. Before I could draw a breath to call a spell in my own defense, one of them punched me."

And hurt his hand, no doubt, Manus thought darkly, for he knew Maeve had never been frail.

"Where are Ginny and Fafne?"

"I . . . I don't know," she said. "But I think Thistle followed them . . ."

Manus hissed an oath. He would get nothing more, and he knew it. With a snarl, he charged out of the cottage, whipping into the air and following the distant howl that he now realized was his moor terrier.

He found Thistle just outside the northern edge of the forest that bordered Ghloelea. The moor terrier was racing around a spot and baying like one of the Wild Kin. Manus landed in the center of the circle the moor terrier ran and felt the coppery taint of bloodmagic in the weaving of a spell.

Gated away! But where? Or did he really need to ask, for knowing who the Nidubh called mistress, there was only one place they could possibly have gone.

Dun Elwyn, like as not. Though what he was going to do about it in his present state of existence was not a question he cared to ponder. He had no form to fight them like a man, and no flesh to let him cast spells. About as useful as the wind, he was.

And less so, he came to realize. For even as he stood in the circle, he saw the faint rime of a new dawn casting grey and pink on the horizon. The cock would crow, and there was naught he could do but find his cairn stone in the rubble of Auntie Maeve's hut.

"Thistle, wheesht!" he shouted in a voice that brooked

no argument. "Come, you mangy little burr bogie!"

It might have been the power that raged in his voice. Whatever the case, Thistle snapped to attention and followed Manus as he made his way overland towards Maeve's cottage.

Naught he could do until he had rested briefly in his stone.

And even after that, he didn't know what he was going to do to rescue Ginny and the lad. He could only hope the lass was working out her own plan.

Chapter Fifteen

Was I dreaming? Ginny thought as the dull throb of pain slowly pressed into her awareness. The back of her head hurt horribly. The world smelled rank as she took her first deep breath, and the surface on which she lay hardly felt like a comfortable pallet. With a moan, she opened her eyes and tried to move and spit out the corner of the blanket that had somehow gotten stuffed into her mouth. But her arms would not draw forward, and her eyes only perceived darkness that tickled her lashes. As for the blanket, it was firmly anchored into her mouth with a strip of cloth.

What in the name of Cernunnos . . .

She tried to move again, to no avail. Her legs felt free, but lying as she was and hampered by her own divided skirt, she found she couldn't do anything remotely graceful. Still, knowing Manus would have attributed it to a stubborn streak that he often compared to Thistle's, she got her knees under her and was able to shift herself upright. Kneeling in what felt like old reeds and soft dirt, she decided to rest a moment and let mage senses search the unknown around her.

As near as she could tell, she was alone in the immediate area, and by the odor and the general chill, she was likely in some sort of dungeon cell. Where, however, was another matter. She felt nothing remotely familiar within her first exploration, but here and there, her senses brushed a hint of bloodmagic's copper taint. One such brush felt like some sort of ward. Another seemed to be a spell of misdirection.

All carefully laid and ancient in texture. She pushed farther, hoping to find something she could anchor on and orient herself, when she touched an essence that recoiled in surprise before sending flashes of pain back to strike her. With a hiss, Ginny broke off the search, quickly drawing her mage senses back.

Horns, now they'll know I'm awake! she thought, and for some reason that frightened her. And it was in that moment of heightened perception that she began to recall just how she came to be in this terrible state.

Thistle's high-pitched ranting was the first clear impression to fall into place, for it had jerked her out of sleep. Muffled under slumber's weighty cloak, she had struggled to rise and put an end to the noise, only to learn the purpose behind it. The sharp sting of static gave her the first clue. Someone was casting a powerful spell that conjured lightning to strike one end of the cottage and shatter the wall.

After that, chaos reigned. Several men, cloaked in darkness so that Ginny could not even be certain they were real, poured through the gap that was left, accompanied by a pack of savage dogs. Auntie Maeve shouted in anger as Ginny tried to cast spells to deter both men and dogs. She worried about doing harm to the latter until one of the beasts lunged for her and gave her a look at the spiked collar around its thick neck. These were not the hounds that plagued Ardagh, but animals trained to hunt and kill. They would have torn her to shreds too, but Thistle made his little presence known by snapping jaws on a hamstring. The attacking animal yelped horribly and was flung off course by pain. Unfortunately, Thistle was flung off as well. But once he was clear, Ginny felt no compunction about throwing magebolts at these dogs and their masters.

Numbers, however, seemed to be on their side, and for some reason they did not fear her magic. For every magebolt she cast, there were two men unharmed who would move in to take the place of the fallen attacker. Soon enough, there was little she could do in her own defense, and to make matters worse, she heard Fafne cry out as he was cornered and seized. Auntie Maeve went to assist the lad, speaking the words of a spell, but before she could finish, one of the men struck her a hard blow to the face with his fist. Ginny cried out as the old woman was thrown to the ground, where she lay unmoving. With a snarl, the man finished by shoving the table over onto the old woman.

Ginny forgot her own danger then, shrieking in anger and fighting to reach Auntie Maeve's side. Alas, the men were on her before she could cross the jumbled room. She kicked and screamed, recalling that her own fists were hurting from battering against their leather armor. They merely forced her to the floor, pinning her there as she struggled like a wounded badger. Several healthy curses were spent against her, but in the end, she could not fight them. They shoved a lump of cloth into her mouth to bind her tongue. A blindfold was placed over her eyes and her wrists were bound together at her back. Traditional ways of subduing mageborn, she grimly noted, most of whom needed tongues to speak the words and hands to gesture in order to cast spells. Kicking proved useless, for though she still had her clothes on, she had removed her boots to sleep. Someone jerked her off the floor and flung her over his shoulders like a sack of wheat.

From there, she was carried off over rough terrain. She had the impression that Thistle was following, snapping at the heels of their attackers, and more than once, she heard the moor terrier yelp when he was cruelly kicked away.

Briefly, she even wondered where Manus had gotten himself off to, not that his spirit would have been able to assist her.

She was dumped on her feet then, staggering for balance and feeling the stiffness of heather and peat under her stockings. One of her captors seized her arm and started hauling her up a rise. It was then that she felt the prickly stab of fear. The taint of bloodmagic was suddenly around her. She could hear a woman's voice whispering the words of a spell with which Ginny was unfamiliar. And yet, a few of the words told her all she needed to know. A gate spell was being laid and she was being taken to another place. There was little doubt in Ginny's mind that it was a place she did not want to be, so in desperation, she jerked free of her captor's hand. Blind though she was, she threw herself at the source of the spell, hoping to distract the caster before she could finish the words.

Her guard, however, was not so appreciative of the trouble his diminutive prisoner caused. A heavy fist pounded the back of her head with one swift blow, and Ginny fell, getting lost in the dark realm of unconsciousness.

From there, all memories were faint, thought she did know one thing for sure. The magical essence that had cast the gate spell belonged to the one that had just meted swift retaliation against Ginny's search.

Oh, Blessed Arianrhod, Bright Lady of the Silver Wheel. What am I to do?

The heavy thunder of a metal bar thrown back and the groan of hinges long exposed to moisture knelled on her ears. "Will ye look at that, Seamus," a man said with a gruff chuckle. "Our little sparrow hawk has awakened."

Ginny reached out with mage senses, touching mortal

male essence. Of course, she could smell them as well, sweat and musk and leather mixed under ale. Two men entered her cell, and the thought was not pleasing to her. She heard them clump across the reeds towards her.

"All trussed up and waiting for us, Oran," the one she assumed was Seamus replied.

"I dunno," Oran said. "I could swear I heard the mistress say we was not to touch her."

"I'm wearing gauntlets, and so are you," Seamus said.

The words sent a chill flushing through Ginny. She sought to protest with a shout, but could manage no more than a muffled yell. A gloved hand latched onto her arm and pulled her off the ground. She started to kick at the owner, but they were shoving her back until she felt herself pressed against a damp stone wall. Every part of her protested the rough hands that began to course up and down her. One of them reached up and drew the blindfold up, giving her a glimpse of a rugged face under a thick beard. His partner was a round-faced youth.

"Better put that back," the latter said cautiously, and she recognized him as Oran. "She looks like she could burn you with her eyes."

"I doubt that," Seamus said, and his searching hand grew more aggressive. Ginny closed her eyes, fear tightening every fiber of her being in protest. *How dare they! What right did they have?*

None, she quickly realized, for tense as she was, she could not fail to sense the unseelie darkness that swelled behind them. She opened her eyes in time to see the Nidubh rearing over both men in some half-form with a hideous hound's head on a more humanoid female torso covered with black scales that glistened like obsidian. Ginny would have screamed if it were possible. Her sudden fright went unnoticed by Seamus and Oran, at least until claws seized each of them by the back of the neck and flung them both aside as though they were no more than a child's moppet. Ginny dropped to the floor and stared up at the back of the monstrous demon that turned, twitching a tail with a barbed end.

"SHE IS NOT FOR YOU!" the Nidubh howled.

Both men were scrambling now. One jerked his long dagger from its sheath and slashed at the Nidubh's frightful form. A claw snatched the blade from his grasp and flung it away. Ginny flinched as the steel struck the wall near her and ricocheted into the reeds. By then, both men were running for the dungeon door. They never made it. That sinuous tail lashed out, split and ensnared their legs like ropes, jerking them into the air and dangling them so their common plaids fluttered in the way of their flailing hands. Ginny watched the creature's tail continue to stretch and split as though it had no limit to the configurations it could perform. Thin strips suddenly wrapped about the men's upper bodies, hauling them around so the Nidubh was half an arm's length from each man's head. Ginny watched as those clawed hands lashed out like brigand's blades, razoring each man's throat in turn and drinking the blood.

She thought she would vomit and, with the gag in her mouth, Ginny knew she would choke. She closed her eyes, unable to watch the demon feast, wondering if that was to be her own fate. Her body convulsed in protest of the horrors she had witnessed. In spite of the anger she felt against these men, they did not deserve such a terrible fate.

A hand grasped her shoulder to steady her as she retched, and the gag was released, allowing air to enter her lungs more freely. She hunched forward, retching and sobbing until her stomach cramped and her mouth burned with bile.

"Get rid of them," a woman whispered.

Ginny slowly reared upright again and found a face before her that held a strange beauty in the cold features. Alabaster skin and white hair were a startling a contrast to the black linen gown and the strip of MacElwyn marriage plaid about slender shoulders, but not so much as the glacier blue eyes that bore into Ginny.

"I have already touched your mage essence, and I know the limits of your power," the woman said gently. "I will leave you ungagged and unbound, because I know you will be unable to escape this place unaided."

Ginny stared at the woman as she drew a small dagger from her ornate belt and cut the gag, then the ropes at Ginny's wrists. Pain flooded her limbs as her arms were finally returned to a normal position. She sat rubbing them and her aching jaw while watching the beautiful creature before her.

"Are you . . . the one they call Lady Edain?" Ginny asked, her own voice harsh from retching.

The icy glance narrowed over a faint slash of a smile. "Yes, not that the knowledge will serve you in any way you might find useful."

"Where's Fafne?"

"Fafne? Is that his name?"

"Yes," Ginny said. She could see the Nidubh slowly shrinking to become the black hound with the fiery eyes again. Of the men, there were no signs, leaving her to wonder if the creature had devoured them. She had heard that demons did that sometimes.

"You need not concern yourself with the lad," Edain said. "I will not kill him, for it would serve no purpose."

"But you will finish what you started and make him one of the hounds of Ardagh?"

"In time," Edain said, drawing back. "For now, I have other matters to attend. You need not worry about the men. Nidubh will see that they do not bother you again."

"Why protect me?" Ginny asked. "Why even keep me alive if I am a danger to your precious plan to sacrifice your husband to Arawn?"

Edain actually looked surprised. "How did you know of this?" she asked.

Ginny kept her mouth clamped tight, unwilling to give Manus away, but Edain merely nodded.

"The spirit mage," Edain said and smiled. "I thought I felt his presence at Dun Ardagh that night. Well, it does not matter anyway. Your knowledge cannot stop me."

"Then why waste dungeon space on the likes of me?" Ginny said as coldly as she dared.

"I have my reasons," Edain said as she started out of the cell. "Capturing the mage spirit will not be so easy. These matters must be done with every detail in place."

"Then, I am to be the bait?" Ginny said, trying to keep a hint of hope out of her voice. Manus was still free, and that might well be her only salvation.

"In a sense," Edain agreed. "Besides, to kill you now would merely give me power that will eventually be gone. But to give you to Arawn and your spirit mage friend to the Nidubh in one swift moment . . . that will buy me many years of Arawn's favor. And such sacrifices must be made in their proper time to reap the greatest benefit possible."

She slipped out of the dungeon, followed by the Nidubh. The door closed, the bolt clattered and Ginny was alone in silence.

A fine mess, she thought, straightening her disheveled clothes and looking for a more comfortable place, preferably away from where the Nidubh had killed the men, since

Ginny could still feel a hint of their deaths hovering on the stagnant air. The cell lacked a pallet on which to finish her sleep, so she pressed herself into a corner to keep her upright and allow her to watch the door.

Hopeless. As hopeless as the prospect of escape, it would seem.

Just where in the name of Cernunnos was Manus, anyway?

And how was Ginny going to warn him of the trap Edain had set for him?

Chapter Sixteen

Cock's crow came and passed, and Manus waited in the depths of the cairn stone, contemplating what had to be done. Find Ginny, for starters. And Fafne before the bloodmage was able to finish what she started with the lad. Simple matters for an ordinary man, who would merely have gathered a rank of his friends and stormed the countryside in search of the maid to rescue her. Not so simple for a spirit, even one with Manus' determination. His existence was strictured by powerful limitations. Besides, he'd never been all that good with a blade. Elsewise, he would have been less likely to die as he had on a bandit's rusty auld dagger.

As soon as he was able to rise from his stone, he set out to scour the countryside, but he was not so eager to let his presence be detected, so he dove underground and swam the murky depths of soil as though it were no more than water in a loch. Besides, it was the only way he could keep Thistle from following him. The moor terrier knew which hand fed him and was just as eager as Manus to see the lass again.

Auntie Maeve, in the meantime, headed for nearest croft to beg assistance of the men there to get her cottage back in order. And to get one of them to take a message south to a mageborn she knew lived in Alansglen who would be able to report the grave matters here to the Council of Mageborn in Caer Keltora. Three days there by foot or horse. Manus could have swiftly taken his incorporeal form to Alansglen and back, but he disliked the thought of straying so far from his cairn stone before the next cock's crow. As it was, he risked being out of range by going northwest towards Dun Elwyn, especially if the Nidubh or its mistress captured his essence. But that risk had to be taken if he was to find out where Ginny had gone. Her death would not do his conscience any good. Besides, the Nidubh was apparently not fond of light, so he doubted the demon would be out and about in the bright hours of day.

At length, Manus allowed himself to lift his head above the ground—invisibly, so as not to startle anyone. He had reached one of the outer holdings seated about Dun Elwyn, and the sun was straight overhead. All around him were sheep, and he admitted to himself that wet, muddy wool was one odor he gratefully did not miss in this afterlife. Cautiously, he lifted his essence higher, putting his head and shoulders above the animals grazing about, oblivious to his presence. Off to one side, he spotted the shepherd in charge of the lazy flock. A brief scry with mage senses—one of the few abilities left to him in death—assured him that the lad possessed no power to sense mageborn, dead or otherwise. Manus dared to move through the flock then, and noticed that some of the sheep tensed as he passed, but they did not panic and give away his presence. Too stupid, for which he was grateful.

He saw the distant structure of the old dun on a hill overlooking this green. It was a grim-faced configuration, the sort of keep intended to frighten those who dwelled about it into obedience. Manus rose into the air and flew around the glen that surrounded it, keeping a wary eye out for the dark presence that wanted his life. With each sweep, he drew closer to the walls, always alert to the danger he faced. But if his enemies were about, they were not keeping watch, or they believed he was a prisoner of the night.

At last, he was just outside the walls of the dun. Massive stones rose to end in crenellations like broken teeth across the top. Manus lay hands on them . . . or rather inside them. They were cold and tinged with death, and the sensations they invoked in his spirit essence brought him no pleasure. The burn of bloodmagic was everywhere. He sensed wards and deceptions, and at the center of it all, a presence that reeked of death.

He pulled back his hands and looked at the structure with a frown. Though he could have easily stepped through the wall and entered it, he was cautious. The Nidubh would likely be hoping for that very rashness from him. He could sense her demon essence in the spells that guarded this place as much as the essence of her mistress. He just wished he could sense where Ginny was being held.

To find her, I'll have to go inside.

Well, he would not do so as they expected, and with a sigh, he sank into the ground once more, going deep and being grateful that death meant he did not need to breathe.

Claustrophobic darkness surrounded him, broken by an underground stream. He glided through it until he found a stone substructure that was likely the foundation of the old hillfort that had occupied this tor before the coming of the keep. There were many such places throughout Keltora and the rest of Ard-Taebh. Some were thought to have been the dwellings of the Old Ones. Others defied even that explanation. When he first apprenticed to his own uncle, Manus remembered the man talking of the ancient days before the Great Cataclysm, and of the races of man and seelie who dwelled side by side. Man was an innocent then, according to his uncle. But Manus had cared not for such histories as a lad. All he wanted was to understand why this power was his and what he could do with it. He never realized until he was older that the tales his uncle related of the past were meant to give Manus that knowledge. To remind him that power had a price and the heritage of magic was not to be taken lightly.

Magic had betrayed the Old Ones. They who had been its greatest masters had, in the end, fallen to its power. For it was said they had meddled in nature beyond reasonable cause and brought about the very destruction that tore the world asunder. The Great Cataclysm that remade all the lands.

Manus was passing through the stone foundations when he sensed that matters were not right in this place. A tingle swept his frame, creeping into his essence. Magic, he realized, was here in the depths of the earth itself, and it took him but a moment to realize that what he felt brushing his spirit essence was a ley line, one of the many lines of natural power that stretched about the world. In his life, he had tapped such things for the magical essence they could afford him to use in spell craft. Ley lines were not particular where they ran, and this one seemed to stretch for a great distance in either direction underground. He had heard of such. Ley lines had no physical presence, and were not restricted by the barriers of nature. They could be found in the bottom of lochs and at the tops of mountains, and some of them formed a grid through the very air itself. Mageborn could use them for everything from guiding gate spells to feeding the fury of the elements . . . sort of like what the Old Ones did before they threw the balance of the world into chaos.

The power in this line flowed over his spirit essence like a refreshing bath. He paused for a moment to wallow in one of the few sensations he could still enjoy, momentarily forgetting the danger such power presented.

He got a swift reminder when he felt the surge of bloodmagic's taint stretching into the ley, reaching for him like an eager hand. *Horns,* he thought and jerked himself out of range, and though he evaded what he knew was nothing less than an attempt to capture his essence, he cursed himself to realize that, like a fool, he had given himself away.

He fled towards the stone foundations, seeking to get out of this depth before they could ring him in some manner of wards, but as soon as he reached the foundations, he knew he had tarried too long. His essence met the stone as a solid mass that would not let him pass. Where he touched it, he sensed that the bloodmage was once more trying to tighten her ring of wards about him to hold him captive.

He could not let that happen . . . not now.

Quickly, he dove deeper underground, stretching his senses to find an opening in the ever-widening web of power reaching for him. But it was growing harder to find those gaps. The magical net was tightening about him, shortening the distance he could move.

NO! he thought frantically, cursing himself for the folly of his careless nature. He had not made this many mistakes as a man alive under the influence of the sweet heather ale that had been his weakness.

His senses told him there was but one glimmer of hope still remaining to him . . . the underground stream.

He charged towards it, gliding into the water and mingling his essence with the liquid. Like a strong breeze, it scattered his essence into tiny sparkles, each one almost a separate entity. And that scattering was just what he needed to slip through the net. The bloodmage was seeking a whole essence, not one that had been broken into many tiny fragments. He could sense her anger lashing, but striking water was useless. Bits of Manus slipped through the magical net, following the flow of the stream for quite some ways before it spat him out in some well.

He jerked his essence back into one form, only to realize he was rising out of the well. Then it hit him as he detected iron and wood. Part of his essence had just been seized up by a bucket and the rest of him followed. He was drawn up into daylight just as a woman reached for the bucket. She screamed at the sight of the sodden spirit who dangled from her rope, and threw the whole contraption back into the well, charging away.

Horns! Manus thought as he shifted himself into invisibility and surged out of the well, making for the safety of Auntie Maeve's cottage.

The last thing he saw as he flew over the land was the frantic woman who raced for the small gathering of crofter huts surrounding the well, screaming that she had just seen a kelpie.

"I've been accounted for as worse," Manus muttered, and reflected that Ginny would have accused him of starting trouble just for the sheer pleasure of it.

Then again, it would be nice if Ginny were here to scold him.

As it was, he would have to find another time to slip back to Dun Elwyn and look for her.

And this time, he doubted the bloodmage or the Nidubh would give him the opportunity to escape the trap they obviously had waiting for him.

Chapter Seventeen

Ginny awoke with the sense of dread one often felt in strange surroundings. She had no concept of time for there were no windows in this place. Only the amber glare of torches flickering through the small window on her cell door afforded any source of light. Of course, mageborn were blessed with the sight of a cat when they were in the dark, and the chamber was clear to Ginny's gaze. Nitre-glazed stone walls, old reeds on the floor, rows of rusty shackles . . . she could see them all and the vision was not pleasant.

She could also see that she was alone.

Slowly, her mind reformulated where she was and how she got there. She closed her eyes, took several deep breaths and reached out with mage senses to check the limitations of her prison. Magic with the taint of death in its weave formed walls about the place. Upward and outward, it was strongest. Below, however, there seemed an absence of the barriers she felt elsewhere. An oversight? A gap? Surely not. The Lady Edain did not strike Ginny as such a fool.

Ginny reached downward with her senses, seeping them into the dirt and rock that formed the foundation of this keep. She felt cold water's rush. Earth's warm embrace. The tingle of a ley line passing under the structure. And a hint of essence that was more than familiar.

Manus?

What was he doing down there? It seemed as though he were swimming through the dirt, only to pause when he found the ley. Ginny sighed. Just like Manus to seek a back way in, though she was grateful for the effort. She had vaguely hoped that he would think of something.

Then, horror of horror, she felt the burn of bloodmagic sinking into the ground. Manus tried to flee, but the foundations became solid barriers against his ethereal form. Ginny sensed the sudden appearance of an invisible net of power stretching into the soil in an attempt to enclose him. She gasped as he dove into the stream of underground water and scattered into fragments, then disappeared.

Manus? Had be been sundered? The thought tightened her chest with grief as she drew back to herself, bowing her head.

If Manus was lost to her, what hope did she have now? He knew more of matters concerning bloodmagic than Ginny ever would.

How was she to stop Edain?

As though I am in a position to stop her. I cannot gate out of this place. And if I start striking out at the mortalborn with my magic, what purpose would that serve?

Ginny sank back against the wall and crossed her arms over her chest, drawing her knees to her. Horns, this was a dilemma, and she had no way of knowing if she could get herself out of it alone.

But sitting here brooding would not help.

She had to think of something.

With a snarl, she rose and began to pace about the cell. It had no purpose other than to help keep the inherent chill such dungeons had from setting into her limbs and get her blood circulating. Walking was something she often did to clear her head for thinking. As a child, she had frequently slipped away from her sisters to go wandering the moor about her father's croft. There, she would have no other

119

presence but the cattle as her company. The solitude of her nature used to vex her family, but they could not begin to understand what the mage power was doing to her heart and soul. From the very first hint of its existence, she had felt isolated and alone from those who surrounded her. Only her mother seemed to understand the agony that inflamed Ginny. At least, out alone on the moors like a wild child, she felt at peace.

There had been a favorite place too, high on an old tor. There, she found the shade of an ancient oak that had long ago grown up to wrap roots around the base of a single monolith of blue stone mottled with moss. Between stone and tree, there was a space where she could sit and watch the moors below. She would talk to the tree, telling it her troubles as though it were a kind old grandmother. And sometimes, she would study the stone, tracing fingers over its surface where she had found marks that meant nothing to her then. Now, she knew they were warding marks placed there by an Old One. Strange, but her presence never seemed to disturb their elemental power. Still, she had felt it was there even then, had noticed the strange song that would shiver her with its ethereal beauty, never knowing then that she was touching magic and it was alive within the stone and the tree that she came to think of as her only friends.

Ginny shook her head. Childhood memories were not going to get her out of this dungeon cell. How could she be so wasteful of her time? There was likely precious little of it left to waste, considering Edain's plan to sacrifice Ginny to Arawn. In anger, Ginny kicked at the reeds, scattering them, when her stocking-shod toe contacted something less giving.

"Horns!" she hissed. A stone, like as not . . .

. . . or a weapon.

She went to her knees in a flash, pushing aside the reeds to find the offending, precious rock. But instead, she found the heavy pommel of a man's long dirk. Her hand closed about the grip and drew its length from the floor.

A weapon, indeed. But how . . .

Then she remembered, the men who had come into this cell to torment her. The men who fed the demon their lives. One of them had tried to strike the Nidubh with this very knife, only to have it thrown from his hand. In her fright of the terrible moments, she had not noticed, but now, as she held steel, she realized there might yet be a way to gain her freedom and that of the boy.

She was staring at the blade when she heard the clatter of a bolt thrown on her prison door. With a gasp, she backed into the corner where she'd slept, standing sideways so the loose material of her divided skirt covered the knife.

The door opened to reveal a guard with a tray.

"Here," he said gruffly, not coming any farther than the door. "Mistress says you're to have this."

He held forth the tray.

Ginny held her place.

"Well, come on," he snapped. "I haven't got all day!"

"Leave it by the door," she said, keeping the long dirk hidden in her skirts. Taking enough steps forward to be just out of reach, she cocked her head. "I'll fetch it once you've left."

A sneer raised one corner of his mouth. "Afraid of me, lass?" he asked.

"No," she said with a sigh. "But I'm not foolish enough to trust you either. No more than I would trust that dark creature that stands behind you."

With a gasp, the man turned as though expecting the shadows to spit forth the demon creature that had ended

121

the lives of his fellow warriors.

Ginny stepped forward while bringing the dagger around, pommel first, and clouting it stoutly against the back of his head. He jerked, then crumpled to the floor in a heap, the tray throwing its contents across the reeds. Ginny frowned in disgust at the sight of the oatmeal mush. Tasteless stuff. She'd never been fond of it.

She laid the dagger aside long enough to drag the man into the cell, straining against the unwieldy weight of leather armor, muscles and weaponry. At least, he wasn't one of the fat ones . . . and his feet were small, she gleefully discovered as she deprived him of his boots. It took no more than a wad of cloth torn from his jerkin to improve the fit, while other strips provided her with a means of securing his hands, ankles and tongue should he awaken before Ginny made good her escape. She dragged his short sword from its sheath as well, hiding it under the reeds close to the door.

Once she was satisfied that her prisoner was well secured and had no means of assisting in his own escape, she collected the long dirk, slipped it into her belt and peered out at the length of the corridor. No one in sight in any of the scattered wells of torchlight that glimmered throughout the dark. She stepped outside, drew the cell door shut and shot the bolt, then carefully made her way along among the shadows.

Now to find Fafne and get both of them out of this dreadful place before something else could happen.

Chapter Eighteen

Ginny met no one as she traversed the length of the dungeon corridor, which puzzled her greatly. She would have expected a regular contingent of guards posted to look after the prisoners, though as far as she could tell, she was the only one. Had Edain decided Ginny was so little threat to the bloodmage, she was not worthy of a regular guard? Or perhaps the "bait" was best left alone to make the trap more appealing.

Whatever the reason, she made her way from one end of the dungeon to the other unchallenged. Along the way, she stopped long enough to peer into cells, only to find them devoid of company. Either MacElwyn had few thieves and murderers to contend with in his clan territory, or he was such a terror to his people, they stayed out of trouble on principle. Ginny wasn't sure she wanted to know which, for either answer could easily imply a certain fearsome nature was attached to MacElwyn.

Besides, she was nearly at the end. There were but a few more cells to search, and she had yet to find any sign of Fafne.

Or so she thought. Up until now, all the cells she had explored were either sitting wide open or shut and left unbolted. But at the very end, she found one cell bolted and padlocked against intrusion and escape. This door had a sliding plate window as well. Ginny pushed it aside, dreading the shriek that never came, then stood up on her toes to look inside.

Barely any light crept through the gap, but her mage sight quickly adjusted to the shadows, revealing the hunkered form crouched against the far wall. Red-gold pelt, long hair and a remnant of a familiar plaidie greeted her.

"Fafne?" she called as quietly as she could.

The hair at the side of the head moved as though the ear beneath it were pricking in response. *But his ears didn't do that before,* she thought.

"Fafne?" she repeated.

He stirred slowly, and she heard the ominous rattle of a chain as his head swiveled around in her direction. A tear-stained, grimy face greeted her. Pain flooded his eyes, and the sight of it jabbed her heart with remorse, for around his neck, he wore a shackle much like the collar of a dog.

"Oh, Fafne," she said and reached for the padlock, intending to use her magic to release the mechanism.

But before she touched it, static burned the tips of her fingers. Ginny jerked her hand back with a gasp. Magic! The padlock contained a ward set specifically against the touch of a mage.

"Horns," she hissed. "Clever creature . . ."

Ginny drew a deep breath, stilling the anger at nearly letting her own guard down, and sent mage senses to brush the lock. Its spell-bound aura blossomed before her mageborn vision, revealing a faint sphere of crackling red lights that stretched tiny dagger-like tendrils to undulate about the surface of the padlock. A pain spell. Ginny deepened her concentration, trying to read the padlock itself. Invisible runes revealed themselves to her mage senses: another ward, and this one set to warn the caster should magical tampering occur. Ginny studied each mark in turn, satisfied that she had not disturbed the latter even though the former had lashed at her so abruptly. Both were attuned specifically to mage essence.

For me, like as not, Ginny thought darkly. Had she not felt the faint touch of the pain spell so soon, she might well have brought Edain and the Nidubh down here in the blink of an eye, spoiling all hope of escape.

But someone must be able to pass this . . . to feed him.

Like a mortal man with a key.

She shook her head. The guard she left bound in her cell had not carried such implements as keys. Only his armor and weapons and the tray . . .

Ginny made a face and hurried back up to her own cell. Her prisoner was still unconscious. She opened the door and slipped in cautiously. He did not stir until she started to remove the gauntlets tucked into his belt. The abrupt movement nearly spilled her back. He sought to push himself upright, rolling side to side. Throwing his head back and forth and arching his back, he struggled against the bonds, making a feeble effort to voice his anger.

"Stop that," Ginny ordered, and for good measure, she picked up the tray and clipped the back of his head with it. He cursed through the gag, and though the word was not clear, she could guess it all the same.

"Be quiet, or I'll tear your life out of you!" she said, knowing full well the threat was naught but air. She could no more commit such an act of bloodmagic than she could command Thistle. But the man knew mageborn had that power, for he suddenly quieted and lay still. "That's better," she said and continued to pull the gauntlets from his belt.

Once she had them on her hands and collected his sword from under the reeds, she hurried back to the far end and Fafne's cell. The lad was still crouched against the wall, but now he had turned to look in her direction.

"I'll have you out as quick as you can recite your ances-tors," she said.

Hopefully, that was a long enough list to keep him from getting impatient. She wasn't totally sure this plan would work. She could not risk touching the lock with her hands, or disturbing it with magic. Still, the sword would likely break the lock without disturbing the wards, but she couldn't be sure whether or not steel would transmit magic to her. She hoped wearing the guard's sweaty gauntlets would keep the spell from recognizing her.

During her training, Manus once told her that magic could be foiled by the strangest things. He'd spend days trying to learn how to cast a magebolt through a pair of gauntlets, but the leather would foil him every time, leaving him with blistered fingers and making the uncle who trained him laugh. What Manus had finally learned was that a magebolt stopped the moment it struck an object, be it leather, stone, wood, metal or flesh, and that in order to cast one while wearing gauntlets, he had to draw the power for the bolt from an outside source other than his own mage essence and cause it to form beyond the gauntlet itself so the bolt could fly at its intended target.

Ginny was hoping now that theory worked in reverse. At worst, she might still get burned by the pain spell. She took a deep breath, rearing back with the sword as though it were an axe, and bringing it down across the shanks of the padlock where it held the bolt.

There was a flash of sparks as steel met iron, and the flickers of light that started up the blade startled Ginny. She dropped the sword, throwing herself back across the cor-ridor to escape the fiery flashes that lashed towards the hilt with blinding speed. The pain spell engulfed the sword, then faded. Cautiously, she reached for the hilt, hesitating to seize it at first. But the blade remained calm, and she was able to lift it without any hint of danger.

Her gaze quickly shifted to the padlock itself. It hung crooked now, one of the shanks shattered by the blow. She carefully took the sword and used it to push the padlock out of the bolt. The fiery display greeted her again, but not before she saw the padlock tumble to the ground. Once more, she let the sword fall before the aggressive spell could reach her, then leaned across and avoided both as she took hold of the bolt and threw it open . . .

Pain lashed her directly this time, and threw her back across the corridor to strike the wall and drop to the floor in a heap. Horns, she thought, groggily pushing herself upright and shoving her hair out of her face. She should have known there was likely to be a second trap on the door.

No time to worry now. If she had alerted Edain, there would be time enough to reflect later, but only if they got out of this place now. Ginny thrust herself off the floor. She had managed to unbolt the door, and it fell in at the barest application of a heel. She cursed Edain's cleverness under her breath as she rushed into the cell.

Fafne reacted like a whipped cur, throwing himself against the wall and whimpering as though he expected some terrible retribution.

"It's all right, Fafne," Ginny said. "I'll have you free in a moment."

The pin holding the shackle about his neck was a simpler affair to foil with the long dagger she carried. Within moments, she had him free and dragged him towards the cell door. At first, he pulled back like a reluctant hound being taken to a bath, but Ginny kept a steady grasp on him and coaxed him as though he were a frightened hound.

"Come on, lad. Easy, that's it. I won't hurt you . . . easy.

127

That's a good lad . . ."

Ginny repeated the phrases over and over, hoping to register with her voice that she was not going to harm him. He stopped tugging against her and began to move with her as she started up the spiral of stairs that led out of the dungeons.

There was a guard room at the top, curiously empty, which only added to Ginny's sense of dread. Where had everyone gone? Surely Edain had not turned her own people into hounds as she had Fafne's family. That would mean a lot more explaining than one bloodmage could handle. Folks were bound to notice if more than one dun was overrun by a horde of mysterious hounds.

Again, she told herself she would ponder these matters later. It was important that she and the lad get out of this place now.

The guard room opened out into a long corridor that ended with the choice of stairs going up and a doorway to the left. Ginny chose the latter and pushed it open to find herself in small courtyard on ground level. Washing hung about, and there were tubs of water in various stages of use, but no sign of the maids and lads who should have been managing them.

Where is everyone? she thought once more, crossing the yard and making for a door that led into a short hall and a kitchen. Here, she saw no one tending the bread that was burning in the ovens or basting the portion of beef roasting on a spit. She could, however, hear a rabble of voices, and though the best route looked to be a door that would likely open into another yard, curiosity wormed its way past her better judgment. Firmly holding Fafne, she crept over to the door that led down a corridor and opened out into a great hall.

There she learned the real reason the keep seemed deserted. Every single member of the household proper must have been crowded into that chamber, all pointing towards the rafters. Ginny pulled Fafne along, keeping to the walls in hopes that they could slip by the crowd unnoticed, and allowing her gaze to flit up at whatever had their attention above.

She froze, for up on the rafters was a man in MacElwyn tartan. And from the wild look of him, he was not in possession of all his wits.

Chapter Nineteen

"Cowards!" Rory MacElwyn snarled from his precarious perch. "Ye have betrayed me! Ye have sent my son to the axeman's block!"

"My Lord, please come down!" more than one voice implored.

Ginny listened to the shouts as she continued to make her way along the wall for the main doors. If they could just get out while all this distraction was taking place. She briefly glanced about, hoping to catch a glimpse of Edain, and the search was rewarded. The Lady MacElwyn stood on the dais, the black Keltoran staghound at her side and men-at-arms around her. She stared up at her mad husband, wringing her hands, and in that moment, Ginny realized how this lady had deceived all who served her.

"Rory, please," she called. "Please, my lord, come down before you do yourself harm."

"Betrayed!" MacElwyn replied, shaking his head. "My line is dead! My son's head will decorate the walls of Caer Keltora, and I will have no heir."

The Nidubh shifted its gaze but slightly, as though weighing some possibility. Ginny felt impelled to draw herself and Fafne behind one of the carved pillars supporting the gallery above, and not without good cause. Those eyes might look normal now as they scanned the mass of servants and kin who swarmed the chamber, but Ginny could feel the power in them. If the Nidubh should see her or Fafne, all would be lost.

Then again, if Edain's true self was unknown to these people, then so was that of her beast, and to reveal itself in this crowd would not serve the bloodmage's plans. With luck, neither Edain nor the Nidubh could risk that revelation at this point.

Ginny waited a few moments, then peered around the pillar at the dais. The Nidubh was not looking in their direction. Indeed, all eyes were on the gallery. Ginny took Fafne's arm firmly and started moving again, glancing towards the gallery in time to see men clambering over the rail and making for the beams on which the master precariously balanced. MacElwyn had pressed his face to one of the supports, eyes closed.

"All is lost," he groaned. "There is nothing left . . ."

"My Lord, please," Edain said fearfully.

Someone must have given away the plan, for MacElwyn suddenly whipped a dagger from the back of his belt and wrenched around towards the nearest man trying to crawl across the beam.

"Traitor!" the Laird shouted. "I'll have your tripes for garters!"

The guard was forced to draw back as the blade lashed at his face, and he nearly lost his balance in the process. The crowd gasped as one. Ginny felt her own stomach twinge in uncertainty. The main doors were but a few man-lengths away and she had yet to be challenged.

"Traitors!" MacElwyn shouted. "Ye have taken my son, but ye'll not take me!"

He struck at the young guard again, and this time, his dagger found a gap in the leather curraise. Someone screamed. The young guard nearly lost his balance, grappling to maintain his grip on the beam. He was in no position to draw a weapon to defend himself. Ginny could see

131

this as she and Fafne reached the doors.

She felt torn. She had the means and power to save the young man and his crazed master, but she dared not use the power lest her escape be foiled. If only Manus were here to provide a distraction, but there was no use in wishing for that assistance. Besides, she could hear the clang of a blade on a targe, and a quick glance up showed her that the next guard had made it forward enough to throw his targe in the path of the master's slashing dagger. Surely, they would manage to stop him now. She seized the edge of the door, looking out into a corridor that led for the stairs and would take her down to the stableyard and freedom.

And they probably would have made it, had Fafne not tripped where his plaidie was slipping loose and trailing the ground. He stumbled with a yelp that brought several pairs of eyes swinging around his way. A woman screamed, and her voiced wrenched through the hall as sharp as a knife, attracting the attention of a pair of eyes Ginny had hoped to avoid.

"Stop her!" Edain cried.

So much for subtlety, Ginny grimly noted. She might as well have painted herself blue and danced naked through the crowd for all the attention that suddenly turned her way. Which meant she had no excuse for hiding what she was.

Ginny raised her hand and shouted, *"Loisg!"* Fire filled her palm, causing those around her—mostly unarmed servants she was grateful to realize—to scatter like rats surprised in a granary. That confusion was to her advantage, or so she hoped. She seized Fafne's arm and pushed him towards the door, backing that way herself.

Alas, she should have made certain her own path was clear. She heard Fafne cry out too late. There were still guards outside, and they had seized the lad. Another was rearing back with his fist to strike at Ginny. She managed to dodge the blow, but rather than risk hurting him with the fire, she threw it at his feet where it caught the reeds. He danced back like a puppet being jerked about on its strings, stagger-stepping to avoid the flames.

A brief victory, she sadly noted. Another man was already there, catching Ginny's arm and wrenching it back at a painful angle. She screamed and hammered his shins with the hard heels of her stolen boots as his other arm closed around her neck to subdue her. She stretched her free hand out and hissed, *"Solus!"* filling it with light that she tossed back over her shoulder into the guard's face. Alas, he must have known the spell was harmless, for he only shouted and jerked her arm harder until she feared he would break it. The pain sent flashed across her vision and set her head to swimming. She nearly fainted then and there from the fire that rushed through her nerves and sickened her stomach. There was nothing she could do as he wrenched her around and pushed her back into the great hall.

We will die now for certain, she thought.

The chaos of her own defiance had briefly distracted attention from another conflict. A man shouted from the rafter, clearly a cry of rage. Other voices joined the rabble. Ginny's captor stopped so that she was able to look up.

A struggle was ensuing now. More men were on the rafters, and MacElwyn was trapped between two sets of his own guards who were defending themselves against his savage blows with their targes while making their way across the beam in an attempt to seize him.

"NO!" he shouted. "Back, ye knaves, or I'll kill every last man of ye!"

They crowded him so he had no way to turn. Or so they thought.

For just as they were about to lay hands on him, the Laird MacElwyn decided his honor and reputation could never survive the capture. Before any man among them could stop him, he thrust his own blade into his barrel-thick chest.

"NO!" Edain shrieked.

The move so stunned his own men, they ceased their attempt to seize him, watching as he tottered on the beam, glowering at them like a crazed prophet. Then slowly, as though practiced a thousand times, he leaned out and gently curved his body as though diving into water. There were screams a hundred times louder than before as the Laird MacElwyn fell off the beam and crashed like a stone onto the surface on a table. The wood shattered under his weight, scattering food and platters and blood across the reeds.

Murmurs of shock began to buzz. Lady Edain screamed and threw herself from the dais in some mockery of remorse. She pushed her way through the throng that gathered about the body of her husband, tumbling to her knees with such believable sobs, Ginny felt her own throat tighten in sympathy.

"It was not his time," Edain wailed, seizing his blood-soaked plaidie.

Hands took her gently, pulling her from the body as though fearing the sight would undo her. Only Ginny saw the glacial blue gaze that flitted in her direction full of anger beneath the tears, and only Ginny felt the sting of another mage ripping into her thoughts.

"You have undone all my plans!" the angry voice hissed inside Ginny's head. *"Now you and the lad shall take his place!"*

Those words burned themselves into Ginny's mind, whipping about like a scourge as she was once more bound and gagged to prevent her from casting spells. Then she and Fafne were dragged back to the dungeon to be returned to the cells they had only recently escaped.

Chapter Twenty

Though they took the dagger from Ginny, they failed to notice the stolen boots as they shackled her to the wall in the same cell with Fafne. The boy was hooked to a wall on the opposite side, and they were left alone to ponder their fates. Ginny felt furious at herself as much as at Edain. *I should have been more cautious. Should have taken a less obvious route.*

Hindsight! Not terribly useful just now.

She wished they hadn't gagged her. It would have been nice to be able to ask Fafne if he was all right. The poor lad was whimpering like a terrified pup, and the noise was a bit unnerving. But there wasn't anything she could do, not bound as she was.

A right royal mess. And she couldn't even blame Manus, wherever he was.

She wondered how long it would be before she and the lad were sacrificed and how Edain would convince the folk here that the sacrifice was necessary, when the cell door opened and a figure draped in a mourning plaid filled the gap. Edain. Her pale blue eyes held a fire that tied Ginny's stomach into a knot. The bloodmage stepped into the cell, gracefully crossing the reeds. Behind her came the Nidubh and two guards, but as soon as the dog was inside the cell, Edain waved the latter away.

"I wish to speak to her alone," she said.

The guards looked reluctant to obey at first. "But my lady, if she is a bloodmage, as you have said . . ."

Ginny felt her own outrage burning on her cheeks. *I am no filthy bloodmage!* she thought. How dare this brazen creature tell her people such a lie!

"I will be safe so long as she remains bound and gagged," Edain said. "Leave us and close the cell door."

The guards exchanged looks, then shrugged and stepped out of the cell, closing the door in their wake. Edain took a deep breath, closing her eyes in concentration, and Ginny felt the faint brush of power being drawn from her own essence. Just a wisp, but it startled her so, she gasped.

After a moment, Edain opened her eyes. "They are away," she said, glancing at the Nidubh. The staghound's eyes shifted to burning coals, and its face seemed to remold itself in some hideous parody of a hound.

Edain moved her hand and whispered a few spell words, and the reeds rose to form a chair. The bloodmage walked around and fastidiously brushed the seat with the end of her mourning plaid before she sat down facing Ginny.

"You have undone years of work, my dear," Edain said. "Never in the decades that I've seen have I ever had my plans ruined so brilliantly. I worked so hard to keep Rory alive before the time of sacrifice, and if you had not distracted everyone by trying to escape, the men would have been able to fetch him down. For that, I cannot forgive you. However, you shall have the opportunity to make good your folly before you die."

Ginny glowered furiously at the bloodmage.

"Oh, I am sorry," Edain said, and glanced at the Nidubh. "Would you, my precious?"

The hound shifted even more, revealing the scaly hands that had lifted two men before they lost their lives. Ginny drew back against the wall, uncertain as those fingers elongated and reached around her head to loosen the gag.

137

"Better?" the Nidubh asked.

Ginny held her tongue. The demon merely grinned its hound-like parody of a smile and drew the appendages back to itself, where they returned to their animal shape.

"Now, as I was saying, you shall have a chance to redeem yourself, though it shall be a very short redemption."

"No," Ginny said.

"No?" Edain said softly. "You have not heard my proposal."

"I know what you want," Ginny retorted. "My life, the lad's . . . and Manus."

"Well, actually, I don't care a fig for the lad's life. It means nothing to my well-being, and once I complete his transformation, I'll set him free, and no one will be the wiser."

"Do you mean to say that what you have done to Fafne and his family was nothing more than a whim?"

"Oh, no. There was a purpose in my actions," Edain said. "Survival. It's very important to me that I survive."

"And you are willing to sacrifice others to assure that," Ginny said.

"Yes."

"But why?"

"I would think that even a mageborn would understand," Edain said. "I was never such a powerful bloodmage until I offered my soul to Arawn. In exchange, he gave me great powers and the Nidubh as my familiar, but there was also a price. At the end of seven years, Arawn would claim my soul—unless I was able to provide him with another. And so long as every seven years, I continue to provide a soul for his Cauldron of Doom, I may keep my own. Because Arawn needs warriors for his final battle, I have always selected men who extol the virtues held sacred by our ancestors. Generosity, perfection of form and courage. Rory has all these . . . or did. Alas, I never thought his love for his wayward son would drive him to such madness."

"And leave you without a sacrifice." Ginny made sure her tone reeked of contempt.

"It goes further than that," Edain said and smiled. "I don't mind telling you because I know you will not be telling anyone else. When Tomis was taken, he threatened to reveal who and what I was if I did not assure his freedom."

"I don't understand," Ginny said.

"He has only to tell the King that I, a bloodmage, bewitched him into his treasonous plot, and I would be unable to find the peace and prosperity of which I have grown fond. I cannot afford such to risk that."

"But the MacArdaghs . . ."

"Were the only witnesses to his treason. So I had to get rid of them, but I knew I couldn't just kill them off without someone noticing, especially after I learned that the lad's father had sung his song of triumph to every ear within his household. I had no choice but to make them all disappear without a trace."

"There are hounds ravaging the countryside, and you think no one will notice?" Ginny said. "The word that Dun Ardagh is under a curse has already traveled far and away."

"Ah, but the manner of the curse will confuse them for generations to come."

"They've only to send a mageborn from Caer Keltora to look into the matter," Ginny insisted.

"Yes, I realize that. But by the time such word gets to them, I shall be long gone from this place. Of course, there is still the matter of dealing with you and your ethereal friend."

"No," Ginny repeated. "I will not help you."

Edain frowned. "You're a very stubborn creature for one who has no immediate future. I cannot have you or that crafty mageborn spirit of yours bolting about the countryside telling others about me before I have finished what I have begun. But I am willing to offer you a swift death in exchange for a little assistance from you."

"Assistance to do what?" Ginny insisted.

"I want the mageborn spirit's soul for Arawn . . ."

"But Mistress, you said I could . . ." the Nidubh began.

Edain turned a hard look upon the hound-like demon. "Matters have changed," she said firmly. "I have need of his soul now. Without it, I have nothing with which to keep my bargain. Rory is dead, and as a dead man, he is of no use to me now. Since I cannot find a man of virtue, I shall have to make do with the sweet essence of a mageborn instead."

"You could give her to the Dark Lord of Annwn," the Nidubh said most sullenly.

"No. His spirit would be a better sacrifice, and you shall have her in his place . . . but only if you promise to make her death swift and painless. And you must not sully her flesh, Nidubh. Take the essence, but leave the body, for I will have need of it as well."

Ginny glowered. She had never been fond of being talked about as though she was not present. "What do you mean?" she insisted angrily. "What use would my corpse be to you?"

"Ah, well, you see, Rory's untimely death has left me with a small problem. In the past, I always left on the day of the funeral . . . two days after Solstice, as a rule. I would pretend to take my own life in a moment of grief, thus leaving kith and kin to marvel at the strength of love and no room to question my true reason for leaving. Only Rory will be placed in his cairn before the coming Solstice, leaving me unable to go away, with loose ends such as yourself and the lad still alive. So, I have a unique problem. *Where* I give Arawn the sacrificed soul is of little consequence, though *when* is vitally important. I will have to leave here before Solstice and make the sacrifice elsewhere . . . which is why you and I are going to trade places."

"We can't trade places," Ginny retorted. "Folk will notice."

"Will they?" Edain said with a smile. She lowered her head, putting her hands to her face, and Ginny felt power reaching out to consume a bit of her own essence once more. *"Bi ann Ginny,"* Edain whispered and raised her face.

Except it wasn't her face, but Ginny's.

"How . . . ?" Ginny's jaw practically touched her chest. Never before had she witnessed such a display of power.

"It's an old spell," Edain said. "And with it, I shall leave, taking you along, disguised as me, of course. No one will be the wiser. They will believe the bloodmage we captured at my husband's death escaped and conjured a demon to take me prisoner. And when they find a corpse wearing my wedding plaid, they will know the creature murdered me and look for her instead. So, all I need is your assistance to capture the mage spirit, and the rest will be simple."

"No!" Ginny said even more firmly than before. "If you want Manus' soul, you'll have to take it without my help!"

Edain shifted back to her own features and smiled. "My dear. Your presence here is all the help I will need. Your friend has already made one attempt to enter this place. He does not strike me as a man who would give up so easily.

141

Laura J. Underwood

Manus . . . what a nice name. It shall come in useful when I set forth the spells to trap him."

She rose from the chair.

"Now, if you'll excuse me, I must go back to playing the grieving widow for my husband's kinsmen, who are likely already trying to decide who among them I will hand the reins of power to. Fortunately, they cannot approach me about the matter until after he is placed in his cairn, and quite frankly, I think they'd be rather put out to learn Rory thought very little of them all."

"Just as he thought so much of his son," Ginny said.

"Yes, well, there really wasn't anything I could do about that. Tomis was headstrong and foolish."

"And a better lover than his father, I imagine?"

"That is an opinion I do not wish to debate," Edain said. "He was, like many young men, too sure of himself. And too quick for his own good. Had he thought out his plans of treason instead of telling them to the wrong sets of ears, he might have proven successful in his venture to overthrow the throne of Keltora and return the crown to the MacPhearsons."

"I'm surprised that plan didn't suit you," Ginny said.

"I have no interest in politics," Edain said. "Only in survival. It is why I have lived a long life, my dear. Too bad you will not have that privilege, but then, if you had kept to your own business instead of meddling in mine . . ."

"I did keep to my own business until you wrought havoc at Dun Ardagh," Ginny said. "It's your failure that has brought you to this point, not my meddling."

Edain stiffened and the glacial eyes grew hard as diamonds. "Have care, little mageborn," she said darkly. "My power may be a secret but, as I am sure you have discovered, it extends quite far, and I have no fear of using it here,

142

where there would be no one to hear your screams of pain."

"You can kill me if you like," Ginny said, "but don't think you'll be safe from discovery. Others out there already know what you are."

"Who?" Edain said darkly. "That dotty old woman in Ghloelea? I have no reason to fear her. Her magic is fading. She can't even plant a proper ward anymore. If she could, those men I conjured to tear down her cottage would have turned back into willow trees."

"But her tongue is still strong," Ginny said. "And she has a far reach too. Even as we speak, she has messengers out seeking other mageborn to warn them about you. Soon, everyone in Keltora will know the truth."

Edain jerked her hand, and the Nidubh once more formed hands with which to put Ginny's gag back in place.

"Funerals are boring enough without this useless conversation," Edain said. "Count your days carefully, my dear. You will soon be leaving this world. And I'll send your old woman on her way as well, if I must." Another gesture, and the reed chair fell apart, flumping to the ground. Edain went over to the door, never bothering to call out. The men beyond opened the door as though expecting her all along, and stood back as she stepped through the gap.

Ginny glowered as the Nidubh turned dark, hound-like eyes back over one shoulder and gave her a teasing smirk before loping after the disappearing bloodmage.

The door closed, its echo ringing on Ginny's ears. She took a deep breath to calm her tense nerves.

A terrible mess, indeed.

Oh, Manus, she thought darkly. *I should have thrown my fears to the wind and let you use me to make the gate.*

Hindsight. Useless now.

Chapter Twenty-One

There were farm lads hauling stone and thatch when Manus returned to Ghloelea. He spied Auntie Maeve in the middle of it all, conducting repairs with her usual aplomb.

"No, not that stone, lad," she groused as she stopped a worker and snatched a potato-sized rock from his hand. "That's auld Manus' cairn stone, and shall have no place in my wall! Last thing I need is his mageborn spirit having free rein to come and go as he pleases."

Manus sighed. Why did everyone regret his company so? Invisibly, he slipped up beside the old woman while the worker shook his head in dismay and headed elsewhere. Auntie Maeve juggled the stone in one hand, then turned towards Manus with a frown.

"Like now?" he asked.

" 'Bout time ye got back, lad," she said. "Any luck?"

Manus frowned. "Do ye really want to look daft in front of these lads?" he asked, using a low voice that only mage hearing could detect.

As if they heard their cue, a couple of the workmen had paused and glanced towards her in uncertainty. She fixed them with a surly glower.

"Well, what are you looking at?" she asked.

They quickly ducked their heads and went back to the chore of gathering rubble to rebuild her wall. Auntie Maeve snorted and walked out of the cottage, still weighing the cairn stone in one hand. Manus followed her as she made her way to a stone bench under a willow tree and seated herself. He glided his invisible form into the space at her side.

"So, did ye find poor Ginny and the lad?" she asked, watching the distance with a squint.

"No, I couldn't get into Dun Elwyn," Manus said bitterly, crossing his arms in frustration over his failure.

"Got the place warded, has she?"

"Like a ground spider's nest," he said. "The whole exterior is housed inside a web of wards, all interconnected and impassable for me."

"Did you try going underground?" Auntie Maeve asked.

"Aye, and nearly fell into her trap. There's an underground ley line, and she's got her awareness attached to it."

"They usually do."

"Which is why I need your help," Manus said.

Silence fell over the old woman like a cloak. She continued to stare at the willows surrounding her lovely cottage, shoulders hunched and stiff.

"Well?" he asked. "Will ye help me?"

"You know I want to, Manus," she said with a grim sigh, "but my powers are not what they once were. Those men who came last night . . . I should have sensed them because some of them weren't real men, but conjurlings. Transformed trees. Willow men."

"Willow men?"

"Aye, it's an old spell. There used to be a tale that said willows walked when the Old Ones were young, and that the souls of trees can be turned to men who have hearts of wood."

"Bogie tales to frighten children," Manus said.

"Every tale has its origin," she said. "Not that it matters now. The point is, I should have sensed them, and my wards should have kept them out, but my magic has grown

145

feeble over the years. I'm not the mageborn I once was."

"I don't need your magic, old woman," he said and leaned over to kiss her cheek, a useless gesture since his lips just surged unhampered through her flesh. He drew back, clearing his throat. "I need your body . . ."

"I'm too old for that, ye randy little . . ."

"Ye know what I mean," Manus said. "I have to get into that keep. I can't just wander in. I need to be carried in."

"In my body?" she asked.

"Nay, woman. In my cairn stone."

"But I'm an old woman! I can't walk that far."

"Ye won't have to. I'll share yer flesh long enough to open us a gate to Dun Elwyn."

"And once we're there?"

"Ye must carry my stone inside the keep and past the wards."

Auntie Maeve sighed. "What about yer dog?"

"Thistle will have to stay here until we're done."

The old woman wore a dubious frown.

"Yer my only hope, Maeve," Manus said softly. "If I lose Ginny now, 'twill ne'er let my heart rest in peace . . . and then I'll just have to find another place to hang around, and since you're the only other mageborn for several leagues . . ."

"Oh, don't you threaten me, Manus MacGreeley," she hissed. "I'll do what I can, and if it means sharing bodies with ye for a brief time, then let's waste no more breath blathering about it. But once yer in the stone, how am I to get back here?"

"Ye can walk," he said.

She struck at him with one hand, a useless gesture of rage for it passed right through him, but he flinched back all the same, and laughed at her surly glower.

"Look, as soon as I get Ginny out of that dreadful place, I'll gate us all back here. All right?"

"Oh, get on with it before I change my mind," she said.

Manus stood as Maeve closed her eyes, remaining on the bench. He'd never actually tried this before, but he knew it was supposed to work. He had only to attach himself to the core of power that was at the heart of Auntie Maeve's mage essence, and her awareness and flesh would become as his own.

Carefully, he seated himself within the old woman who gave a little shudder as his awareness stroked her own. There was a moment of uncertainty, of darkness and disjointedness, then her eyes opened and revealed to him the world as she saw it.

The first thing he noticed was that she was going myopic, and that impairment took him by surprise.

"How do ye see?" he cried from within her.

"With my eyes," she said. "I told ye I was getting feeble."

"All right," he said. "Just relax and let me manage affairs for a bit to orient myself."

"If ye insist," she said with a sigh. Slowly, Manus felt a range of senses becoming his own. Sight, hearing, smell, touch . . . He felt the weight of the stone in his hand and the gentle push of the breeze through her hair. All sensations he missed. Carefully, he sought to manipulate the limbs and pull her off the bench. At first, the body seemed leaden, then it responded, moving with no immediate urgency and a little bit of discomfort.

"Yer back's going bad too, I see," he said.

"Oh, stop nattering and get on with it."

"Well, first, I think we should move into a more private place to open the gate," Manus said. "No use in frightening the lads."

He felt her head nod in agreement. "This way," she said and a hand rose awkwardly in a gesture of direction. "There's a grove over there where we'll be less obvious."

They started across the ground, Manus wryly noting the lack of spring in Auntie Maeve's step. If this was the price of being an old mage, maybe he was not so bad off in this otherworld existence he led. At least he would never know the infirmities of age.

Or the pleasures of love, he grimly noted.

"Stop thinking such randy things," Auntie Maeve insisted.

"Sorry," he said.

They entered a grove where enough willow fronds formed curtains of pale green between them and the cottage. Manus closed his eyes, stretching mage senses and reveling in the power that responded to his magical call. He felt it feeding into him, washing through him as the ley line had. Horns, he did miss that, the sense that he and the world were one.

Power welled around him as he thought of the field road just beyond the keep.

"Farther back, or she'll know yer coming," Auntie Maeve said.

"All right," he hissed. "Ye're interfering with my concentration, auld woman."

"Don't forget the strictures," she said. "We don't want her or the beast to know we're coming."

"I'm stricturing, woman! Let me concentrate!"

"So where are yer cloaking wards?" she went on, purposely ignoring his plea. "Without the cloaking wards, every mage in Keltora will know what ye're about."

"If ye don't be quiet, ye auld banshee, and let me concentrate on this spell, I'll send yer essence into that fat cat of yers and fetch Thistle to deal with the beast."

"Ye've no respect for yer elders, lad. When I was your age . . ."

"The Old Ones walked," he finished. "Wheesht, or we'll never find Ginny alive!"

He heard her grumble something unkind in the back of her mind, and couldn't stop a smile from stretching her lips under his command. Then, he sighed, closing his eyes and concentrating on the crofts just back of the keep. In fact, the place where he first came near the sheep. Carefully, he moved his hands to form glyphs in the air that would give the spell its cloak and keep it from being sensed on the other end.

Softly, Manus whispered the gate spell, watching as power formed a whorl before him and opened a rift in the fabric of the world. Beyond, he could see the fields and the distant walls of the keep. He stepped through the gate and into a field where the ground felt soft as butter.

"Horns," Auntie Maeve hissed. "Look what ye've gone and done."

Manus looked down to find he'd firmly planted her feet in a large pile of fresh sheep droppings.

Chapter Twenty-Two

"Ye big oaf," Auntie Maeve groused. "Couldn't take time to concentrate on the ground, could ye?"

" 'Tis a wonder I could get us here safely at all, what with the way ye were nattering at me, auld woman," Manus retorted.

"Well, get us out of this mess!"

Manus heaved a sigh that expanded her massive chest, and stepped out of the manure, shaking off her feet. Horns, if he didn't need her now . . .

"I'll never get the smell off my boots," she groused.

Indeed, now that he was using Maeve's nose, Manus could smell the heady musk odor of the sheep, and the oily lanolin smell of wool. He turned to glance around, and sure enough, there was a small herd moving ahead of a young shepherd who had his back to Manus and Auntie Maeve. Might be best, then, if they moved along, lest the lad give them away. He urged her body forward, secretly cursing the ungainly bulk that could not swing along at a more masculine gait.

"You just wait until you're old," she scoffed.

"I don't think I have to worry about that," he said.

"Jackanapes," she muttered with her own lips.

It was getting on in the afternoon by the time they trudged up the road to where farms were more abundant. Manus noted a clear bit of activity around the keep. The mournful cry of pipes played a dirge-like song that floated across the fields to their ears.

"Funeral pibroch," Auntie Maeve said softly. "A MacElwyn has died."

Manus frowned. "But it's not Solstice."

"Mayhaps it's for the son," she suggested.

He waited until they were just outside the main gates before he slipped free of Maeve's flesh and fled for the darkness of his cairn stone. Even this far outside the keep, he sensed a faint scratch of the bloodmage's power. In the cairn stone, he was still aware of it, but it was as though his stone muted the effect on his essence.

Maeve ambled towards the gate, glancing about at the crowds of folk gathering there. A cart loaded with baskets of vegetables, mostly turnips and potatoes, was rumbling up the road to her back. Ahead were the gates and the guards who stood watch. Auntie Maeve was practically at the entrance when one of them stepped forward to stop her.

"Here, where do you think you're going, old woman?" he asked.

Auntie Maeve hesitated only a whit before fixing a stern matronly glower on the man. "Why, to the market," she said.

"The market's closed today," he said. "The Laird of MacElwyn is dead and all are in mourning."

"Dead?" she said. "How?"

" 'Tis no matter. None may enter what don't have proper business within, so be off with ye."

"How dare you . . ." Auntie Maeve began, and Manus sensed that another guard was about to approach. Fortunately, she had her hand on the stone in her pouch, and he pushed his awareness into her.

"Don't push them, old woman!" he wind whispered to her. "We'll find another way in."

The cart of vegetables rumbled up to the gate as Auntie

Maeve muttered a curse on all young men and turned away.

"So how am I to get you inside?" she muttered, clutching the stone.

"Toss me into the cart," Manus replied.

"What?"

"Put me with the tatties," he said.

She made a face, but ambled around behind the cart all the same and, with a quick glance at the guards who were now occupied with stopping an old beggar and his child, she tossed the stone into the back of the cartload.

"Good luck," Manus heard her mutter.

I'll need it, he thought as the cart rolled on in unchallenged. Nor could he believe his fortune when the cart went straight for the inner gates of the keep proper. This load must have been meant for the kitchen.

Of course, if MacElwyn really is dead, they'd be preparing a feast for his wake. Nor was it lost on Manus that the Laird's death could mean worse trouble for Ginny. The sooner he got inside, the better.

The cart rumbled on into the yard, where several lads charged out to seize up the wares. Lasses rushed about finishing laundry that flapped on the line to dry. The basket filled with potatoes and Manus' cairn stone was taken into the kitchen scullery and dumped unceremoniously on the stone floor. Though Manus could not see, he sensed a hulking presence that exuded something of an ox-like temperament. Cautiously, he opened one eye and pushed it beyond the limitations of the stone.

A scullion sat on a small stool, a huge lad whose girth outreached the basket his massive hand reached into to snatch up a potato. With a surly look, the lad trimmed away the skin of the potato and tossed it into a bowl, reaching into the basket to seize up another . . .

152

Alas, the potato he grabbed was Manus' cairn stone. *Horns,* Manus thought as he felt his stone lifted. He was not afraid of being hurt, for he was beyond mortal damage, but the experience was not one he wanted to remember, especially when the lad pressed the blade of his small paring knife against the surface. Steel skittered across the stone, raising sparks just before the blade snapped.

"Horns!" the lad shouted and threw the cairn stone out the nearest window. Manus became airborne, tumbling from the opening. And just when he feared his stone would be shattered on the cobbles of the yard, it landed in a pile of bed linens where it was quickly covered by a blanket being pulled from the drying line. The basket of laundry was quickly hoisted and borne back inside on the hip of a maid.

"Look at me hands," she complained to another. "They's all knots and wrinkled from all this washing. I tell ye, I should have listened to me mother and gone off with that tinker lad."

"Which tinker lad would that be?" the other asked. "The one what they wanted to hang?"

"Nay, this one was the tinker what came from up north, the one with the blue eyes."

"Didn't think much of him," the other said with a sigh. "He was kissing all the lasses before the stable lads sent him packing."

"Oh, you wish."

Manus wanted to scream at them, but he suspected if the laundry started to talk, he would not get much farther.

They seemed to wander a goodly ways before the basket thumped to the floor. "Coming," the lass called, and her complaints about never having one task finished but for another being thrown at her faded in the distance.

At last, Manus thought and carefully eased out of his

cairn stone, staying invisible as he stretched his awareness to test his surroundings. He appeared to be in a storage closet with no windows. Not a problem, he decided, and slipped his essence through the closed door to peer out at the room. A back hall greeted him. He stretched his senses even farther, waiting to find some hint of the bloodmage's web of power, but none came into immediate range. *Good.* The only hint of power in range was that down at the far end of this hall. The doorway there bore her blood taint.

Best not go that way then, he told himself and headed in the opposite direction, for it was apt as not to be the Lady Edain's lair. And where that lady rested, most likely so did the Nidubh. Carefully, always aware that there could be some among these folk who carried mage blood enough to sense him and give him away, Manus made his way through the keep, sliding from room to room until he came to a large chamber that must have belonged to the Laird MacElwyn. There, stretched out on a large bed with the three remaining double ells of his plaidie cleaned and neatly folded, lay the Laird himself. Around him were women folk who carefully washed his body in preparation for placing it into a cairn.

Manus wandered around among the living, hoping to tell if there was a hint of magic in this death, but there was none that he could find. He leaned closer to the corpse to study the flesh. A silver plate of salt had been placed on the barrel chest, an old custom that Manus recalled was intended to keep the spirit from getting back into the body. Folk of lesser means used a clod of earth instead, unable to afford the luxury of wasting good seasoning.

So there was no magic involved, which meant the Laird MacElwyn had not been properly sacrificed to Arawn. Manus leaned closer, only to have one of the women step through him. The disconcerting sense of her presence made him shudder, and she, in turn, gave a gasp and whispered, "I felt a chill."

The other women looked about in uncertainty. One quickly shifted the plate of salt as though that move would rid them of whatever ill luck they thought had come to visit them here, and the movement allowed Manus to clearly see the knife wound in the Laird's chest. Stabbed to death. The memory of meeting such a death himself made him want to be elsewhere.

Best he get on with finding Ginny.

Of course, what he was going to do when he found her was another matter all together. He had no power to release her from her prison.

All hope lay in Ginny herself. If she would just let him share her flesh, all would be well.

He pondered these matters as he slipped out of the Laird's chambers and made his way to another section of the keep. And he was going to start downward into the lower regions when he sensed that something was amiss. As though some hand had touched a part of him.

The cairn stone!

Manus whipped back towards the storage chamber where, much to his chagrin, he found the basket had been removed.

As to where his stone was, he had no idea.

I won't need it before the dawn, he told himself in hopes of keeping his courage intact. By then, he could likely have Ginny out of this place and be back at Tamhasg Wood.

At least, he sincerely hoped so.

Chapter Twenty-Three

In the past, desperation had driven Ginny to act rashly on her own behalf. Running away from home, living with Manus to learn her craft in spite of the fact that his lust for heather ale made him impossible to deal with at times. Had he cared for her half as much as he cared for his precious brew, her life might not be about to end so ignominiously.

That anger spurred her even now, and she fought to push it aside. Concentration was what she needed. She had learned it over the years. That and the fact that mageborn did not always need tongues to cast spells.

"It would seem that you are one of those rare mageborn who can cast spells with your emotions as well as your words," Manus once told her when she had described her supernatural experiences as a child. "That would explain why hearth fires and crockery reacted to your presence as they did."

"But why, if mageborn must learn the spell tongue to cast magic?" she had asked.

"Well, I'm no scholar," Manus said, "but I was told, when I was a lad and mage sign first manifested in me, that in the days when the Old Ones walked among men, there was no mage tongue. The Old Ones and the magic were one with each other and the world, and they needed only their wills to work the wonders of the craft. But when the Great Cataclysm shook the world and left but a few of the Old Ones to tarry, they knew that in order to pass the magic on to mortalkind so that the world could survive, there would have to be a tongue, for they learned that when they mixed their immortal blood with our own, it was weakened. So they gave words to the spells that humankind blessed with mage blood could use that power. But according to the Great Uncle what taught me the craft, ye dinna always have to speak the spells if yer will and the blood of the Old Ones you carry is strong."

Ginny had wondered about that most of her life. She remembered the tales of the Old Ones and their power, and how they had meddled too much with nature, causing the Great Cataclysm that brought about their eventual doom. She also recalled all those times as a child when she felt so closely tied to the world around her, it was as though she could sense every tree, every rock and every blade of grass in her blood. Those were the days when she would sit alone in the woods and on the moors and listen to the whisper of the wind. The days when she felt that she and the world were one. All it had taken was silence and concentration.

Of course, it had been years since she sent hearth fires blazing. Manus had taught her the stricturing of her power so she could freely express feelings of ire without risking the roof over their heads. But now, if she could just lay those strictures aside in her mind. Break the fetters on her magic and reach out with the raw force that had blossomed in her from early on, and perhaps then she could free herself and the lad curled in a wretched knot across the cell.

Ginny closed her eyes and sought the silence within. She let her senses drift, reaching into the ground beneath her first to find what essence waited there. The web of Edain's blood taint could be felt in much of it, but here and there, Ginny found patches of power that were clean of Edain's foul touch. These, she carefully gathered to her, drawing them into the core of mage essence that filled her soul and sang in her blood.

Once she felt enough essence to spare, she shifted her concentration. Where she leaned against the wall, she let her senses drift into the stone, touching it with her mage essence, sending tendrils of awareness to slip through the stone and head for the wall mounts of iron. As soon as she touched them, she felt their age. Old iron that had been here since the keep was first built. Rusty iron, weakened through years of deterioration.

Ginny clung to that, letting her mage senses seep into every weak crack of the metal. Where the rust had eaten the metal, she pushed harder with the essence she had stored in herself, tapping away with the patience of a stonecutter. And with each push, she felt the essence of iron grow weaker and weaker. Brittle as thin ice on a pond.

Her head started to swim with the effort, but she would not give up now. The iron was fracturing. She sensed it crumbling, felt it giving way. She took a deep breath and pulled as hard as she was physically able to on the shackles themselves, and was satisfied to feel them shatter and shower her head with bits of metallic debris. The chains thumped the reeds as her arms dropped to her sides. She was free.

Ginny tore the gag from her mouth, spitting out the dry cloth. Then she worried the shackle bands until they fell from her wrists. Quickly, she pushed herself off the floor and reached for Fafne.

He started as she touched him, looking up at her with animal fright in his eyes.

"It's all right," she whispered and worked on the shackles that held him, weaving bits of magic into the metal to weaken it so it fell open and set him free.

"How will we get out?" he asked as she pulled him to his

feet and made for the door.

"With even more difficulty than before," she said. She put hands out to test the wood, and even before her fingers brushed its mitred surface, she felt the wards that had been laid on the wood. Edain was taking no chances. Ginny sighed, backing away and crossing her arms. Free and yet still a prisoner. Horns.

"What now?" Fafne asked.

"Let me think," Ginny said. The gate spell was still out. And digging was impossible without a shovel and a sense of direction.

"Well, ten feet down and then take a westerly turn, and ye might get there by Winter Feast," a familiar voice rang through the air.

"Manus?" Ginny turned around, looking about.

"In spirit, if not in flesh," he said, and manifested by sliding up through the floor reeds.

Had he not been incorporeal, she would have thrown arms around him for joy just to see him. Then again, she quickly reminded herself that he'd given her enough grief to last a lifetime, but she was grateful to see him all the same, for it meant he was all right.

"Where have you been?" she found herself snapping at him out of habit.

"Trying to find a door that wasn't barred by magic and demon spit," he replied. "It's good to see you're alive and well, lass, but I think now we'd best concentrate on getting you and the lad out of here."

"How?" she said. "The door is blocked and I can't gate myself . . ."

He cocked his head sideways as she spoke, mischief swelling in his eyes. "Well, I know of only one way to remedy that, lass."

"I . . ." she hesitated, the old uncertainty rising to cloud her thoughts.

"Ginny," he said gently, his whole demeanor changing as he moved closer. "What are ye afraid of?"

"I'm not afraid of anything," she said, turning away.

"Oh, yes you are," he said. "I sense it in you even now."

"I just don't like the idea of having your spirit inside me," she said.

"Neither did Auntie Maeve, but she cooperated enough to let me gate her here and get my cairn stone into the keep," Manus said.

"What?" Ginny turned back.

"My stone was the only way I could get in," he replied. "Lady Edain has this keep saturated with wards and traps, and I knew I'd never be able to gate straight in without setting off all manner of magical bells and whistles. As it is, getting out will be tricky. We can gate out, but she's likely to put the Nidubh on as we do. Mageborn can be foiled from following gate spells, but demons have an uncanny way of catching a magical trail that has been scattered and still finding the source."

"Then it would be useless for us to try and gate ourselves out of this place," she said.

"Out of Dun Elwyn, aye. Stealth 'twill be our best tool. Out of this cell, however . . ."

Ginny frowned and looked at Fafne. The lad was watching them with a mask of uncertainty that mirrored the feelings she was trying to keep hidden.

"Ginny," Manus said. "I don't want to hurt ye, lass. I've grown far too fond of ye."

"You should have thought of that the night you went wandering the moors full of heather ale and perished," she blurted, then took a deep breath and closed her eyes.

"What?"

"You know perfectly well what I mean," she said, turning back to glower at him.

But puzzlement had taken the usual shine from his gaze. "What are ye saying, lass?"

"If you had really cared as much for me as you claim now, you would have stopped drinking and wandering the moors and leaving me alone to worry about ye so . . ." She paused, looking down, not sure why the words were sticking in her throat.

"Ginny?" he said softly. "Lass, I . . . I never knew. Ye ne'er gave me a sign of how ye felt then."

"I was afraid to," she whispered. "Every man in my life proved a traitor to me. Even you with your drinking and wandering and blethering. Of course, what should I have expected? You had a wife and loved her dearly. There was no room for anyone else in your heart."

"In my heart?" he said. "Ginny, I would have dumped every keg of heather ale in the world for a sweet word from you. When you first came, I thought ye were a gift from the gods to comfort me for my loss, but ye were so cold to me then. When I wandered, it was just as much to curse those who had hurt ye and made yer heart stone as it was to mourn my own loss."

She turned away once more, throat thick with pain. *Why? Why hadn't he said something then?* "I would have given anything for a sign that you truly cared," she said. "And that is why I fear having you in me now. I never knew your touch when you were alive. How can I bear it now that you are dead?"

A long, slow sound like a sigh escaped him.

"We can't unmake the past, Ginny," Manus said. "It's a bit late for that now. And unless you put the past aside and

161

let me help you now, 'twill be no future for either of us or the lad."

Ginny glanced at Fafne, then back at Manus.

"Ye have my word, Ginny Ni Cooley," Manus said with a gentle smile. "I'll give ye back yer body as soon as we're out of this cell . . . and I won't land ye in a pile of sheep droppings like I did Auntie Maeve."

She blinked at him. "You put that dear old woman into sheep droppings?"

He shrugged. "Aye, well, there's none of that in the upper halls where I plan to take us . . . if ye'll let me."

Ginny nodded, slowly. "What must I do?"

"Sit yerself down and relax, lass, and I'll manage the rest," he said.

She nodded again, sinking to the ground, and closing her eyes.

A faint breeze seemed to tickle her as his essence sank into her. At first, there was the sense of losing all control, and she panicked, taking a sharp breath at the sensation.

"Relax," he repeated, his voice warm and soothing within her.

Ginny took a deep breath and obeyed. Masculine essence spread through her limbs, vibrant with strength and magic.

"There now, that was simple enough," he said.

They rose as one, standing in the cell. She was not in charge of herself as she motioned Fafne to her side. Her arms spread wide and she heard herself whispering spell words as she drew power to her from the very stones and ground on which she stood. Blue light flashed before her, a whorl that spread wide and showed her a corridor where torches and candles blazed.

Magic flared within her as she stepped into the blue whorl and entered another place.

162

Chapter Twenty-Four

The warmth that Manus' essence sent rippling through every inch of Ginny's being sloughed off like water as he drew his spirit out of her body. For a moment, she was left staggering under a strange sense of loss and longing.

"Are ye all right, lass?" Manus said softly from close behind her.

Horns, she thought and took a deep breath before she turned to face him and nodded. "I'm fine," she said. Except for the flush of her cheeks and the patter of her heart. She had not felt such a sensation since she was fourteen and a handsome, older cousin had bowed to her and kissed her hand. Of course, later, she had seen him do likewise to her elder sister with the same charming smile, and that was when she first came to realize some young men looked upon gaining the favor of as many females as possible as a manly challenge. That often, their flattery was nothing more than a ruse to wrap their plaidie about the lass. "I'm just a little dizzy, that's all."

"The gate spell can do that to ye if yer not used to it," Manus agreed with a nod. "Is that why ye were frowning?"

Ginny blinked, realizing she must have allowed her thoughts to mar her features. "Just thinking," she said.

"Not about me, I hope," he quipped.

She made a face at him to assure him otherwise, and glanced over to where Fafne crouched on his haunches. He was scratching the back of his ear with one hand. Horns, she hoped the lad wasn't getting fleas. She crossed the room, taking firm hold of his arm and drawing him to his feet.

"Which way?" she asked Manus.

"Well, that way lies the bloodmage's lair, so I don't recommend it as a path we want to take," he said, gesturing in one direction, "while that corridor leads to the master chambers and the Laird's corpse." His arm shifted. "I think that way, mayhaps. There are back stairs leading down to the servants' quarters and the kitchen wing. But before we can take any path, we need to find my cairn stone."

"Where did you leave it?" Ginny asked.

"Well, I last saw it in a laundry basket in the linen closet," he said, "but after I went exploring a bit and before I found you, I came back to seek my stone and found it missing."

"Someone took it, perhaps?" she suggested, not liking the thought.

" 'Twould seem so," he said with a frown.

"It could have been the servant who was doing the laundry," Ginny said. "If I were putting away linens and found a stone, I would probably toss it out."

"Aye," Manus said. "Assuming it was a servant that found it."

"Can you sense it?" Ginny asked.

Manus shook his head. Ginny sighed and closed her eyes, fixing the image of the cairn stone and its essence within her mind. Once the image was clear, she sent mage senses stretching out around her, carefully probing for the stone as she avoided the marks of the Nidubh and Edain's bloodmagic taint. But the stone was nowhere in the immediate vicinity. Ginny pushed farther out, and the effort was rewarded.

"Oh, dear," she muttered.

"What?" Manus asked.

"It's with the corpse," she said darkly.

Manus frowned. "Why would they put it there?" he muttered.

"Come on," Ginny said, taking Fafne's arm and starting in the direction of the master chambers.

" 'Twill be auld women in there," Manus said. "They might not take kindly to your intrusion on their grief."

"We can't leave the stone here," Ginny said. "If Edain finds it, she'll use it to capture you."

"Well, you've a point there," Manus agreed.

"Besides, I can always spell the women into leaving with misdirection."

"Ye'd better stricture it well, or the Lady will sense ye," Manus said with a shudder.

Ginny nodded and started Fafne down the corridor. Manus followed them invisibly, though she could still sense him, and having had his essence in her seemed to sharpen her awareness of his presence.

At a turn in the corridor, they paused. Ginny whispered, *"Faic mi cha,"* being careful to draw the spell essence from herself as she leaned around the corner to glance down the way.

Two men draped in mourning plaid with sword and targe at the ready stood before the door that centered the corridor. *Horns,* Ginny thought as she drew back. The stone was in that very chamber. She glanced back towards where she sensed Manus waiting.

"No auld women," she whispered. "Just two guards."

"I'll handle them," Manus said, materializing just enough for her to see the sparkle of mischief she always dreaded.

"Just don't be too obvious," she said.

165

His smile was the last part of him to fade. Ginny wanted to shout in rage, for she knew that look too well. Instead, she gritted her teeth, and speaking the spell of misdirection once more, she peered around the corner.

A faint moan whimpered from the far end of the corridor where another door was. The guards traded uneasy glances with one another, then cast a look back at the room they guarded.

"I cannot find my plaidie," a voice whispered from down the way. "How can I be buried if I cannot find my plaidie?"

From down the way, a faint figure materialized, a naked man wearing the visage of the Laird MacElwyn.

"Where is my plaidie," he moaned softly. "You must find my plaidie for me, please. I cannot cross to the Summerland unclothed . . ."

Apparently, dealing with spirit folk was not part of their manly training. Still, one of the guards drew his dagger and with a shout, he pointed it at the spirit.

"Begone, creature of the nether realms!" he cried.

"You would betray me?" the spirit said, its face contorting into something more horrifying. "Then you will join me in Annwn!"

The spirit lunged at them, and that was all it took to turn brave men into children. The guards turned and ran towards Ginny, and she barely pulled back, whispering, *"Faic mi cha!"* before they flashed past her and went racing for the stairs.

"Brilliant, Manus!" Ginny hissed in anger as she raced into the corridor and headed for the master chamber. "There will be a score of guards up here before you could say your own name."

"More than enough time," the spirit replied and shifted back into his old familiar form. "Let's fetch my stone and get out of here before they get their kilts and their courage back in order."

She suppressed an angry oath, quickly trying the door to the master chamber. All was quiet within. The washing women had apparently finished their chore. Laird MacElwyn lay covered in his precious plaidie, a silver plate of salt on his chest. A few candle stands had been placed about, their flames sending darkness gliding about the edges of the room where the windows were shuttered. Black cloth had been draped over the headboard and the furniture, giving the whole room an eerie sense of doom. Ginny slipped inside, pulling Fafne with her and closing the door even as Manus stepped blithely through the wood.

"I was convincing, wasn't I?" he asked.

Ginny rolled her eyes. "Boast later," she said. "Let's find your stone."

They scanned the room, and Ginny once more closed her eyes, using her mage senses to scry for the bit of rock. She quickly found it, sitting on a table over by the shadowy wall. Quickly, she crossed the room, reaching for the bit of rock, eager to be away from this place.

"Ginny!" Manus cried.

She felt the surge of darkness even as he shouted. Instinct more than anything made her throw herself back as the very ebon cloth on the table swelled into a hideous shape and dove at her with a snarl. Demon essence surrounded Ginny. She felt hot breath and jaws snapping just inches from her face as she tumbled backwards. An involuntary shriek escaped her lungs as she hit the floor. Large black paws planted themselves on either side of her head. She found herself looking into fiery eyes and a maw of sharp fangs.

"NO!" Manus shouted and charged forward.

Before Ginny could wonder what he was about, she felt his mage essence collide with her own. Blackness surged across her vision briefly as Manus attached his awareness to hers. She heard herself shout in a gruff manner, felt her fist fly up of its own accord, and yelped when it slammed into the soft part of the Nidubh's canine nose. The black hound gave a howl of pain and jerked away, and Ginny was free to charge to her feet.

"*Gath saighead buail!*" she snapped, and sent a magebolt at the monster with startling speed. The demon dog howled again, and Ginny felt Manus preparing for another strike.

"Behind you!" Fafne shouted in a frightened voice.

Too late did Ginny start to turn. The weight of a small stone clutched in a fist snapped into the side of her head. Sharp pain sent flashes of red across her vision as she fell to the reed-strewn floor.

"I cannot believe I underestimated you two again . . ."

Ginny rolled onto her back and found herself looking up at the white-haired bloodmage who balanced Manus' cairn stone deftly in the palm of her hand as she glowered.

The stone! She has the stone! Ginny didn't know if that was her thought or Manus', but she felt herself urgently fighting nausea and pain to rise and reclaim it. But before she could even get off the floor, Lady Edain held forth the cairn stone and hissed, "*Le mo toil mi ceangal thu dhuibh clach!*"

If Ginny thought she hurt before, she realized the sensation was mild compared to the new agony that sent fire to sear her nerves. Manus' essence was torn from her body, and it burned so much, she had to scream. And somewhere in the midst of the pain, she thought she heard him shrieking as well.

Voices suddenly filled the corridor outside the door.

Ginny felt the last of Manus ripped from her as shouts of men filtered through her pain. The guards were returning, and they were not alone.

"*Mistress, we are undone if they find us here!*" the Nidubh shouted.

"Not yet!" Edain snapped. "*Mo bi ann Ginny . . . Ginny bi ann mo!*"

Bodies were rushing into the chamber as Ginny felt more magic sweep over her. She was vaguely aware of the sense that something foul cloaked her own flesh. The Nidubh threw off its animal guise for one closer to its true shape. Its whip of a tail stretched to seize Ginny up off the floor. She could do no more than dangle helplessly in that grasp as the creature snagged Fafne as well. His voice filled the chamber with short-high-pitched yelps.

But it was hearing the sound of her own voice shouting from another place that threw confusion into Ginny's muddled senses.

"Stay back, all of you, or the Lady Edain will die!"

What? Ginny thought, struggling to open her eyes and push white hair from her face . . . *My hair isn't . . .* From her lofty perch, she could see well enough the figure on the floor holding fire in one hand. *That looks like me!*

She started to shout, "She is deceiving you!" but part of the demon's scaly tail turned into a hand that clamped hard over her mouth. Ginny struggled, but her head was still swimming, and her body still ached from the trauma of having Manus' essence jerked out of her.

Then Lady Edain, in Ginny's voice, began the words of a gate spell.

But she told them I couldn't cast such a spell, Ginny thought. *She told me when they were taking me back to the dungeon that I was a weak little mage . . .*

169

And yet, here she was casting greater spells in Ginny's form.

Blackness swirled into a mouth as the gate spell opened a dark rift in the world. The demon moved into it first, carrying Ginny and Fafne along. In desperation, Ginny bit at the appendage covering her mouth. The Nidubh merely laughed and released her mouth . . .

Your mistake, Ginny thought, raising her hand. *"Loisg!"* she said and threw white fire into those red eyes.

The demon shrieked and practically threw Ginny into the void of darkness. She struck what felt like a wall of stone before all awareness fled, though just before she fainted, she swore she heard someone in the master chamber shout, "The Lady Edain is mageborn too!"

Chapter Twenty-Five

When Edain cast her spell to bind Manus to his cairn stone, his first instinct was to throw every ounce of his will into fighting the call. He would not let her imprison him so, not while he had an ounce of freedom, and as a result, he tried desperately to weave his essence into Ginny's to keep himself a part of her. But then he heard her screams of pain, and found himself echoing the cry as he shared her awareness of agony. The spell was literally ripping him out of her, and the very act of tearing their souls apart was going to kill her if he did not let go.

So he did, and felt himself thrown into the depths of the small cairn stone. His essence slammed into it as surely as he'd been tossed against a wall, shooting more pain into non-existing nerves. He nearly lost all awareness at that moment.

Then the agony abated, and he found himself battering the walls of his prison in a foolish rage. How could he let this happen? How could he have failed Ginny this way? He had allowed a mere bloodmage to deceive him in the worst way . . . to trap him as though he were no more than an insignificant insect.

He would gladly have thrown his anger at her, but now that he lacked corporeal flesh, he was helpless.

Besides, there was an awful lot of magic being bandied about outside his stone. Magic of a proportion that caused his curiosity to burn his anger away. A mixture of blood and demon magic, sharp as new blades.

171

Eagerly, Manus pressed himself to the edge of his cairn stone. A prisoner he might be, but he still had sight and hearing.

At first, it revealed only darkness. *So change directions, ye gormless gyte,* he scolded himself, and moved to the opposite side to peer out at the world.

The eye of his essence perceived fingers and a hand. Beyond that, he saw the Nidubh had switched back to its less desirable true shape. Black and scaly with a canine head, it stood upright, revealing a hag's wretched body. Horns, he'd never seen anything so ugly in his whole life. No wonder demonkind shapeshifted so much. Probably couldn't stand the sight of their true selves. Its tail had stretched and split into appendages, one part of which was wrapped about Edain's waist.

Edain? How?

He shifted again to look the other way. The hand that held him was attached to a very familiar shape. *Ginny?* She was speaking harshly to an ever-growing crowd of men and women gathering in the chamber, threatening to kill the Lady Edain if any among them were so foolish as to try and stop her. Then she started the words of a gate spell and opened a black rift in the fabric of the world. Towing Fafne and carrying Edain, the Nidubh started towards that hole.

But Ginny couldn't cast a gate spell. It took moons of practice to learn and time to perfect, for it was one of the most dangerous spells any mageborn could work. Manus had taken moons to learn it, and he always practiced with the guidance of his master. He'd been practicing for nearly a year before he tried it on his own. There was no way she could have learned it in the short time he had shared her flesh.

On the other hand, the Nidubh would never have followed Ginny anywhere with such docility.

Edain! Had to be. There was no other explanation.

We destroyed your safe haven, he thought. *They must know your true nature now.*

He drew back from the stone as he felt it moving for the gate. There was the tingle of magic's blood essence touching his awareness, then a quiet that set ill with him. He didn't like being helpless this way.

At length, magic folded around him again. Someone was weaving spells in a circular pattern. He pressed himself once more to the edge and saw that his stone had been placed on a larger one, and by shifting around, he could see the woman kneeling a short ways off. Her moon-white hair brushed the ground as she marked a circle about him. He could not tell where they were, but he got the vague impression of an old stone hall that had fallen into misuse, for above there were portions of sky visible. Edain continued to draw the circle around him, whispering spell words as she made marks on the flagstones.

Where in the name of Cernunnos are we?

She glanced up towards him, and a faint smile stretched fey lips. "Well, so you can see, can you?" she said.

"Which means you can hear me," he said darkly.

"Why, yes, I can. You are a very strong presence. Arawn should be pleased."

"What do you mean?"

"Oh, you needn't pretend ignorance of the fate I've chosen for you," she said.

"Maybe I wasn't paying attention," he said flatly.

"Indeed," she said, and continued her task. "Then all will be revealed in due time. We've still one more night before the Solstice, and I am making sure you stay put until then."

"But you've lost your sacrifice, haven't ye?" he said. "That means yer bargain with Arawn is broken."

"Not necessarily," she said. "It is true that I have lost the prepared sacrifice to a little oversight, and that I have lost the comfort of my life before I was ready to relinquish it, but I have not lost my soul yet because I have something just as pleasing for the Dark Lord's Cauldron of Doom."

Manus frowned, though he knew she could not see the expression. "Where's Ginny?" he asked. "And the lad?"

Edain fixed him with a hard look. "In due time," she said. "Now, please be quiet before I am tempted to throw silence over your stone. I need all my concentration to finish this little task, and then I will be happy to fill your last hours with all the answers I can."

Manus held his tongue and watched as Edain finished the spell work. He knew now what she was about. She was sealing his stone within the same sort of circle one used to bind otherworld elements when summoning them. He didn't like the look of that.

At length, she ceased to mark the ground and whispered a spell while touching the circle she'd made. He had to admit, her skill was admirable for one who had turned her life into a path of darkness. And all for what? Power? She had that. Money? She seemed disinterested there.

All to save her own life, he thought.

The spell wove around him, burning the edges of his essence with its presence. He watched as a sphere of power formed, encasing his stone and the ground.

"All right, now," she said. "You can come out of your stone."

"Not exactly," he said.

"Le mo toil, mi saor thu a do clach," she said with a smile, gesturing almost tiredly with one hand.

174

Manus felt the spell binding him into the stone wash cold from his essence. With a gasp, he practically dove out of the stone, only to tumble back when his exuberant exit tossed him against the colorful lines of the sphere. With a yelp, he fell back, landing on the flagstones. Fortunately, the only thing hurt was his pride, though the sphere did have quite a sting. He pulled himself to his feet in a weary fashion, straightening his plaidie and crossing his arms to glower at the bloodmage.

"All right, now where is Ginny?" he insisted in a firm voice that might have had more effect had he been free. Edain merely cocked her head.

"She and the lad are with the Nidubh in another portion of this old place," Edain said.

"Where are we?"

"This place?" she said and gestured around her. "This is the plot of land that started all the blood feuds between MacArdagh and MacElwyn so many generations ago, no one can remember."

He glanced about, better able to perceive that his surrounding was an old hall.

"They say this rath was once the home of Old Ones," she said. "There's a line of power passing over it, and another crossing under. One north to south, one east to west . . . and I don't have to tell you what that means."

"This place is a portal," Manus said.

"Yes, and I have been preparing it for some time," Edain said. "I had planned to bring Rory here for a romantic evening alone."

"That would have ended in his death, I imagine."

"Of course, but I would have seen to it that the death looked innocent enough. That's why I always choose vigorous old men for this. No one questions their passing. I

175

would have rushed back to Dun Elwyn in tears, declaring that my Laird died in my arms in a moment of passion that proved more than his old, weakened heart could take."

"How convenient," Manus said. "Too bad he took his own life."

"Yes, well, even I could not see the extent of his madness over Tomis' capture and conviction," she said. "Personally, I would have thought he would have been furious at the shame his son brought on his name."

"One never knows what a man is really thinking," Manus said. "Or where his true loyalties lie."

"This is true, and matters were starting to look a bit bleak at first. I saw you and the little hedge witch as nothing more than an inconvenience to my secrets, easily eliminated under the right circumstances. But then, Rory had to go and ruin everything, all because he loved his son better than I could have imagined. Fortunately, your interference has also provided me with the means to fulfill my bargain with Arawn."

"Why?"

"Why what?"

"Why give me to him?" Manus said. "Why not try to defeat him instead?"

"Surely, you jest," she said.

"It could be done," Manus said. "Ginny and I could help you break free of him."

"Could you, now?" Edain said. "Such a generous offer from one who has so little time. No, I think not. Why should I let you help me, then risk having you go to the Mage Council and tell them about me? This way is better. You shall be my sacrifice to Arawn. Your little Ginny will feed her essence to the Nidubh, and her body will be left in my form to fool the masses into believing I died by that terrible creature's hand."

"And the lad?"

"He will spend the rest of his days as his family shall. The Hounds of Ardagh will be meat for stories for generations to come. And not one drop of MacArdagh blood will have been shed to tell the great Council of Mageborn the true tale."

"Yer a heartless lass, ye know," Manus said.

"Yes, that is true," she said. "I value my life and I want to keep it, and if being heartless is the way to keep it, so be it. Is that so wrong? Wanting to live and survive to see another dawn?"

"It is if it means others must suffer so you can survive," Manus said.

"Pity," she said. "I thought you would understand, being mageborn yourself . . . and dead. Life is a precious thing, and even those of us who are blessed with more of it than mortalkind can appreciate that. I plan to keep living as long as possible, and I plan to keep my soul in the bargain."

She started away from him.

"Don't even think about trying to escape the sphere," she said. "It would burn your essence quite painfully."

"I'll remember that," he said. "But tell me, where will you go once we are gone?"

"I think Yewer will be my next home," she said. "There's a certain baron there who recently lost his wife and is seeking another."

She disappeared into the shadows at the far end. Manus frowned and looked around.

There didn't seem to be any sign of weakness in the sphere.

Horns, he thought, and hoped Ginny was thinking of a plan.

Chapter Twenty-Six

"Wake up . . ."

Those words filtered through the muddle of Ginny's brain, a sweet coo that reminded her of when she was small and her mother would come in to rouse her for the day. And yet, there was something more sinister underlying the gentle call that took her a moment to fathom.

Ginny opened her eyes to find the glacial stare of the bloodmage quite close.

"Had a nice nap?" Edain said. "Oh, don't bother trying to answer."

The gag did nothing to hide Ginny's glower. Edain smiled and sat back. Off to one side, Ginny could hear lapping sounds, and when she shifted her head, she found Fafne close at her side, hunched over a bowl of thin soup which he slurped up with his tongue. Furtive eyes rose to greet her stare, like a beast fearing it would lose its meal to a greater predator.

"He's getting to be quite good at that," Edain said cheerfully. "Very little effort on my part will be needed to change him completely."

Had her tongue been free, Ginny would have let it lash at the bloodmage for her cruel jest. She wolfed back the desire, though, eager to learn where she had been taken. Her gaze wandered around at what looked like ruins. Broken walls and open windows through which a pale bit of gloaming was still visible. And around Ginny; she sensed old magic faintly permeating the stones.

"I think its ancient name was Dun Daileban," Edain said as though understanding the meaning of the glance. "Old Ones once lived here. MacArdagh and MacElwyn fought for this land. A pity that neither of them really understood the value of it."

Which is? Ginny wondered.

"Can you feel the ley lines?" Edain asked.

Ginny closed her eyes and stretched mage senses. White fire surrounded her, two lines of power running from cardinal points.

"Before the Great Cataclysm, this place was thought to be a seat of power used by the Old Ones, a gateway to many worlds beyond our imagining," Edain said. "Now, it is little more than a haven for mice and stoats and ravens, but still, the power lingers. Here, I shall call forth the Dark Lord of Annwn, and give him the soul of your dead mage friend. I'm sure Arawn will be pleased."

As Ginny opened her eyes, her foot twitched with the need to plant it firmly in Edain's pretty face. The bloodmage must have suspected as much for she drew back, rising to her feet to tower over Ginny and smile.

"Enjoy your last evening," Edain said. "Tomorrow night is the Solstice and, when the dark hour reigns, Manus will be given to Arawn's Cauldron of Doom, the lad shall be a hound and your spirit essence will feed the Nidubh. And this time, I promise you will not escape."

She gestured off towards the patch of shadows that formed in one corner of the room. A hideous shape, half-hound and half-woman with fiery eyes, watched Ginny from the inky protection of growing night.

"The Nidubh will see to it that you are no more trouble to me," Edain said. "After all, if you escape again, the demon will have lost a fine meal. Now, I must begin the

179

final preparations to properly greet the Dark Lord's coming." She cast a glance at the Nidubh. "And I will not be disturbed under any circumstances, is that understood?"

"As you will," the Nidubh said in its true voice.

With those words, Edain slipped away like a shadow.

Horns, Ginny thought. This time, she'd been bound with her hands behind her back, and as near as she could feel, the knots were tight. Besides, the moment she showed any sign of trying to struggle, the Nidubh lunged just to the edge of the shadows and snarled a warning. Fafne quickly pulled back against the wall, leaning over his precious dish of soup, and Ginny smelled enough of it to wish she could have a share. Her stomach was empty of anything decent.

A fine mess, she thought darkly. Where was Manus? Still in his stone, like as not. Poor Manus. Trapped and unable to assist in any fashion. Not that he would have been able to help her if he were free. For that matter, she could easily blame this mess on him. If he hadn't tried to frighten the guards as he did . . .

No, she couldn't really throw all the blame on him. Edain had already made her plans clear. Ginny should have thought out her own escape a little more carefully the first time. Then she would have been well outside the walls of Dun Elwyn before Edain knew Ginny and the lad were gone.

Fafne finished the last of his soup and crawled over to Ginny's side, leaning against her as though eager to share warmth. The scent of his pelt made her wonder if Thistle was all right. As near as she knew, she'd last seen him wandering the woods of Ghloelea, chasing Ginny's captors. She did hope he was all right. At least, Auntie Maeve could take care of him . . .

But Auntie Maeve is still back at Dun Elwyn, Ginny thought and made a face. So the old woman was nowhere near her own home and would likely have no way of knowing what had become of Manus and Ginny. And since Auntie Maeve could not use the gate spell, that meant there was no one to look after the moor terrier. Granted, Thistle could take care of himself. *Better than I obviously can.* He would just go find some small game, oblivious to his mistress' fate. The thought that he would not even care did occur to her as well, and the advent of such a thought tightened her throat with despair.

No one will ever know what has become of me, she thought darkly. The villagers at Conorscroft would likely miss their mage when wells and cattle ran dry, and the mischievous bogies of Tamhasg Wood started to invade their hen houses and granaries and stores. The hob would likely finish off all of Ginny's hens before taking after someone else's flock. Eventually, the villagers would tire of the mess, cursing Ginny's lack of concern as they approached the Council of Mageborn to find them another to live in their area and look after their magical needs.

The shadows were lengthening, and the Nidubh braved the center of the floor now. As near as Ginny could tell, this was some sort of kitchen, for mage sight revealed a large fireplace and several overturned tables of stone. She ignored the demon and stretched mage senses once more, determined to explore as much as she could. She touched power here and there, little wisps of old magic that was as soft and feathery as that she had found in the lea stone as a child. Then she found something much stronger, a spell woven with the essence of blood and death. It was so alien to this place, she knew it had to be something Edain had set. And if Ginny pushed at it hard enough, she felt something else as well, something strong and familiar.

Manus . . .

Whatever the blood spell was, he was trapped within it. At least, he's still alive . . . or unsundered, she corrected herself.

"Stop that!" the Nidubh hissed in a gravel-like voice, and Ginny felt the hot breath of the demon practically in her face. She opened her eyes to find the distorted canine countenance close, and Fafne cowering behind her.

I'm not doing anything wrong! she thought angrily, and to make that point clear, she shoved her foot into the stomach of the cadaverous-shaped beast. The Nidubh lurched back and snarled, saliva dripping from the jaws.

Fafne suddenly yelped and hid his face in Ginny's hair. The cowardly reaction seemed to amuse the Nidubh, for a grin spread across its face, sharp and toothy.

"What's the matter, little pup?" the demon said in a teasing manner. *"Are you frightened of me?"*

The Nidubh's tail stretched and reached around to nudge the lad, who yelped again and clung to Ginny. The tail pushed again, and Ginny watched helplessly, cursing herself for being unable to assist the poor lad. Her anger welled. *He's done nothing to deserve this!* Had she hands and a tongue, she would have burned the evil beast to teach it better manners. But she could no more have stopped the sun from setting outside the broken window, where cool wind was whipping the limbs of trees and rattling old shutters.

The Nidubh split its tail this time, sending a tendril around both sides of Ginny. Those ends poked and prodded the lad, caressing his hair, pulling his tail.

"What's wrong, whelp?" the Nidubh continued. *"Where's your courage?"*

Leave him alone! Ginny screamed in her head, and once more she lashed at the Nidubh with her feet. It was dangerous to strike at a demon, and she knew the Nidubh could just as easily slash Ginny's throat with one of those talons, but the demon seemed more intent on tormenting the lad. With a snarl, the creature shoved Ginny out of the way, throwing her over to one side.

"You, I will deal with in due time," the demon said and rose to tower over the cowering lad.

Horns! Ginny struggled against her ropes, seeking to free her hands. The rough hemp rubbed and burned, but anger was giving her the courage to keep fighting.

Fafne sprang away with high-pitched yips, scrambling for any route of escape. But every way he turned, the Nidubh was there, cutting off his escape, sometimes with its tail, sometimes with a claw. And still others, the demon would elongate its neck and snap jaws at the lad, sending him scurrying another way. Ginny saw it all as she got her knees under her and glanced around at the room.

The fireplace was long ago abandoned, and with it, bits of iron that had once formed pokers and grates. Ginny crawled to her feet and used the demon's distraction to race towards those. She sank down at the end of a broken grate and began to rub the ropes against it. Rusty bits of iron crumbled, but there were edges too. She tried to ignore the thought that cutting herself on iron could lead to poisoning of the blood if the wound were not treated. Besides, the ropes were starting to fray, and loosened enough that she could get her hands free. She reached up and snatched the gag from her mouth and turned . . .

A long black tail knotted like a fist slammed Ginny off to one side. She hit the edge of the fireplace hard, tumbling in a daze.

"It's not as easy as that," the Nidubh said, rearing over Ginny. Talons seized her shoulders and dragged her up-

right. *"There is no way I am going to let you spoil the mistress' plans, little mage. If I must claim your essence now, so be it!"*

The hideous face leaned close, its rank breath burning Ginny's nose. Fiery eyes blazed over a hideous grin. Ginny looked at the fangs and wondered which would be the quicker death—to be rent or sundered.

"NO!" a youthful voice shrieked, and with its cry, the air became a chorus of hounds howling in response.

The Nidubh barely turned its head in time to see the iron poker that bashed into its nose, and though its flesh was impervious to the cut of mortal steel, the poker had apparently been forged in Old Ones' fire. The demon shrieked in pain from the well-aimed blow. Ginny fell as those talons released her, dropping her carelessly to the hearth. She struggled upright in time to see Fafne dropping the poker and running across the kitchen.

Five long strides were all he managed. The Nidubh roared in anger, lashing out with its tail. At first, Ginny feared the beast would inflict a wound with its poisonous barb, but the Nidubh seemed more eager to enact other forms of revenge. Clearly, it had forgotten Edain's orders that the lad was not to be harmed. The demon wrapped its tail around the lad's neck, jerking him back.

Ginny struggled to get her feet under her. Struggled to find a source of power when she touched the ley line. *Yes!* she thought and jerked it to her, filling her mage essence with its fire.

And with a shout, she turned that fire on the back of the beast, praying that she did not harm the lad as well. White fire wrapped around the dark demon like a cloak. The Nidubh screamed as its flesh was seared from its bones. It dropped Fafne to the ground and turned for Ginny.

She hit it again, feeling the sear of those ancient flames

coursing through her mage blood. Every bit of anger she could muster went with the strike. It was as if she was back in her father's house, rousing the hearth fires with her wrath. But those fires were mere candlewicks compared to the conflagration she unleashed now.

The Nidubh gave one more hideous scream before it was totally consumed.

And out in the dark, the Hounds of Ardagh sang its death to the cold night.

Chapter Twenty-Seven

The demon's fiery destruction left a sulfurous stench hanging in the air. Ginny let the passing of the white fire's power glide away from her and began searching the smoldering ash for a sign of life. As the stinking black dust settled, she spied a hunched form bent over on the floor.

"Fafne?" she said and bolted around the pile of demon ashes to reach him.

Tiny whimpers marked each panting breath that shook his trembling frame as she knelt at his side. His pelt was singed, which was far better than Ginny had feared, considering she'd had no time to properly stricture the wildfire spell. Fortunately, the demon had absorbed the worst of those flames, for which Ginny was grateful. To have killed the lad with such unbridled power would have done her heart no good.

"Fafne," she repeated. "Come on, sit up, lad, and let me have a look at you."

His face was dark with ashes tracked here and there by the trickle of tears. "I tried to stop it," he whimpered. "I tried . . ."

"And you did very well," she assured him. "Had you not been so brave and distracted it as you did, I would not have lived to stop it from hurting you."

"I was brave?" he said warily.

"Very brave," she assured him, "and I know you'll be braver yet, for we cannot stay here."

"Why not?"

"I killed the Nidubh, and Edain will know," Ginny said. "Now, come on. Let's get out of here before she catches us and destroys us in a fit of temper."

She took his arm, guiding him upright, and noticing grimly that he tended to walk with more of a hunch than before. *Horns, I've got to find someone who can help him,* she thought. But before she could do that, she needed to get him and herself out of this place alive.

Ginny guided Fafne toward the open windows and broken walls. A quick glance revealed that the ground outside was close enough for a safe little drop. Together, they scrambled over the rough opening and made the descent with as much grace as their hurry would allow. Ginny knew this was no time to tarry. Edain would likely be close.

Once outside, Ginny saw that the outer walls had long ago crumbled away. She was afforded a grand view of a slope that led down to a track of heavy forest that surrounded the old mound on which Dun Daileban had been built. *Good. Cover,* she thought, and hurried the lad along. If they could make that stand of trees . . . She practically carried him over those broken walls and made for nearest path her mage sight could detect in the dark.

Behind her, Ginny heard a shout of rage. A woman's cry of anger whipped through the ruins. There was no time to turn back. She knew precisely what she would see. Edain, standing over the ashes of her demon.

"Keep going," Ginny said to Fafne instead, hoping she could keep him from stumbling around too much.

Alas, the hill was steep enough to make that task difficult. Fafne staggered and bumped into her with every other step. She feared she would be dragging him before it was done, but her urgency to reach the protective haven of the trees kept her from reducing her pace for his comfort.

The slope became a little steeper just as they reached the edge of the forest. Ginny made out a ditch, likely an old moat. She stumbled on the rough slope herself while trying to keep Fafne upright, and the pair of them tumbled into it, rolling in dirt. *At least it was dry,* she wryly reassured herself. She scrambled to her feet and hauled Fafne towards the far bank.

"Come back here, or I'll destroy Manus' soul now!" came Edain's angry shout echoing from the edge of the ruins.

Manus, Ginny thought, her heart catching in her throat. No, she couldn't stop even for that threat. She had to keep going or else they all would die. And besides, she reminded herself, Manus was already dead. The loss of his spirit would be no small grief, but she had to get Fafne to safety, and prayed that Edain's threat was no more than air. After all, if the bloodmage sundered Manus' mage spirit now, whose soul would she have to trade to Arawn for her own?

Right, keep telling yourself that, she scolded quietly. *Practical to the end.*

They surmounted the hummock on the far side when Ginny sensed the first blast of a magebolt heading their way. She threw herself and the lad to the ground as it shattered on the nearest tree. *Horns, that was too close.* They needed to be deeper into the forest. Edain was apparently braving the slope to follow them, for Ginny heard a dislodged stone tumble down into the moat, and a woman's healthy curse blessed mageborn ears as clear as a shout.

Ginny grabbed Fafne again and pulled him to his feet. Towing him in her wake, she wove an erratic path through the scattering of trees, making for the heavy thickets. Another magebolt slammed the tree nearest them. Edain was getting closer. Not a comforting thought, in Ginny's opinion. Alone, she could have easily outrun the blood-mage, for bolting through forests was something she did often enough as a child. But the lad's condition gave him no such fleetness. If he could just drop to all fours now, but she doubted his partial transformation would allow him that luxury yet.

They practically threw themselves into the thicket. Fafne thrashed and floundered at the sting of twigs lashing them on their rapid flight. He was making far too much noise, and Ginny feared the sounds would let Edain know which way they traveled. She wanted to stop and cast silence on him to see if that would help, but the shouts of the bloodmage on their heels meant she was still too close for Ginny's comfort. Besides, such a spell would be like a lamp in the dark to one born to steal essence from others to work her spells.

They pushed through a particularly thick hedge that snagged Ginny's hair and clothes and nearly snatched off Fafne's plaidie when the thicket gave way to a clearing where a stream of water trickled peacefully to form a pool. Ginny halted, and Fafne almost tumbled her as he blundered into her.

The clearing was far from empty. A pack of red-gold hounds were gathered there, and at the sight of Ginny and the lad, they sprang to their feet.

Horns! She'd forgotten the hounds, in spite of hearing them baying when the Nidubh died.

She turned and tried to push Fafne back for safety, but before they could even make the thicket, more of the hounds emerged. They were surrounded by thirty or so of the beasts, ranging in size from gangly pups to several large males.

Warily, the hounds approached, and Ginny pulled Fafne

with her as she backed towards the stream. She could have used light to frighten them away, but that would let Edain know where they were. *As if these beasts have not already told her that,* Ginny thought.

They would have to run, but which way?

The larger of the beasts began to close slowly, heads lowered as though uncertain as to how she would react. Slowly, the circle closed on them. Horns, she had to try something. What if the hounds attacked?

But if I use magic, Edain will find us . . .

Everything had hinged on just being able to outdistance the bloodmage, but now the tables looked as though they had turned.

Some of the younger hounds began to circle closer a little more rapidly than the elder beasts. One playfully dropped its chest to the ground, tail high and wagging, and another followed suit.

What?

Carefully, Ginny put her hand out, palm down. The elder dogs stayed back, but the younger ones came almost eagerly to accept her touch. They sniffed her and Fafne, who stood quite still, his entire body rigid with uncertainty. Then one of them leaped forward and lapped at Fafne's face. He yelped and dropped, rolling onto his side in a submissive gesture.

"Why aren't they attacking?" Ginny muttered.

"They're my family," Fafne said in a small voice. "They know me as I know them. Father wants us to go to the ground."

She blinked and glanced at the lad. "What?"

"Father wants us to lie down," Fafne said, gesturing to the huge male who was now approaching with dignity. "He knows you're trying to help me, and he wants to help us."

"What do you mean?"

"She's coming."

Edain! Ginny carefully cast out with mage senses, and felt the edge of a blood-hue aura quite close. *Horns.* Edain was coming.

"Father says we must lie on the ground."

Ginny eyed the lad with uncertainty, but even as she did, several of the older hounds had now moved in to snag her sleeves in gentle mouths and tug her down.

This is insane, she told herself, but she dropped to the ground all the same, with Fafne close to her. And as she did, the hounds gathered their number close, some of the younger ones settling on her back while others lay against her and the lad.

And not a moment too soon, it would seem, for Ginny had hardly lowered her head when she sensed a raging presence coming. There was a blast of wind that parted the thicket and opened a path for the moon-haired figure to enter the clearing through. Peering through spindly legs, Ginny watched as Edain strode into the clearing.

"Where are they?" the bloodmage demanded, looking rapidly around.

The pack held its place, watching her with wary eyes.

"Well?" she hissed, then snarled an oath. "Why am I wasting my time with you lot?" she said. "The Nidubh is dead and no longer has you under its power."

She started forward as though searching, but the eldest hound growled a warning, and Edain stopped, fixing him with a surly glare.

"I should turn you into a tree, Gabhan MacArdagh," Edain muttered, "but I've better things to do with my time."

Ginny held her breath. *Oh, please, go away,* she thought

191

and wished she dared a hint of a misdirection spell. But Edain merely shook her head and started off in another direction of her own accord. Apparently, the hounds were of no interest to her now.

Ginny stayed where she was for what seemed like forever, the odor of loam and the musky scent of the hounds filling every breath she quietly drew. Then, at last, when silence seemed to prevail and the sound of Edain's passing became no more than a whisper, Ginny sat up to look around.

At once, several of the hounds began to lick her face. She carefully pushed them away, petting as many as she could as she rose to her feet.

"We have to find shelter," she said.

"Father says there's an old croft less than a quarter of a league in that direction," Fafne said, gesturing in the opposite direction from that which Edain took. "It's MacArdagh land, and we'll be safe enough there."

"Oh, really," Ginny said, giving the large hound a dubious look.

"He says the man's name is Corbin MacLean," Fafne added, "and that he has a fondness for a good tale. Ours should keep him entertained for the night."

Ginny nodded, and wondered what Master MacLean would think about a mageborn woman and a half-transformed lad traveling through the dark in the company of so many hounds.

That the curse of Dun Ardagh had come to his door, like as not.

Chapter Twenty-Eight

Manus had been pondering the architecture of his magical prison when he felt power surging through the ley lines as its essence was summoned for a spell. *Horns!* He knew that essence, and it wasn't the blood stench of the Lady Edain.

Ginny! Good lass! It felt as though she was summoning a fire spell.

Manus would have cheered, but a shriek distracted him then. Edain's howl of rage echoed from some distant space where she laired.

No! he thought. *Flee, lass!*

The scream died as its owner moved swiftly out of his hearing range. Manus would have held his breath, had he needed it, for he sensed nothing save silence and solitude . . . and a faint whisper of a demon's death.

Horns, Ginny. What have ye gone and done, lass?

Alas, he would obviously have to wait for the answer, so he turned his attention once more to his prison's magical structure. He probed it carefully for weakness, or for any gap that he might be able to slip through. But Edain had woven it tighter than a goatskin on a bodhran. She knew too well what she was doing. *What would you expect from a bloodmage who has lived so long?* This sphere would keep him from escaping.

He was also aware that it would keep something far more powerful than he from getting free. The marks Edain had placed about the circle were familiar to Manus. He followed the edge, reading them from his side and shook his head in dismay. This sphere was more than his prison. It was meant to assure her that what she planned to summon to take his soul could not break the bargain and claim hers as well.

Arawn.

Manus' essence shivered. He had never been fond of meeting evil gods out in the open. The idea of being cooped up in this tiny place with the master of Annwn was not the least bit pleasant.

Which means she has no intention of pulling me out of here to fulfill her bargain.

The marks clearly showed Manus that here in this circle lay the thin veil of the portal she would pull aside to summon the Dark Lord. Manus tried to recall what the god would look like, remembering some boring old tome forced on him when he was a lad. A history of the gods of Ard-Taebh that his uncle once made Manus read.

. . . he comes clothed in midnight, his face pale and gaunt as death. They called him the Champion of Shadows, and swore that his mother was a dragon. His armor is said to have been forged from a black demon's hide when the world was new. His steel is covered in the shadows of despair and the blood of those whom he has claimed for his realm, and any man who is touched by the blade dies of the wound, no matter how slight it may be. On his heels are said to run the Wild Kin, and at his side, Black Hunters, the Nidubh. His army is made up of the damned and the cursed, of Dark Ones and minions of the demon-kin. To look too long upon him and his evil host as they ride across the moonless moors in search of souls to fill his Cauldron of Doom is to tempt the call of death . . .

Manus made a face. This was certainly not going to be

the most pleasant experience of his incorporeal life. He wondered if it was hot in the Cauldron of Doom. Or did one just swirl around in a void of nonexistence?

He was pondering that dilemma, oblivious to the passage of time, when he heard the thunder of heels crossing the floor. Manus looked up in time to see Edain striding into the hall, white hair whipping like the tail of an agitated horse at the gallop. She did not stop her angry march until she was almost upon the sphere, and even then she kept moving, circling him like a predator. From this range, he could see that her clothing was disheveled and the marriage plaid for which she had no respect looked to have picked up a few burrs and twigs and fresh rents.

"Been running with the Wild Kin, have ye, woman?" he quipped.

"Silence!" Edain snapped.

"What's got yer kilt in a bit of a twist . . . ?"

"I said silence!" Edain roared, and though Manus had no cause to fear physical pain from her, he stepped back all the same, especially when the sphere of binding began to hum and grow warm around him.

Edain drew a deep breath, reaching for some vestige of self-control. She threw back her shoulders and fixed Manus with a wintry stare.

"Your precious Ginny has escaped," Edain said. "Both she and the lad got away."

"So," Manus said. "You'll just send the Nidubh to fetch them back and . . ."

"The Nidubh has been sundered by White Fire!"

"Howt Awa," Manus said. "That won't set well with Arawn. After all, he gave ye the beast to increase yer power, and without the Nidubh, ye've nothing to draw strength from . . ."

"Mock all you like, *Manus,*" she said, and his name sent a slight quiver through his mage essence as it rolled off her angry tongue. "You are still in my power, and come the Dark Hour tomorrow night, your soul shall belong to Arawn!"

"That doesn't matter to me anymore," Manus said with a sigh of resignation. "I've lived my life and beyond. There's no reason for me to tarry in this mortal realm any longer, though it does grieve me to think I shall spend my eternity serving such an evil god. But all that really matters here is that Ginny and the lad got away. So no matter what ye do to me now, yer still doomed."

"We shall see," Edain said. "Or do you really believe your little hedge witch would desert you to such a terrible fate?"

Manus frowned. "Ginny's a practical lass, and I've been naught but grief and woe to her all these years since I left my flesh on the moors that ill-fated night."

"Bravo," Edain said. "You should have been a bard, and I will believe that she has left you to your fate when I see it. After all, it's apparent to me that she cares about you. I can see it in her eyes."

Manus said nothing, and Edain merely smiled.

"Whether or not she chooses to come rescue you," she said softly, "does not matter to me in the least either. One way or another, I shall hunt her down and put an end to her meddling in my affairs. If I must seek her to the very ends of the earth, I will make her pay for interfering in my plans. And as for you . . . count your last hours carefully, spirit. You will suffer the anticipation of your demise before the Cauldron of Doom claims your miserable soul. That I can promise."

She turned on her heels and marched away, becoming

one with the shadows. Still, he heard the echo of her departure for moments after.

Manus blinked and turned away. His courage had held him up well, but now it was sliding from him as new anxieties came to take its place.

Horns, Ginny, he thought. *Please, whatever you do, don't try to come back for me. Get yourself and the lad to Caer Keltora by whatever means you can, lass, but don't be so foolish as to waste your own life trying to rescue me.*

He prayed that she would be practical as ever, and leave him to his fate.

Chapter Twenty-Nine

A little more than an hour of stumbling through the dark woods brought Ginny and Fafne to the edge of a rolling moor and a stone wall surrounding a small croft. Ginny stopped at the gate, peering warily at the small building. Goats bleated in a pen, and a little roost for the hens graced one corner. Smoke drifted from the chimney, and a glim of firelight peeped through wooden shutters to indicate someone might still be up and about. *That could be good . . . or not,* she thought warily, and cast a glance over the silent pack lingering at her heels. How was she going to explain all these hounds?

"Father says ye've naught to worry where Master MacLean is concerned," Fafne said softly. "He's a good man, fair and honest."

"Why was he not at your father's keep that night?" she asked.

"Ye'll see," Fafne said, and without a hint of unease, he strode up to the wooden door, laying a firm fist against it repeatedly. Ginny hurried up the path to join him, ready in case there was to be trouble.

"Who's there?" a deep voice called.

" 'Tis Fafne MacArdagh, Master MacLean," Fafne replied.

The thump of a heavy bar being moved aside resounded within the cottage before the door swung wide. Light flooded forth, silhouetting the tall, thick-shouldered figure of a man kilted and cloaked in his full plaidie. Mage sight revealed to Ginny that he had red hair and a rugged face, and that his eyes were opaque moons. He reached out with one hand and said. "Come closer, lad, and who is this lass with ye?"

Fafne obeyed and, as Ginny watched, Master MacLean gently touched fingers to Fafne's features.

" 'Tis Mistress Ginny," Fafne replied.

"Come here, lass," Master MacLean said. "Ye've naught to fear from an auld blind man, have ye?"

"No, sir," Ginny said and moved closer so he could touch her face as well. He smelled of berries and herbs and wool and more masculine scents, and she was quick to notice that around his neck he wore a small stone of green with a hole in the middle. As she stared at it, Master MacLean smiled.

"A right handsome little wren," he said, "and mageborn as well."

"How can you tell?" Ginny asked, unable to keep the dubious air out of her voice.

"That yer a mageborn? I have an auld auntie many times removed who was one, lass," MacLean said. "I ken the touch of a mageborn. 'Tis always like putting yer hand near cold running water . . . it tickles. As to yer braw looks, my bonny lass, I've put my hand to many a face, and know the difference between one that be well-formed and one that is not. Besides, can't an old man dream?"

Ginny laughed and nodded, understanding. Manus once told her there were some folk in Keltora who possessed the ability to sense a mageborn's essence or magic's touch because the blood was in them, but that they did not always manifest the power, or even reveal its legacy in their own blood.

"Come in, though I fear ye must leave the dogs outside,"

he went on. "I've little enough room as it is."

Ginny glanced back at the hounds. Granted, he could probably smell the pack, but how could he know there were so many? She was tempted to scry him and see what secrets he hid, but Fafne touched her arm, distracting her.

"Father says they'll stay within the wall and keep watch," Fafne said.

She sighed and followed as Master MacLean allowed them the freedom of entering his croft.

"Take the bench by the fire," he said. "There's soup still in the kettle, if ye've no fear of what a blind man eats."

"I didn't know being blind made a difference in the taste of food," Ginny said and eagerly helped herself to a portion. It smelled wonderful, and she realized, as she began to devour it with as much enthusiasm as Fafne, she had not eaten since that night at Auntie Maeve's cottage.

MacLean chuckled. "A wise choice of words, lass," he said. "So what brings the pair of ye out so late at night?"

"You can tell day from night, then?" she asked between bites.

"I may no longer be able to see the sun, lass, but I do recall how it feels," MacLean said. "And night smells different from day. Now, if I may know your tale?"

"Well, where to begin," Ginny said. "But a few nights ago, I was enjoying peace and quiet in Tamhasg Wood when Fafne showed up with the Nidubh on his heels and a terrible story about what became of his family."

"What?" MacLean leaned forward. "Has something happened at Dun Ardagh?"

"The entire household, save poor Fafne here, have been turned into hounds," Ginny said.

"By whom?"

"By the Lady Edain of Dun Elwyn," Ginny replied.

"She's a bloodmage, and cast the spell to keep them from testifying against Rory MacElwyn's son, who was taken for a traitor."

"Aye, well, I heard that bit o' news," MacLean said. "And there's been rumor that some curse had fallen on Dun Ardagh. Hounds, they say, have been ravaging the countryside all around it, and no one seems to know where the wretched beasts came from."

"They came from the household," Ginny said.

"This Lady Edain must be a powerful mageborn then."

"She's a bloodmage," Ginny said, "and she'd been doing all this just to keep Rory's son from interfering in her plans to sacrifice Rory MacElwyn to Arawn."

"Someone must warn him, then . . ."

"It's too late for that," Ginny said. "Rory took his own life, and now Edain intends to sacrifice someone I . . . care about in his place." She decided it might not be wise to mention that someone was already dead.

"Horns, lass, how can I help ye?"

"Well, I really don't think you want to get involved . . ."

"Lass, I owe my loyalty to the Laird of Dun Ardagh, and if stopping this dreadful creature from trading someone else to Arawn for her own soul means avenging the terrible curse she had put upon the MacArdaghs, so be it. You have my word, I will do what I can to assist you."

"What I need," Ginny said, "is a safe place for Fafne to remain. You see, he is suffering from the same curse as his family, but the transformation on him is not complete. He must be taken to Caer Keltora where the Council of Mageborn can help him and them . . ."

"That's a long ways for an old blind man to travel, lass," MacLean said and grinned, "but I'll gladly see what I can do to help the lad get there."

"Good," Ginny said. "Now, if you don't mind, the soup was very good, and I am very tired."

"Of course," MacLean said. "There are blankets in that chest under the table. You and the lad are welcome to the warmth of the hearth."

"Thank you," she said and went to the chest, drawing out several blankets. She handed two to Fafne and held two for herself. Horns, but she was tired. She laid herself out near the hearth, only to pause when she saw that MacLean did not seek out a bed.

"Are you planning to sit a while, sir?" she asked. "The hounds will warn us if there is danger."

"I have not slept on a bed since I lost my sight, lass," MacLean said. "Too many bad memories come with the pillow."

"I don't understand."

"My blindness was brought on me by love," he said.

"What?"

MacLean grinned. " 'Tis a long tale, lass."

"You listened to mine," she said softly.

"Well, years ago before you were born and I was crofter to another, I was in love with a lass from the north. She was the fairest ere I'd seen, and I thought myself fortunate when she actually returned my affection, but her father did not take so kindly to my company. He did all that was in his earthly power to stop us from meeting, but love knows no barriers, and we always found ways to surmount them.

"My lass and I were determined that we would wed and secretly planned to elope, since her father would not give his consent. Alas, our plans became known to him through the wicked wagging of the tongue of a jealous servant lass. And on the night that my lass and I planned to flee, her father locked her in the dungeon cells of his keep, and in her

202

stead, he sent a dark creature with whom he had made a bargain."

"The servant lass?" Ginny asked.

"No, I think I could have managed her. Oh, no, he made a bargain with a bogie fiend . . . a *Fuath!*"

Ginny's eyes widened. She glanced at Fafne for a moment, but the lad was already curled fast asleep in his blankets. "But isn't that a water bogie?"

"Aye, a malicious creature too, and always eager to claim the blood of a strong man. Apparently, my love's father knew where such a creature could be found. He trapped it with steel, then threatened its destruction before he offered it a sweet bargain. He would leave the bogie creature be and set it free, if it would come to me in the guise of his daughter and slay me.

"Well, naturally, the Fuath agreed, and on the very night of the aforementioned tryst, it met me on the bank of the river, wearing her beautiful face and speaking to me of love. It stretched arms towards me as though eager to enfold me in a kiss, and I would have given over to the invitation, but as it came closer, I could smell the rotten carnage that was its breath and see that its clothes and hair were damp. I jerked my dagger free and thrust my steel at it, and it changed into a hideous creature and threw itself at me with a howl. Horns, I fought it with all my strength, and at length it seemed to flee. Exhausted, I went home, unable to understand what had happened, and after fixing my doors and windows with iron, I lay on my bed in thought . . .

"That was when it started to rain, and there was a leak in the thatch of my old place that long needed repair. Water began to trickle through quite suddenly, splattering on me as I lay in the bed. I opened my eyes, and there it was, the Fuath, sliding through the thatch of the roof with the water.

It came at me, extending claws and raking at my face, and though I tried to throw myself out of its way, it managed to scratch my eyes. The poison in its claws blinded me, and I am as you see me today."

"But how did you escape it?" Ginny insisted. "If it blinded you . . ."

"The bane of water is fire, lass, and though I could not see, I could feel the fire even in my pain. I seized the creature as it tried to claw me again, and thrust it into the hearth. There was a terrible shriek, and a shattering force that threw me back. Next thing I knew, the cottage was burning, and I was running blindly for my life. I fell, exhausted, at the gate of a healer's home. He took me in and did what he could for me, then brought me to Dun Ardagh where a True Healer happened to be visiting at the time. They healed me as best they could, and the Laird of Dun Ardagh offered me this croft. His followers visit me and see to my needs, and in turn, I tend a small herd of goats as my simple duty."

Ginny sighed. "A very sad tale," she said. "You are a brave man to have kept going as you have."

"I sense, lass, that you have more courage than I could ever muster," he said softly. "After all, you are mageborn, and fulfilling the legacy of your power takes more courage than any could imagine. Now, I fear I grow weary, lass. An old blind man needs his sleep."

"Thank you," Ginny said and settled down on her blankets.

"For what?" he asked.

"For being in such a convenient spot," she replied. "And for being such a kind and generous host."

"I do what I can," he said. "Good night, lass."

"Good night, sir," she replied and closed her eyes to let

exhaustion take its toll. And as sleep claimed her, she promised herself that should she survive this ordeal, she would make an effort to do some great kindness for Master MacLean.

Chapter Thirty

Dawn had yet to make its presence known when Ginny awoke. She rose quietly, warming herself before the fire as she took a moment to study her newest benefactor. Master MacLean still sat upright in his chair, head lolled against his chest and sightless eyes closed. Asleep, he looked a handsome, muckle man; though his age was obvious in the faint streaks of grey-blond that were shot through the rich Keltoran auburn locks. She faintly smiled to recall Manus saying those unfortunate enough to live elsewhere in Ard-Taebh were wont to claim that every Keltoran was cousin to the other, since nearly all of them possessed fiery clay- or copper-colored hair.

She rose from the hearth after a time and silently crept to the door. In a way, she felt a little like a thief, slipping out of the cottage before first light could burn the dew from the grass, but she felt such a departure was necessary. She did not wish to have Master MacLean or Fafne follow her back into such danger.

She had to return to Dun Daileban and save Manus.

But moreover, to stop Edain.

In truth, she did feel that the former reason was more important to her. And she did care what happened to Manus now. He had, after all, done much for her, and she owed him that. *I know what I am because of you. You sheltered me when you could have turned me away. And you never forced me into anything against my will. You gave me the freedom of choice, and you respected my wishes in spite of the fact that I was never truly kind to you.*

Granted, she would admit that he had more often than not vexed her in life and in death, but there was a small part of her that could not deny that she had wanted to love him, and had wanted him to return those feelings, and only to herself would she ever admit that the feelings had frightened her.

Besides, it would take time to get Fafne into more capably trained mageborn hands than her own, and there was precious little of that remaining now. For if Edain succeeded by the next Dark Hour in sacrificing Manus' soul to keep her own, she would be gone and there would be very little chance of Ginny finding the creature afterwards.

At least, not until she chose to strike again.

Like she would really just disappear and leave me to my peace and freedom. No, Edain would not be so foolish or neglectful as to leave such a powerful loose end behind. Not when Ginny and Fafne could both reveal Edain's presence and deeds to the Council of Mageborn. The Council would likely hunt Edain down and sunder her powers before they would execute her. They had long ago declared all bloodmagic to be forbidden, and any mageborn who broke their vow to the Council was subject to such punishments as sundering or even death, depending on the crimes.

On the other hand, there were some who theorized that bloodmages were another breed of being altogether. That they were descended from the Dark Ones, the ancient enemies of the Old Ones, and that bloodmages had evolved after the Great Cataclysm for the same reason—to keep the darker side of magic alive and maintain the balance of the world.

The magic can only survive so long as we survive, Ginny thought as she stepped out of the cottage and glanced around the darkness of the yard within the stone walls. Several sets of eyes turned her way. The hounds of Ardagh had ranged themselves about the yard, and as Ginny stepped among them on her way to the gate, several sprang to their feet and came at her. Wagging tails and lolling tongues assured her they meant her no harm. She tried to pet as many of them as she could, making for the gate, but they insisted on crowding around her.

"Wheesht," she said softly so as not to disturb those within the croft. "Away with you. Go on . . ."

She might as well have talked to the ground. She decided then to just ignore them, pushing through the small part of the pack that swarmed cheerfully in her wake. She opened the gate and slipped outside, closing it behind her. Much to her chagrin, however, several of the hounds managed to slip through with her, and a few others leaped over the wall as graceful as red deer in the Highland Ranges. Ginny rolled her eyes and started back in the direction of the woods. Surely, they would not follow her when the rest of their kith and kin seemed to stay behind.

If she had thought Thistle was stubborn, these hounds were just as determined. Every time she stopped and tried to shoo them away, they stood at a safe distance, tails wagging. As soon as she started on again, they would ghost after her as though understanding the need for silence on this mission.

At length, she gave up trying to dismiss them. Besides, the great depths of the forest about Dun Daileban lay before her, a growing thickness of charcoal and verde in the morning light. She stopped at its edge, carefully stretching mage senses into its green, and sensed a faint film of magic hovering in the air. A wall of wardings, as near as she could tell, tied to the element of earth.

Wonderful, Edain's marked it with ground wards! Ginny started slowly around the perimeter of the woods, seeking a rift in the elemental carpet that would betray her the moment she touched foot to it. She sensed that it was tied to her own essence. *Of course, she should have that memorized by now*, Ginny fumed. About the only way Ginny could cross that in secret would be if she could fly . . . or ride the back of a horse. But she did not possess either a spell of levitation or a beast of burden in her current state.

The ward seemed to be a band rather than the entire ground. Edain had put it out like a circle, and its width was perhaps two or three ells. Much farther than Ginny could hope to leap. She ruled out climbing trees and clambering from one to the next.

On the other hand, what was to stop her from toppling a tree outside the ring of magic so it formed a bridge?

It could not touch the ground, she reminded herself. If it did, the moment Ginny touched the wood, her presence would likely be sensed. So she had to topple a tree with a heady enough collection of limbs to keep the trunk off the ward circle.

Simple enough, she hoped. With new determination, she began to circle the forest, seeking a tree that suited her. And she found one in a dead oak that looked ready to fall anyway. Standing on the side of the tree away from the warding circle, Ginny called the dogs out of the tree's path.

"Please," she said, hoping they would understand her. "Stay behind me while I do this."

They must have understood, for they all gathered to her back and seated themselves on the ground. *Horns, I wish Thistle was half as cooperative.* And she also hoped the little moor terrier was all right. She sighed and closed her eyes, reaching into herself to find the tranquility within that the spell required of her, and stretched mage senses to explore the ground around the roots.

As she had hoped, they seemed to be retracted enough. She sensed no life in the tree, and went so far as to concentrate on finding any life residing within the branches or the wood itself as well. It would not do to disrupt the spring nests of birds so fond of old trees with their multitude of insects.

There was a squirrel's nest up in the branches, but it was empty. *Good,* she thought and concentrated on drawing power from the earth beneath her feet and loosening the soil around the tree by whispering the words of a spell that came in handy for preparing the ground around her own cottage for turning each spring. She felt the earth heave as the tree moaned and swayed. Shifting her concentration, she called for wind, weaving her own strength into the spell as she thrust it against the trunk. There was a louder moan and the grinding hiss of dirt giving way, followed by a resounding crash and the sharp splintering of weaker wood. Local birds scattered with frightened calls, then all was quiet.

Ginny opened her eyes to find a large spiderweb of broken roots clinging to clumps of rich soil facing her. She leaned a bit to look around the mass and peer at the length of the great tree. It appeared to have landed so that the trunk formed a bridge without touching the ground.

Pleased with the effort, she rolled down her plaid shawl and tied it around her waist to keep it out of her way. Thankfully, she was still wearing a divided skirt, for it saved her having to hitch the material up between her knees as she would have in her youth. Hoyden ways, once learned, her father would say, are difficult to put aside for a lass. Which was why he forbade her to wear anything but proper female attire as a child. It had not stopped her from clambering up trees then, and was certainly not going to keep her grounded now. Using the roots to assist her ascent, she crawled up atop the trunk where she stood poised like a performer on a high rope, waiting for her cue.

Or in this case, her balance. The trunk, though wide, was neither smooth nor straight, and there were lower limbs to negotiate, but she cautiously made her way down its length, casting a glance at the ground . . .

. . . and nearly lost her balance when she heard the snap of smaller branches and felt the wood heave. With a gasp, she slid to her knees, clinging to one of the branches, and froze, glancing towards the ground. The tree had rolled a bit, but as near as she could tell, it still rested off the ground.

Careful, she told herself and began the journey anew. She stayed low this time, crawling on the trunk, maintaining handholds on the branches in passing. Suddenly, confidence in her physical agility deserted her. The fall would not hurt since the trunk was no more than half her own height off the ground at this point. Of course, there was a possibility that the tree might roll on her, but the risk was still great since she was now over the section of ground heavily ensorcelled with Edain's warding spells. If Ginny fell and touched the ground, she would give herself away.

She moved on more slowly as well, inching over the rough bark and feeling a bit of it snag the material of her divided skirt now and again. But she didn't dare hitch the legs up. Her knees would not be able to abide the surface. She crawled farther, selecting her path with care. Again, she felt the tree shift under her, and the lurch would likely have unseated her had she not already wrapped her arms around a limb. She stopped again, wondering if this had been such a great idea after all. Casting mage senses downward told her she was still over the warding circle. She took a deep breath and started on once more.

Ginny glanced to the side when movement caught her attention. Red-gold bodies were traversing the ground on either side of the trunk. The hounds were crossing the circle, and some of them were stopping right next to her to wag tails and dance on their hind legs.

"Horns!" she hissed and cast mage senses around her. What if they were alerting Edain? "Shoo! Go back!" she snapped at them for all the good it served. They raced along, pretending like this was a game. One of them actually tried leaping up beside her, only to miss and fall with a yelp. Horns, she'd better move on before Edain arrived, for surely the bloodmage knew now that Ginny was here . . .

She started to push herself on into the narrower height of the trunk when she felt it shift again. Only this time, it rolled and pitched her sideways in a more violent manner, and for all her efforts, she could not hang on. She was tossed off like a poor rider from a green horse, sent flying a distance before the ground slammed into her back. A "whuff" escaped her lungs as air was forced from them. For a moment, she could not breathe, and to add to her discomfort, several of the hounds bounded over, gleefully applying tongues to her face and flailing arms as she fought to draw a breath.

At last, she was able to catch her breath and swatted the hounds from her as she staggered to her feet, hair and clothes disheveled. Grateful that Manus was not here to tease her for looking like such a sight, she tried to move, but her head spun from the fall and her legs were too soft to co-operate at the moment. She found herself sitting on the ground again.

Horns, she thought and cast mage senses about her, only to sigh.

She had not landed on the warding circle, but just outside its edge. With a quick prayer of gratitude to the Lord Protector and the Lady of the Silver Wheel for keeping her hide intact, Ginny crawled away from the bespelled ground, eager to put some distance between her and it. The dogs cavorted around her as though nothing was the matter. And only then did it occur to her to touch the circle again with mage senses.

Of course, it wasn't set for the hounds, she realized as she brushed the spell that held it there. Only for Ginny's mageborn presence.

She would rest, and then she would move on, pleased to believe that so far she and the hounds had not alerted Edain to their company.

Chapter Thirty-One

Time was irrelevant to Manus, except when the dawn came and sent him back to his cairn stone. He had spent the entire night pacing the perimeter of his prison, unwilling to believe there was not some tiny crack in its fabric that he could slide through and make his escape. He almost envied the tightness with which the spell was woven, but then he recalled that the great uncle who taught Manus the craft once spoke of the differences between women and men who cast spells. Men, it seemed, were rather brutal when they set wards and layers of spells about, while women were neat, always carefully crafting each fiber of the spell. On the other hand, men were better at the aggressive magics, though Manus would admit that after watching Ginny face the troubles of the last few days, he would have counted her just as strong as any man in that area.

Edain did not return for the rest of the night and most of the day. That had not stopped Manus from sensing the magical spell she was laying around the dun the night before. Wards to detect a mageborn's passing. He could even tell whose essence was being tied to the spell.

Ginny, lass, I should have taught ye better. You leave too much of your essence lying about for other mageborn to seek and use. Granted, there was no one but himself to be blamed for that. He had tried so hard to make certain she was well crafted in the fundamentals of control and strictures that he feared he had neglected details like keeping your own essence to yourself without using it. The greater mageborn

214

had learned long ago that the swiftest way to find power was in themselves, but the price of that was to grow weak over time. Therefore, spell essence had to be taken from other sources, such as the elements of nature and living essence from animals. Only bloodmages took that one step further, ripping the life from living creatures to feed their power.

Ginny had learned to take essence from other sources, especially the natural elements, but she had not learned yet to shield her own essence and keep it within her. This was why most young mageborn could be felt spell casting from leagues away by more experienced mageborn. They left bits of their magic everywhere. Such a waste.

The spell Edain had laid about this place would have required a lot of power that Manus doubted the bloodmage had at her immediate disposal. After all, she had no *living* essence to drain to feed it, and without the power of the Nidubh to provide a source of essence that was almost inexhaustible—which was why some bloodmages made a point of trying to capture a demon to serve them—Edain would be forced to seek power from other sources.

So he was not surprised to see her wander into the hall when the sun was high and streaming little slivers of light through the slit windows and broken roof above them, looking as though she had not slept in weeks. Her pale beauty waned, as though the glamorie that kept her youthful was starting to fade. *She must be older than I imagined,* he mused. Much older than himself.

"Ah, if it isn't the glacial flower of the Ice Plains," Manus said as he slipped out of his cairn stone and manifested his incorporeal form inside the sphere. "Life without the Nidubh must be trying for you, lass."

She cast him a foul look that would have sent a demon

215

fleeing. He merely grinned, interested to see just how far he could bait her.

"So where are ye finding essence these days, now that you don't have the Nidubh to feed your power?" he asked.

She waved a hand at nothing in particular.

"From wherever I find it," she said. "There are enough mice and stoats and ravens in this place to use to that end."

"And your own essence . . ."

She frowned. "If you wonder whether or not I will grow weak and lose my grasp on that sphere that holds you, don't hold your breath, my friend—though I doubt that would make any difference in your present state. At any rate, I have tied that spell to the ley lines to keep from draining myself . . . which I have also used to feed my spell work."

"Oh, yes, I had forgotten that," he agreed. "So you're holding up then, lass. No problems?"

"Why do you insist on vexing me with all this idle chatter?" she asked as she conjured a chair from the stones before the hearth, then seated herself there and whispered, *"Loisg,"* at the wood within the grate. Flames sparkled and grew, sending amber light everywhere.

"I merely thought to pass the time in conversation," Manus said. "I've little else to do. So how go your plans for this day?"

She made a face at him. "How could she stand your company?" Edain asked.

"Who?"

"The little hedge sorceress," Edain said contemptuously.

"She's no hedge sorceress," Manus insisted. "Ginny is quite good with her spells."

"I doubt that," Edain hissed. "But you are like some rambling old fool, carrying on with your useless banter from dawn to dusk and around again. How does she bear up to that?"

"She has a good heart, my Ginny," Manus said, and realized he liked the sound of calling her his own. "Strong and brave. And she has the patience of stone, which is good since it kept her from killing me long before I died."

Edain snorted and shook her head wearily. "She would have been better off to sunder you when you did."

"That's your opinion," Manus said. "I've been of aid to her since my death."

"In what way?"

"Advice," he said. "I've worlds of it to offer."

"Oh, I bet you do," Edain said. "Though I would have my doubts as to how much of it I would fancy or tolerate before I sundered you."

"I doubt I would have taken you in," Manus muttered.

"Taken me in?" Edain said and laughed. "Do you mean to say you took her in like some stray cat?"

"Aye," Manus said, "and never regretted it."

"So you do love her," Edain said.

"What do you mean?"

"As I told you before, I could see her fondness for you in her eyes. I sense your fondness for her in your essence. So why didn't the two of you consummate that love?"

"I ne'er thought she truly cared for me," he said with a soft sigh, "and was always finding my solace in the heather ale, which did not set well with her."

"Oh, dear," Edain said in a mocking manner. "Do you mean to say you two have shared a life and never gave love its due?"

"It was not to her liking," Manus said. "She fled a forced marriage to seek her freedom and her rights as one of the mageborn. She ended up on my doorstep at a time when I still lived with the pain of another's loss. But what do you care about all this?"

217

"Absolutely nothing," Edain said with a smile that revealed the viper in her dark soul and sent flutters of dread surging through Manus' essence. "I merely think it is always wise to know your enemies' most intimate secrets, as it gives you a greater advantage over them."

Manus felt his expression harden. Had he power, he would have lashed it at her then and there to punish her for mocking him. *Fool,* he groused. *You just gave the wretched creature a weapon to use against Ginny.*

"She won't come for me," he said in a low voice. "She does not care enough to come for me."

"Oh, I think you are very wrong," Edain said. "It will be but a small matter of time to prove I am right. And if *I'm* wrong, what would I lose? Nothing. The only loss will be your existence when the Dark Hour comes and Arawn claims your soul for his Cauldron this very night. That will certainly put an end to all your chatter. I'm looking forward to a little peace and quiet. And after I have rested, I will simply hunt her down and finish her off. How do you like that?"

Manus turned from her and slipped back into his cairn stone. He was not willing to give her the satisfaction of seeing his anger.

Ginny, don't be a fool, he thought. *Stay away, lass. Stay away!*

Chapter Thirty-Two

As Ginny strode cautiously through the forest around Dun Daileban with her escort of frolicking hounds, she couldn't help noticing the marker stones here and there. Some of them were etched with runes so ancient, she had no idea what they represented. She found old monoliths, dolmens and stacks of cairn stones scattered throughout the forest, all bearing a workmanship Manus once told her was associated with the Old Ones. A few of the stones bore images worn by time and barely visible under cloaks of vines and cowls of moss, while still others had become enshrined in the embrace of a tree growing close to them. As she wandered through them, Ginny began to understand why MacArdagh and MacElwyn had fought so long over this patch of land. It held a power as old as the world, and such power could make the man who held it quite prosperous, provided he knew how to use it.

But as interesting as the landscape might be, Ginny could waste precious little time admiring it. Edain had not made passing through these woods easy enough to enjoy their strange beauty. The warding circle turned out to be only the first obstacle in Ginny's path. By her calculations, she should have been able to reach the keep from the cottage in a couple of hours, but following a straight line proved impossible. Ginny sensed other uses of magic, all of them tied to the ley lines that surrounded this place.

Most of the magical traps were easy enough to avoid. The magic in them gave Ginny plenty of warning, which rather bothered her in a way. Edain's subtlety was absent, as if losing the Nidubh had cost her that skill. Some of the spells had a slapdash weaving to their structure that led Ginny to believe they were tossed off as an afterthought, or put there by some inexperienced mageborn child. A few even possessed a frighteningly childlike malice, as if Edain had chosen them simply to be spiteful. Ginny avoided all of these, though it meant her path was a meandering one, but their blatantly obvious nature made her even more cautious.

At one point, she was wandering through a grove of white birches and remembered an old superstition she heard as a child, that the touch of birch meant death. Manus had told her that the only way birch could kill a man was if it fell on him or his own fright stopped his heart. She shook her head, looking at the pillars of white wood slashed with little tatters of pewter and brown. This place was so peaceful. How could it mean death?

What waited beyond it, however, was a more sinister scene, for the edge of the grove stopped at a patch of boggy ground where the trees seemed wretchedly dead or dying. The path she followed meandered between a pair of monoliths bearing those marks she could not read. It continued on to skirt a stretch of water, its surface still and black with rotting matter. No birds could be heard to sing past those stones, and the dogs at her heels suddenly became as wary as deer.

Ginny paused between the monoliths and let her mage senses reach for the path beyond. It appeared to be safe enough, and she felt no threat on the dry ground, but to its side she sensed a miasma as ancient as the soil beneath her feet and the stones at her sides.

Bogie essence, she thought as she held her place and tried to determine just what kind. Something hidden in the water waited with phenomenal patience. *Fuath?* she wondered. *Or kelpie?* The water seemed too shallow to support a water horse. On the other hand, water bogies were as varied as the stars and as elusive as the wind, and had the power to disguise themselves as part of their surroundings. And a water horse really only needed enough depth and darkness to lie in wait, and could shift itself to suit its surroundings.

So it could have been a kelpie, though she was hard pressed to understand how one could survive so far off the beaten track. She wouldn't have come this way herself if it hadn't been for Edain's little traps . . .

I was driven this way!

That thought surged through Ginny like a flood tide.

Edain wanted me to come this way!

Anger rose in her. She should have realized that she was being herded like some stupid animal. Why else plant such an odd assortment of random but obvious traps? Most of them were perfectly harmless pranks, and her only fear to this point had been that touching one of them might alert the bloodmage. Clearly now, the truth behind their purpose was revealed. She was being driven on a path that would lead her straight to this dreadful place.

So what is hiding in there? Ginny wondered as her mind raced over the multitude of possibilities. A bogie, to be sure, and one of the more malicious ones. Something that had dwelled here a long time, maybe left over from the time of the Great Cataclysm. Ginny glanced up at the stone monoliths, wishing they could provide her with a clue.

This is a waste of time, she scolded herself. *I'll just backtrack and find another path.* That seemed the wisest choice. Let the darkness waiting in the water keep waiting. Ginny turned and started to retrace her steps through the grove of white birch when the hounds growled a warning.

A figure stood in the path of her retreat that had the look of a man to him. But his eyes were the green of birch leaves, and his clothes, skin and hair were silvery-white with tattered spots of tan and grey. She saw too that his fingers were long and twig-like, and that he carried a little dagger of thin white wood.

Horns, a conjurling! She had not heard or sensed him, which meant he had been placed here to wait for Ginny to pass. *And I was fool enough to think the birch grove was peaceful!*

"Stand aside, or I shall burn you," Ginny said, raising one hand.

The figure did not stir, save for the wind that lifted the film of his strange-colored hair.

"Look, I know you are made of wood, and that you have no purpose other than to stop me from going back," Ginny said, "but if you step aside, I promise I will not harm you."

Still, the creature did not move, green eyes fixed in a vague stare.

"You really are a wooden-head," Ginny muttered. "It looks like I shall have to do this the hard way."

She began to draw essence from the air and whispered, *"Loisg!"* Cold fire appeared in the palm of her hand. The birch man did not flicker an eye, still holding his place as the hounds began a frenzy of barking.

"No fire allowed!" a voice gurgled behind her.

Ginny had hardly shifted towards the new threat when a gush of brackish water doused the white fire in her hand. Normal water would not have stilled its flames, but the essence in the water that touched her reeked of magical origin. All around her, the air was damp with the scent of stagnant water. She turned to find a large dark shape at her back, and watched as it slowly shifted into the semblance of a handsome young man with a wild black forelock of hair and luminous ebon eyes. He wore about him a plaidie of brackish leaves and rotted matter.

It was a kelpie after all! She had hardly expressed those thoughts when the creature struck her hard across the cheek. It stung as though she'd been slapped with a wet blanket and sent a splash of water spraying her as she fell between the stones and back into the grove. The kelpie stepped forward, only to stop at the edge as though he could go no farther than those monoliths.

At once, the hounds began to attack the kelpie, rushing it with vicious snarls and snaps, but the creature proved quite adept at avoiding them. It would laugh and become as water so their snapping jaws closed over liquid that would splatter them. With startled yelps, several of the hounds fled.

"Adhar buail!" Ginny shouted, seizing air's essence to feed the spell. She threw it at the kelpie, and it struck him like a fist, smashing him into black globules of liquid that splattered across the boggy ground.

Ginny heard a thump behind her and scrambled to her feet just in time. The birch man's fist slammed the ground where she had been, leaving a deep indentation. With an angry wooden moan, the birch man turned for her, raising its fist to strike.

"Loisg!" Ginny cried, and once more she called forth her flames. But before she could toss them at the birch man, water doused her hard, knocking her to the ground.

Horns! The kelpie had pulled himself together and stood on the path, wearing a gleeful grin. Only now, the handsome face he would have used to lure maidens to watery doom had melted into an equine parody with gnashing teeth and flaming eyes.

"Bring her to me," the kelpie said, gesturing with his hoof-like hand. The birch man stumbled forward to obey. Ginny tried to scuttle backwards, hoping to put some distance between herself and the wooden man as he reached out to grab the hem of her divided skirt. She kicked at him as he tried to haul her back to him, but it was as useless as kicking a tree. The hounds leapt at him to no avail, and two of them even tried chewing his ankles in a futile attempt to stop him. And every time she tried to call fire, the kelpie would dash her with his water.

She was about to believe that there was no hope when she heard a man's fierce battle cry roaring through the air, and saw the blade of an ax swing over her to bite into the birch man's chest. The conjurling moaned in pain and pulled back, followed by the owner of the ax, and giving Ginny a glimpse of the muckle figure of a man who had come to her aid.

MacLean? How? She stared as he jerked the ax free.

"No!" the kelpie screamed like a horse and started to charge, heedless of its limitations.

"Salt, lad!" MacLean cried. "Throw the salt in its path."

Fafne suddenly charged into her line of view, reaching into a large sack and hauling forth a smaller one. With a cry, he flung its white contents at the kelpie who shrieked and pulled away. At the same time, MacLean used his ax to skillfully chop the birch man's legs out from under him. The conjurling fell, hitting the ground with a heavy thud, flailing its arms and trying once more to snag Ginny's hem. She rolled out of reach as MacLean began to chop the birch man into firewood.

There was a guttural scream as the kelpie surged back at them, the black horse shape flinging water in its wake.

"Show it the bridle and rowan, lad!" MacLean shouted.

Fafne reached into the sack again, and came out with a bridle and a rowan switch. He held the bridle aloft and shook it so the silver bells woven into its headband tinkled aloud. The kelpie dug heels into the ground, sliding to a halt just inches from the lad who had moved in between the stones. With a shout, Fafne lashed at the beast with his switch, and where ferlie wood touched bogie flesh, smoke rose. The kelpie screamed and wheeled about to flee. Fafne cut it across the flanks, and that burning pain gave the beast incentive to run faster. It dove straight into the pool and disappeared beneath the muck.

"Hang the bridle upon the stone, lad, and lay the rowan across the path," MacLean said. "The bogie beast will trouble us no more."

Fafne obeyed as Ginny crawled to her feet. For good measure, the lad scattered a handful of iron nails on the ground. His tail was wagging, indicating that he was pleased with himself.

"Are ye all right, lass?" MacLean asked.

"I'm fine," Ginny said, "but what are the pair of you doing out here?"

"We came to help ye, lass."

"But you gave your word that you'd get Fafne to Caer Keltora!" she insisted.

"Aye, well, 'tis a long way for a blind man to go, lass," he said. "And besides, what I gave was my word to look after the lad, and when he insisted on coming after ye, I could hardly break my word to ye and let him go alone, could I?"

"But how did you even find me?"

"The hounds showed us the way," MacLean said.

She shook her head. "You don't understand. This forest

225

is full of magical traps."

"I never noticed any."

"But you must take Fafne out of here," Ginny said.

"We just want to help ye, lass," MacLean said.

"You can help me best by keeping Fafne out of Edain's reach while I destroy her . . ."

"Aye, well, yer a brave lass and all, but I'd be shaming my kilt to let ye go off and face such terrible dangers alone. Besides, it seems to me from what I've seen here, ye could use a bit of help from us menfolk."

"Thank you, but I can take care of myself," Ginny said sharply, only to squeal involuntarily when the wooden hand of the birch man fumbled against her foot. MacLean gave it a kick that sent it flying beyond the stones and into the kelpie's pool with far more accuracy than she would have allowed any blind man.

"I thought you said you couldn't see," she said, waving a hand in front of his eyes.

He caught the hand with practiced ease and squeezed it audaciously. "I can't . . . at least, not with me eyes," he said. "But if ye'll remember, I told ye I have an auld auntie who is one of the mageborn."

"And?"

"She made this for me," he said, releasing her hand to touch the small holey stone that dangled on a cord about his neck. "She said I could only use it between dawn and dusk, as the spell is bound to the light of day."

Ginny brushed the stone with mage senses, and felt the spell wound around it by a faintly familiar essence. "Who is this aunt?" she asked.

"Auld Maeve of Ghloelea," he said proudly.

Ginny felt her mouth fall open. She shut it, shaking her head in wonder. "Auntie Maeve is your auntie?" she said.

"Aye, that's what we call her," he said and grinned. "Now, if we've nothing more to discuss, lass, then we'd best get on with this business of stopping that bloodmage. Surely we can all work together on this. Ye can deal with the magic, while the lad and I will deal with the bogies. I wouldn't be able to call myself a proper Keltoran if I didn't know how."

Or a descendent of Auld Auntie Maeve, Ginny mused to herself. "Well, all right," she said. She might as well yield. It would take too long to escort them from the forest without a proper gate spell, and the day was already wearing on.

Besides, she would only admit it to herself, but in truth, if that last encounter were a sample of what she would be up against, she'd be glad of their company.

Chapter Thirty-Three

Though the traps grew less numerous, they were by no means simple. On more than one occasion, the trio was forced to veer off course when they found themselves pursued by various conjurlings. Always, they found ways to evade or defeat the creatures, most of whom were composed of wood and fell to Master MacLean's ax. Ginny was tiring herself out, using mage senses so heavily, but she was reluctant to touch the magic that was in the ley lines crossing Dun Daileban to feed her spells and save draining herself. Drawing essence from them would have alerted Edain to their company.

As if she does not know we are coming. Clearly Edain expected Ginny to return. *She knows I will not leave him to be sundered by Arawn, no matter how many times I have sworn to do it myself.*

It took them the better part of the afternoon to reach the edge of the rath. The sun angled towards the horizon as Ginny approached the ramparts of the old moat and paused, listening. Around her, the hounds moved quiet as the wind, as though they understood the gravity of the situation.

There were still a few hours before the Dark Hour would arrive. If they could find Manus' cairn stone before then, it would be a simple matter of fleeing. Yet, even as Ginny cautiously stretched mage senses to touch the rath, she felt the power that had been invoked to keep his spirit in place. A sphere of power somewhere within the keep. She sighed and brought her senses back to herself, pushing her hair from her face. There was suddenly a waterskin offered to her by a youthful hand. Fafne seemed to be bearing up right well, and she couldn't help wonder why, considering that he crouched even more than before and his features had taken on a hint of dog-like traits. By the Silver Wheel, if they didn't get him to Caer Keltora soon . . .

"Thank you," she said softly and took the water, drawing enough into her mouth to moisten it.

"You look tired," he said.

"I am, but I can't let that stop me," Ginny replied. "How are you feeling?"

"It's strange," he said. "Since I slept at Master MacLean's, I feel much better."

Ginny wished she could tell him he looked better as well. She glanced at the crofter who carefully walked around a tree as though not sure of his footing or his way. "He has the blood in him," she said.

"What blood?" Fafne asked.

"Mage blood," Ginny replied. "I only hope Edain doesn't notice it."

"Why?"

"She would use his essence against us."

Fafne made a face, scratching behind one ear. Ginny reached out and stopped him.

"You could go back," she said. "Or perhaps, just stay here."

He shook his head. "Why? If you die, I am lost."

"Master MacLean will look after you," she said. "He'll get you to a proper mageborn who has the experience to reverse Edain's spell on you and your family."

"So you're not very powerful," Fafne said.

"Oh, quite the contrary," Ginny said. "I've power

enough, and the will to use it. What I lack is the training to use it well. Manus taught me what he could when he was alive, but some spell work is learning by example as much as knowing the words. Without an experienced mage to teach me, I will never have possession of my full potential."

"Couldn't you find someone to train you?" Fafne insisted. "Like Auntie Maeve?"

"Auntie Maeve can't teach me what she can no longer do herself," Ginny said, then frowned. A movement down in the deep woods was gaining her attention. Some of the hounds were starting to gather as though bothered by a presence she had yet to perceive. They packed together, ears twitching and heads shifting back and forth nervously.

"Oh, dear," Ginny whispered.

"What is it?"

"Master MacLean," Ginny said. "I fear we have more company."

MacLean shifted his head back and forth in much the same manner as the dogs. Whatever was out there, he sensed it as well with the acute hearing of a blind man. Ginny took a deep breath, seeking yet another bit of her own essence to feed her mage senses as she stretched them towards the source of their unease.

A dark mist was starting to glide through the woods, rolling across the carpet of leaves and billowing among the trees. *By the Silver Wheel,* Ginny thought as she stared at this new threat. A wind started to lift her hair, and on it, she caught the scent of decay and death.

"What is that?" Fafne asked, sniffing the air.

"The Mist of Annwn," Ginny said.

"Mist of Annwn?" Fafne repeated fearfully. "What's that?"

"The Mist of Annwn usually comes with the Wild Kin."

MacLean was making his way swiftly towards Ginny and the lad, and the dogs were starting to lope up the slope of the moat in his wake.

"Can't you stop it?" Fafne asked.

Ginny frowned. There was only one way, but that meant drawing from the power of the ley line. She would never be able to gather enough essence from anywhere else.

"I'll try," she said and closed her eyes, reaching within for the calm necessary to work the spell.

Already, she sensed the fetid darkness of evil gathering in the whorl of mist as she pulled essence from the ley line and wove it into a circle of protection. White fire sprang up around them as the mist closed on them. The darkness surged around the perimeter of the light as Ginny opened her eyes.

"Look at them," Fafne said.

In the swirling darkness, Ginny could make out the canine forms of the Wild Kin, but unlike the red-gold hounds of Ardagh, these creatures were black as soot, with fiery eyes. They raced in a circle around the edge of her protection, jaws snapping in anger. Their mournful wail was like the harsh wind of winter screaming over the Keltoran moors. The noise seemed to upset the red-gold hounds, and if Ginny had not been forced to concentrate on maintaining the barrier, she would have called silence as well. She watched in horror as some of the creatures started to leap overhead, as though attempting to cross over the barrier of Ginny's spell from the air. She was forced to close it into a half-sphere.

Angrily, the Wild Kin crossed above until their mist and forms cut out what little sunlight there was. Ginny brightened the white fire that kept them at bay, straining with every fiber of her being to make the spell hold. But she was rapidly tiring, and ley line or not, she felt her sphere shrinking.

"I cannot see without the sun," Master MacLean said. "What's happening, lad?"

"They're all around us," Fafne cried.

"Wild Kin?"

"Aye," the lad said.

"Flint and tinder, lad," MacLean said. "Make torches for me, two of them."

Fafne gathered fallen limbs from the abundance that littered the ground within the sphere and searched through the pack for the flint and tinder. He came forth with lamp oil as well and a rag, and tearing the latter in half, soaked the pieces in oil and wrapped them about the ends of the limbs. Then he took the tinder and flint, striking stone to steel until they sparked and made flames leap from the rags.

I could have done that for them, Ginny thought.

"Give me the torches, lad," Master MacLean said.

Fafne carefully placed them in the crofter's hands, and only then did Ginny realize what he was planning.

"No, don't!" she cried. "We're safe in here!"

But Master MacLean either did not believe her or was practicing stubborn male habits. With a torch in each hand, he shouted as dove through the barrier. It was meant to keep the Wild Kin out, but would not stop mortal flesh from passing through it, and before she could shout again, he had plunged outside its protection.

At once, the Wild Kin surrounded him as he blindly raced off into the trees, waving his torches about him to keep them at bay. And to her surprise, they followed him, chasing him into the trees until he was gone from sight.

"No!" Ginny cried and dropped the barrier to charge after the crofter.

But she never moved more than a few paces before a magebolt struck her in the small of the back. Fafne cried out as she fell to the ground. Pain lanced her tired, frayed nerves, shooting through her until she could not bear it. The blackness swept her exhausted senses, and the last thing she heard was a cold, familiar laugh.

Chapter Thirty-Four

The fiery glow of something akin to torchlight greeted Ginny's gaze as she blinked her eyes and rose from the depths of unconsciousness. Every muscle ached when she stirred, and she moaned as she felt the last dregs of magebolt power faintly stinging her nerves. The bolt had not been meant to kill her, she reflected, or she would have been dead.

So, if I am not dead, where am I?

Obviously not in the forest below Dun Daileban. In fact, she reflected that the uncomfortable surface beneath her felt more like a pallet of wood than the ground. And as her awareness rose more clearly, she realized she was lying on her back, limbs stretched out and shackled to an elevated surface.

Not again, she groaned inwardly, and tried to raise her head to see if she could tell where she was. But something coiled across her throat as well, and the first bit of exertion nearly strangled her. She ceased her struggles and took a deep breath. *Bound, perhaps,* she reflected, *but not gagged.* Which meant that if she could center herself and concentrate on finding a source of essence, she could cast the spells necessary to free herself.

She took more deep breaths to distance her mind from the dull ache that claimed her nerves, then slowly stretched mage senses to find a source of essence. But as she tried to draw it to her, she felt a fire burn her wrists, ankles and throat, distracting her concentration with acute pain. A

234

shriek escaped her lips before she could suppress it.

"Ginny, don't!" she heard Manus cry.

Manus?

The pain slithered away, leaving its ache in her. She closed her eyes, gasping for breath, when she sensed a presence at her side.

"Manus?" she whispered hoarsely.

She opened her eyes to find a glacier stare under arched brows. They were accompanied by a thin red smile that sliced the face leaning over her.

"You really are a stubborn little hedge sorceress," Edain said with a shake of her head.

"So I've been told many times," Ginny said with a shuddering sigh.

"It's an old spell I learned from the bloodmage who sired me," Edain said, not waiting for Ginny to ask the question. "It turns all magic, good or bad, back against the caster in the form of excruciating pain. Quite effective, don't you agree?"

"I suppose," Ginny said. "So what now?"

"Well, the Dark Hour is nearly on us, and since I no longer need you to feed the Nidubh, I suppose I'll just give you to Arawn. After all, you're the one who destroyed his pet demon. He'll be more than happy to accept your soul in trade."

"And Manus?"

"Oh, he's still the official sacrifice. Arawn has this liking for good, strong male essence, especially when it's liberally laced with the blood of a mageborn."

"Manus has no blood," Ginny said. "He's nothing but a spirit."

"The Cauldron needs nothing more."

"And what about Fafne? What will you do with him?"

"Fafne is out scratching fleas with the rest of his family," Edain said, and Ginny bit back the dismay that quickly filled her heart to realize she had failed the poor lad. "I finished his transformation as he so foolishly tried to rescue you, so he and his kin are out in the forest having a grand time chasing rabbits and howling at the moon . . ."

And as if to prove Edain right, the distant mournful song of several hounds filled the lonely night.

"What did I tell you?" Edain said brightly. "All men are such dogs."

"That's a fine observation coming from such a perverse bitch," Manus' voice echoed darkly.

Ginny tried to shift her head so she could see him, but the angle was all wrong.

"We are the witty one," Edain said with a laugh, then whispered a spell word.

Ginny yelped as the wooden surface on which she lay shifted upright to give her a view of the room. She saw that night had fallen beyond the walls of the rath, since only darkness filled the windows above. At the center of what must have once been a grand hall was a glowing red sphere, the source of the crimson light. Centered in that sphere next to a stone table stood a familiar figure. Manus looked angry enough to take on the Nidubh herself as he glowered at the bloodmage.

"Poor Manus," Edain said, and Ginny saw him shudder in revulsion when Edain spoke his name. "Men do hate to be helpless. Seven husbands have taught me that."

"I'd show you helpless if I wasn't in this bloody sphere," he snarled, arms locked across his chest. "If yer as wise as ye pretend to be woman, then ye'll heed my words. Ye let Ginny go free now, or by all the gods, I'll see to it you pay for harming her for the rest of your miserable life."

Edain sauntered over to the sphere, putting one hand on its surface. Ginny felt the magic swell. *"Buail!"* Edain hissed, and shards of red light leapt from the inner surface to strike at Manus' incorporeal form. A useless gesture was Ginny's first impression . . . until she saw the shard strike Manus' essence as thought it were a solid form and knock him to the ground. His cry of pain rang on Ginny's ears. She jerked at her own bonds, for all the good it served.

"Manus!" she cried.

"Your threats are useless," Edain said, her voice spreading winter with every word she spoke. "The Dark Hour is nearly at hand. Resign yourself to your fate. When the twelfth stroke comes, I will open the Gates of Annwn so Arawn may claim you both for his own."

"Unlikely he can claim Ginny, what with her being out there at the moment," Manus said, rubbing his chest as he crawled to his feet. "Unless you're planning to open this sphere and let auld *shadow knickers* out into the world of men, which doesn't seem wise. After all, he's not one for keeping his word if he can get more than he bargained for, and untethered, he's just as apt to claim your soul as well."

"I am perfectly aware of that," Edain said and walked over to look at Ginny. "But I'll not be so foolish as to place *her* in the sphere with you before Arawn claims your soul, Manus. Even I know that you must have flesh to cast spells . . . or the assistance of a willing mageborn host, and I would never be so stupid as to allow you to use poor Ginny to that end."

" 'Twas worth the try," Manus said.

"A waste of good effort," Edain said and moved away from Ginny. "Now, I must make the final preparations. I trust you will entertain one another until I return. Share whatever last words you have for one another and the like.

This is, after all, the last night you'll have together in *this* world, though you may have an eternity together in Arawn's Cauldron of Doom."

Edain's soft chuckle faded as she disappeared into the shadows.

For a moment, Ginny closed her eyes, and when she opened them, she found a softer gaze fixed on her from across the way.

"Ginny," Manus said softly. "Why did ye come back?"

"To stop her," Ginny said.

"From sacrificing me?" he said. "What would be the harm in my loss? I'm already dead, but you . . . you have life in ye still. There was no reason to waste it."

"And what good have I done?" she said. "Fafne is one of the hounds now. I failed him."

"You didn't fail him."

"I promised to help him, and I failed," Ginny said, looking elsewhere. "There's no reason for me to go on. I was a fool to think I had enough power to stand up against Edain. I was a fool not to let you use me to gate us to Caer Keltora from the start."

"Wheesht, lass!" Manus said. "I don't like hearing ye talk such nonsense. We're not finished yet."

"Really, Manus. Sometimes I think you are a fool. You're a spirit with no power, and I might as well be mortalborn for all the good I can do, trapped on this pallet. If I try to cast a spell . . ."

"I know, but I just don't like to hear ye blethering like some sheep going to the slaughter."

"And what would you suggest I do then?" Ginny snapped. "I can't cast spells. Fafne's bolting about the woods like a hound now, and only the gods know what has become of poor Master MacLean."

"MacLean?" Manus repeated. "Blind man? Lives not far from Dun Daileban?"

"Do you know him?"

"Aye. How did you meet him?"

"Fafne led me there when we escaped this place," she said. "MacLean gave us shelter, and I left Fafne under his protection, but for some reason, he and the lad decided to follow me back."

"What happened to him?"

"The last I saw of him, the Wild Kin were chasing him through the forest."

"Aye, well, MacLean always was a bit on the wild side himself. He got blinded by a Fuath and still stands boldly against any bogie that comes his way in threat."

"Well, he's dead now," Ginny said.

"Not MacLean," Manus said. "He can take care of himself."

"What makes you so sure?"

"He's almost as mad as his auld Auntie Maeve," Manus said with a chuckle.

"Auntie Maeve!" Ginny groaned. "She's still back at Dun Elwyn!"

"She'll be fine," Manus said. "It's you I'm more concerned about at the moment. Try worrying the ropes a bit and see if ye can loosen them."

"Manus, I'm tired of struggling and fighting . . ."

"That's not the Ginny I know," Manus said. "She's a bright, bold lass who wadna take telling. And besides, there may still be a chance for ye to undo all this, but first ye've got to free yerself and get out of here. And I'll not hear otherwise. Now worry the ropes, lass, while I think."

Ginny sighed. She hated to think Manus might be right.

239

Chapter Thirty-Five

Once I was flesh
And once I was bone,
But now I am spirit
And oh, so alone . . .

The booming baritone was about to drive Ginny mad.
Manus had spent the last hour composing a ballad about
his life and folly, and repeating it to the point that Ginny
began to wish Edain would get this over with. The song was
making it hard for Ginny to concentrate.

She realized that she had not given up entirely, for she
had spent her time easing her hands back and forth in hopes
of loosening the ropes that held her. There was a strong
part of Ginny that refused to admit defeat now. Granted,
she had been through more trials and tribulations up until
now than she cared to remember. She definitely preferred
for her life to be dull and boring. Unfortunately, with
Manus around, that was not always the case, but for the
most part, she could say her life was justifiably quiet. In
spite of what fate seemed to be holding out to her, she knew
she very much wanted her life to keep going. But she would
have given much for the quiet just now, and not just because of Manus' singing.

The Dark Hour was close at hand. She could feel it in
her bones. The Solstice was nigh, and this was the time
when wicked powers could rise to ravage the world.
Were she home, she would be strengthening wards and

raising a healthy hearth fire.

A stirring in the shadows at the far end of the chamber suddenly caught Ginny's eye. She paused from struggling against her bonds to focus on the motion, and within moments she realized that the creature now approaching was Edain. The bloodmage had adorned herself in a flowing black gown that rippled loosely about her body. She had put aside the marriage plaidie and the trappings of a lady and decked herself in startling simplicity that made her seem all the more beautiful. Her long white hair glided about her shoulders like a moon-white veil bathed in blood as she solemnly emerged into the fiery mage-lit center of the hall. In one hand, she carried a dagger whose steel was as black as its hilt, and the only thing to break that funerary blade was the rust and heather hue of a bloodstone set into its pommel. In the other hand, Edain carried a pure white dove that struggled as futilely as Ginny. Such a serene expression masked Edain's face, revealing nothing, and that stoicism caught Manus' attention. His song fell away, and for the first time, Ginny saw unease on his face.

Oh, Manus, she thought. Grief tightened her throat. She would watch him die first, or at least see him sundered before her, since death had claimed his mortal flesh years ago.

Edain began to circle the sphere, whispering softly. Ginny could not make out the words of the chant, but she knew by its pacing that this quiet cantabile was an invocation. And by the actions, it was likely some final sealing of the circle of power that surrounded Manus before attempting to open the Gates of Annwn.

Manus paced the inside of his sphere as Edain followed the outside perimeter in a counter motion. He stayed with her all the way around, wary as a highland red deer. She ignored him, stopping at each cardinal point to wave the dagger over the dove. At last, she returned to the first point, turning her back to Ginny and facing the sphere.

"Dark Lord of Annwn,
Hear my plea.
Open thy gate and
Come to me."

Ginny held her breath as Edain raised the dagger.

"In blood I summon thee
With Death I conjure thee
These souls I offer thee
That I might keep my own."

With those words, Edain plunged the dagger into the breast of the dove, and Ginny swore she saw Manus flinch as though he had taken that blade. Edain walked around the circle, spilling the blood of the dove upon the ground, and somewhere in the night, hounds began to wail. They sounded so close, just outside the walls. The eerie chorus filled the dark with a mournful song that sent anguish racing through every part of Ginny. Then, at the very edge of mage senses, she felt that the world was yielding to some unnatural force. Felt the burn of fetid magic on her nerves as though she were using her power to fight her bonds.

Manus turned towards the center of the sphere, his face growing tense as a darkness began to form high over the table where his cairn stone sat. At first, it was nothing more than a small slit in the fabric of the world, but beyond it, Ginny could sense such a hideous black. She had never seen the Dark Lord of Annwn, not even in some artistic misconception, and she wasn't sure she wanted to see him now.

Manus drew away from the small dark opening that slowly started to grow, and within the sphere it was as though a wind were battering him. She saw him cover his eyes with his hand as though the ebon opening hurt his gaze.

Edain continued her chant of woe, calling on Arawn to remember their bargain, asking him to accept this gift and the other she would offer as well. The hounds gave voice even louder. Hot wind flowed from that hideous opening. It now resembled a toothless maw, opening wider and wider still. She could sense the entity that filled it with doom and despair. Arawn was coming. The Dark Lord was just beyond that dismal gate. And soon, he would emerge to claim Manus, then herself. Oh, that she had a dagger. Oh, that she dared to cast a magebolt at Edain's exposed back . . .

She felt the hand that took her own and the snick of steel through her bonds before she realized what was happening. Ginny turned with a gasp, only to find a grinning, familiar face leaning around the edge of the table, and though his eyes saw nothing, Master MacLean sported a most mischievous grin. He put a finger to his lips and mouthed, "Sorry it took so long."

Ginny tensed, wondering if the magical quality of the bonds would betray her escape, but the spell was apparently designed to stop magic, and not mortal steel. The snick of the first band did nothing to alert Edain. Ginny glanced back at the bloodmage, but she seemed more intent on watching Manus' fear grow with the opening of that terrible gate to Annwn. Ginny's hand was free and she whispered, "Give me the knife," as softly as she was able.

It came into her free hand, and she quickly used it to sever the band at her throat and free the rest of her limbs. Then she took MacLean's hand and whispered, "How did you escape?"

"Not to worry, lass," he replied quietly. "Wild Kin can't cross running burns. Where's yer friend, and why does this place feel like death?"

"No time," Ginny said and, giving the dagger back to MacLean, she started forward as quickly and quietly as she was able. Alas, it did not prove quiet enough. Edain ceased to chant and turned with a hiss.

"How?" she said fiercely. "How can you keep escaping?"

MacLean chose that moment to rush at Edain, raising his blade with a Keltoran battle cry, but the motion merely served to draw the bloodmage's attention. *"Gath saighead buail!"* she snapped, throwing out her hand. A bolt of blue-white leapt from the fingers.

MacLean must have sensed it coming since he could not see, for he managed to dodge to one side, barely letting the magebolt snap past him. The miss infuriated Edain who shouted, *"Adhar buail!"* This time, there was nothing MacLean could do to dodge the hardened fist of air that slammed into him and threw him back across the room clear into the shadows.

As much as Ginny wanted to run to his aid, she knew she had to think of herself first. Edain, having defeated one enemy, was whirling about to deal with the other, and Ginny knew that only a fool would be thinking of offensive spells at this moment. She jerked essence from the stones at her feet instead and pulled its strength before her to form a shield wall, and in good time too. Edain's next shout brought a gout of fire lashing across the chamber. It splattered over the wall of air.

Edain screamed like a fury and, shouting another spell, she stamped her foot on the floor. There was a rumble as the stones swept at Ginny like a tidal wave and twisted her footing beneath her. She fell back, running for the upright pallet in a futile attempt to escape the rush of stone. And she made it, falling behind the wood just in time. Broken flagstones slammed into its surface, and only the fact that it was held upright by magic protected Ginny. She covered her ears against the clatter. Dust and grit filled the air around her, and she coughed as it filled her mouth and nose.

"Stupid little hedge sorceress!" Edain screamed. "I'll sunder you myself!"

Ginny felt the surge of essence before the wooden pallet was thrown aside by an unseen force. She scrambled to get her footing and run. All thoughts of rescuing others were banished in this moment of realizing she was about to die. She fled across the chamber, seeking some haven of escape, and she could hear the shouts of the bloodmage. *"Dealanach buail!"* rang as a fierce warning and power was gathered from the ley lines, scenting the air with raw magic and nature's fire. Ginny threw herself down when she realized what the spell was. A blade of lightning slammed the wall just in the shadows, cracking stone and sending it crumbling, and as the grit cleared, Ginny found herself looking out at the dark of night.

"Oh, no you don't!" Edain hissed.

"Ginny! Run!" Manus shouted from afar.

She would like to have done nothing better, but his voice stopped her. Manus. How could she leave him now? She turned and started back, only to feel the heat of a magebolt slamming her shoulder and knocking her down. Ginny landed on the heap of rubble from the wall, holding herself in pain. Out in the world, the hounds of Ardagh sang, their cries practically in her ears. She looked up to find Edain standing at the edge of the rubble.

"Mi glac . . ." Edain began, and Ginny sensed the death

in those words, knowing it would take her life. She struggled once more to flee, but the rough ground beneath her
was giving way each time she tried to get her feet under her.

"... *do beatha* ..."

Ginny seized up a stone in one hand.

"... *do biadh* ..."

She threw the stone without really hoping to make it
land, and was satisfied to hear a startled scream break from
Edain's lips, spoiling the life-stealing spell before it could
begin its work. Scrambling, Ginny made for the opening
once more.

"You little hoyden!" an angry voice shrieked. Weight
slammed Ginny's back as Edain threw herself out like a cat
pouncing. She sank talon-like nails into Ginny's shoulders
and pushed down as hard as she could, threatening to
batter Ginny's face against the ragged stones. "I'll kill you!"
Edain screamed.

Ginny fought to get herself over on her back, hoping to
find some means of countering the physical attack, when
she heard snarls from the shadows of night outside the walls
of the ruined hall. Edain froze in the act of lifting a stone to
smash it against the back of Ginny's head.

Out in the night, the hounds of Ardagh formed a semicircle, slowly stalking towards the pair. Uncertain, Edain
crawled off Ginny's back and started to head back into the
hall, but even as Ginny rose to see where the bloodmage
fled, she found that Edain had not gotten far. A tall man
blocked the gap, seizing her wrists, and Edain's scream of
fear first made Ginny believe that they were facing the Dark
Lord himself. But as Ginny squinted, she came to realize
the shadowy figure did not belong to the master of Annwn.

"No place to run, my lady," MacLean said in a dark
voice. "Time to pay the piper's fee."

Edain seemed too startled to understand at first what MacLean meant. And before Ginny could rise to have her say, the blind man proved himself still strong as an ox. He seized the lady Edain around her middle as though she were no more than a doll and, lifting her from the rubble, he shouted and threw her out among the hounds. Before the bloodmage could get to her knees, the hounds of Ardagh were on her, savaging the black cloth and pale skin. Justice would be theirs this night, Ginny realized as she turned from the sight of the hounds tearing Edain's flesh from its bone, and there would be nothing she or anyone could do to stop them now.

Within moments, Edain's hideous screams were gone, only to be replaced by the snarls of hounds worrying rags and meat, and the sudden shout of a man in peril.

"Ginny!" Manus cried. "He's coming! Get out of here! Now!"

Chapter Thirty-Six

Manus' frantic cry spurred Ginny, but instead of fleeing to safety, she scrambled clumsily over the broken rubble to get back into the ruins. Inside, the hall had grown bright with a fiery light. The sphere of power had expanded to twice its previous size. Within that fiery orb, she could see Manus crouching below the great darkness of the whorl opening over him.

Black tendrils of mist were starting to glide out of the gap, searching the confines of the sphere. Each time they came close to Manus, he would be spurred to move elsewhere.

"Manus!" Ginny cried and started across the hall. Pain wracked her limbs. She hobbled, trying to find the strength to stay on her feet in spite of the cuts and bruises left by her battle with Edain.

"No, Ginny! Go back!" he pleaded.

She ignored him, reaching out to touch the sphere and determine the composition of its binding spell. But as her hand brushed the orb, blades of crimson fire lashed at her, burning her nerves and mage senses with frightful pain. Ginny jerked back with a startled gasp.

Damn you, Edain! she thought angrily. *Your magic holds even after death!*

But then, she coldly reminded herself that she should be grateful. Otherwise, there would be nothing to contain the evil Edain had conjured within. Edain knew the risk of opening this gate to Annwn, and would not be a fool.

The gate itself widened enough for Ginny to see into its heart, where a figure cloaked in midnight stood. A blood-red sword was clutched in one hand, and eyes like fire glowed from the beautifully sinister features. The sight alone shivered her to the root of her own essence. Here was the darkness that she had been taught to dread and fear even as a child. Arawn. Dark Lord. Master of Annwn. Bane of Light.

He held forth his empty hand sheathed in a gauntlet of midnight leather said to be the hide of a dragon, and in a voice like thunder, he called, "Come to me, Edain. Your bargain with me is forfeit now. For with your death, you are mine."

Edain? Ginny thought and felt mage senses prickle when a presence began to manifest at her side. She turned in time to see an opaquely visible, shimmering form in tattered black cloth all drenched in blood slowly taking form. Edain no longer wore a stoic mask of beauty. Fear widened her pale eyes to realize that even in death, she had been undone by her own folly.

"No," her otherworldly presence pleaded and attempted to draw out of reach.

Tendrils of darkness reached for her, only to stop at the walls of the sphere. The magic was holding. Arawn could not escape his prison, and that fact seemed to enrage him. The darkness around him swelled with black flames that gave off a ghostly magenta light.

"Come!" he shouted, and the power in his voice trembled the very stones of the ruins. Edain shook her head, her spirit essence drawing back in fear. "By your blood oath, I order you to COME!"

Edain might as well have tried to stop the wind. Ginny felt the bloodmage's cold essence reaching for her as though hoping to find an anchor, but there was no escaping the bargain she had made so long ago. *Your soul belongs to him,* Ginny thought, aware that the hands passing through her arms had no power to cling. Terror tightened Edain's mouth, and then the bloodmage's spirit screamed as the power of his voice seized her soul like some gigantic hand. She was jerked back into the sphere by that binding, and where she passed through its fiery wall, flames of pain splattered outward. Ginny had no choice but to leap back from the pain that tried to burn her again. MacLean, however, did not seem to notice the fire that engulfed him briefly.

"What's happening, lass?" he called, scrounging for something in his sporran.

"Arawn has taken Edain's soul," Ginny said.

She watched in frightened fascination as the black tendrils now reached out to grasp Edain's spirit form and draw her into the maw of the whorl. Arawn's laughter at her pitiful struggles rang through the night, and in response, the chorus of hounds filled the air. Edain managed one last scream as her essence was rapidly torn apart by those misty limbs.

It's over, Ginny thought with a glimmer of hope. *Please, Arianrhod, let it be over now. Arawn has what he wants. Make him leave.*

Alas, it was not a prayer to be fulfilled.

"You, mageborn," the Dark Lord of Annwn hissed as he pointed a finger at Manus. "I will have your soul now."

The tendrils lunged for Manus. Try as he did, he could not evade them. They wrapped thin strips about his ankles and wrists, and began to drag his incorporeal form towards the rift that had swallowed and sundered Edain.

"Manus!" Ginny cried and threw herself at the sphere once more, only to have it lash at her and knock her away.

"No!" she screamed. "Manus!"

MacLean shouted, "Where is he, lass?"

Ginny ignored the blind man, crawling to her feet and seizing up a broken bit of stone. Desperation drove her to throw it into the sphere, aiming for the figure within the whorl, but the stone passed through the magical barrier as though it were not there and smacked into the little table where the cairn stone sat . . .

The cairn stone!

"Master MacLean, touch the sphere," she said and held her breath in fear that she might send him to his death.

"What sphere, lass?" he said, his hands flailing in front of him in vain. And as Ginny watched, he passed them through its fiery edge without any discomfort.

Yes, she thought, her hope renewing. The spell was set specifically to imprison magic and mageborn essence, but it was useless against stopping mortal flesh. The hint of essence in MacLean's blood was too weak for the spell to notice.

"Go straight forward," she cried. "There's a table right ahead of you, and on it sits a small stone. I need that stone, Master MacLean, or all hope is sundered."

As would be Manus, she reflected.

MacLean stumbled forward, passing into the sphere without it stopping him. Manus continued to struggle against the tendrils that drew him towards the Dark Lord's gate. Ginny refrained from screaming at MacLean to hurry, fearing it would throw him off his path. He found the table under the whorl. Wind buffeted him as his hands searched the surface. It seemed to Ginny that he would never find the cairn stone; then all at once, he had it in his hands.

"Is this it?" he called.

"Yes," Ginny said. "Throw it to me. Throw it to my voice!"

MacLean looked dubious at her request, but he swung his arm back all the same. But before he could release the stone, the black mist shot out to seize his wrist, almost jerking him off balance.

"Another soul," Arawn chuckled and his power began to lift MacLean off the floor and drag his mortal body towards the whorl as well.

"No!" Ginny cried. *"Gath saighead buail!"*

She jerked essence from the crossing ley lines to feed the magebolt that fled from her outstretched hand. But it disintegrated as soon as it struck the sphere, and she wanted to shriek in outrage. *Fool! Magic cannot pass through it. You might as well try shooting magebolts through gloves . . .*

Of course, from inside the sphere . . .

Ginny closed her eyes, pulling more essence from the ley line, and concentrated on the air just outside the opening of the whorl.

"Gath saighead buail," she called again, and this time, her magebolt appeared within the sphere, streaking into the opening Arawn's gate. She saw the Dark Lord's eyes burning brighter in his rage, for he was forced to draw away, and that distraction was all it took to loosen the tendrils of mist holding MacLean. The blind man fell to the floor, still managing to clutch the cairn stone in a tight hand. With a shout, he scrambled on all fours until he had thrown himself clear of the magical sphere.

Arawn howled in anger, his voice shaking the very ground. Ginny staggered to keep her balance, and charged over to MacLean's side. She practically tore the cairn stone from his hand.

"By my will, Manus MacGreeley, I bind you to your stone!"

she shouted in the mage tongue.

Manus cried out in pain. His essence was being stretched out between the tendrils and Ginny's spell, and for a moment she feared that she was about to sunder him. *Oh, Manus!* She looked into his eyes, and saw the fear and the agony he was bearing. She might well be destroying his spirit herself, but if she let go, she would be doing that very same thing. *Manus, what should I do?*

MacLean apparently had his own ideas. He gave a shout that nearly cost Ginny her concentration. The blind man reached into his sporran once more and pulled forth a semicircle of iron.

A horseshoe?

Before Ginny's startled gaze, MacLean threw the horseshoe into the sphere, guided by Arawn's angry shouts. Cold iron was once believed the bane of all evil, and though Arawn was no bogie, there were those who said he was closely tied to the old laws of magic, an unseelie monster from ancient times. Cold iron held power against him as surely as it did the Black Hunters and the Wild Kin who served him.

The horseshoe tumbled into the whorl. Arawn's attention was drawn to the metal streaking into his realm. He jerked back, raising his sword to strike the iron aside, and that motion was all the distraction Ginny could hope for. She strengthened her magical hold even as the Dark Lord weakened his to defend himself from the metal born of the earth. Manus was practically ripped out of the tendrils. Ginny heard him howl in pain as he passed through the walls of the sphere. His essence was thrown at her so hard, it smacked into the cairn stone, only to disappear.

At the same moment, Arawn's anger got the better of him. The Dark Lord tried to throw a black magebolt at

Ginny, and her first instinct was to throw up her arms, but it struck the inner wall of the sphere imprisoning him and exploded, filling the inside of the sphere with an indigo fire. Magic screamed throughout the air, the wailing of thousands of anguished tongues as a hot wind tore about the hall, knocking Ginny and MacLean back. The keening cut her ears so fiercely, she dropped the cairn stone as she fell and covered her ears with her hands, crouching low to the floor in hopes of escaping whatever backlash was about to occur.

But then, the furies faded, the wind was gone and eerie silence filled the air.

Slowly, Ginny pushed herself upright. The sphere of warding was gone, though she could faintly feel the remains of its presence drifting about in the air, sending static to crackle across her hair and tickle her skin. The gate was gone as well, and where both had been was a thick layer of black ash that reeked of death and decay.

Ginny blinked, sending mage senses to search the area around her. Nothing. No sign of Arawn. Oh, she doubted he had been destroyed in that cataclysmic blast of power, for he was not of mortal flesh at all. But the only hint of magic still remaining in this place was the hum of the ley lines, and that had muted down to a normal flow, meaning that the gate to Annwn was once more closed.

"Master MacLean?" she said softly.

"I'm here, lass," he said, and she saw him rising to sit where he too had thrown himself on the ground. "But where's yer friend?"

Ginny quickly scanned the floor amidst the rubble until she found the cairn stone. Reverently, she cradled it in her hands, touching it with mage senses as well.

"Manus?" she whispered.

There was no response. Briefly, her throat constricted. Had she truly failed? Or had the power she conjured in an attempt to save his life sundered him without her realizing it?

"Manus?" she repeated quietly. "Please . . ."

She felt warmth stir within the stone. A tiny tag of essence brushed the surface against her hands as gentle as a lover's caress, and familiar warmth flooded her with that faint contact.

"Manus? Are you all right?"

"I've been better, lass," his ethereal voice whispered back. "Could ye possibly find the power to let me out, Ginny? I'm feeling a bit cramped in this wee stone just now."

Tears and laughter alternately flooded from Ginny, and then she found the strength to whisper the spell that would release Manus' spirit.

Chapter Thirty-Seven

They reached Master MacLean's croft just before dawn could rime the horizon. All the way, the pack of red-gold hounds rushed about and frolicked, and Ginny could not help but wonder how much they knew of what had occurred. Would they remember their ordeal when they were finally restored?

She was too exhausted to care or do more than throw herself on a pallet and drift into deep sleep. By the time she awoke again, it was nearly midday. Master MacLean was feeding the hounds out in his yard, and he promised her that he would look after the pack until she sent word or returned. For that she was grateful, and she sought out the young hound she knew was Fafne. He licked her face and hands, and she swore his eyes welled with tears as she told him she was sorry, and that she would see to it all was made right.

With Manus sliding his spirit into her flesh and his cairn stone firmly resting in her belt pouch, Ginny allowed him to gate them both to Caer Keltora to report matters to the Council of Mageborn. The High Mage, Turlough Greenfyn, listened with a solemn face while Ginny related the events of the last few days. He assured her that she had done right to come to the Council with this news, for the traitor MacElwyn had indeed confessed that he had an accomplice in his trade, and that the accomplice was none other than the Lady Edain, who was a bloodmage. The Council would find the means to reverse the spells and re-

store the MacArdagh clan, and assured Ginny she would
not need to live in fear of her life. That a King's representa-
tive who was trusted in those parts would be sent to inform
the people of Dun Elwyn what had truly occurred. That relieved Ginny. She had not cared for the idea that she might
have to spend several generations avoiding the clan, should
they come seeking retribution.

At Manus' suggestion, they made their next stop Auntie
Maeve's cottage to collect poor Thistle. The moor terrier
was thrilled to see them, though Ginny noted it would likely
take her two moons to clean all the burrs and briars from
his coat. To their surprise, Auntie Maeve was safely home,
and she told a tale over tea of hitching a ride on a farmer's
cart. She was pleased to know Manus and Ginny had sur-
vived, and a little proud to hear of Master MacLean's part
in the whole affair.

At last, Ginny had nothing more to detain her, and she
insisted they return to Tamhasg Wood. Once she was
home, Manus released her flesh, thanking her for the loan
in a teasing manner, and where normally she would have
given in to a fierce retort, she merely smiled and said,
"Thank you," instead. She had more important chores to
concern her now.

Straight away, Ginny went out and counted the hens,
and was pleased to find them all present and accounted for.
However, she was forced to send Thistle to chase off the
hob when the little bogie decided to renege on their bargain
and try to claim more eggs than he was due.

Her life finally returned to its quiet ways. The folk of
Conorscroft, pleased to have their mageborn back, began to
visit her with their requests. A farmwife wanted a charm to
keep mice from the pantry. Ginny suggested a cat, and then
promised to "charm" the creature so that it would chase the

vermin. *As though it would not do so otherwise,* she mused. Some of the locals came to ask for "luck blessings" and Ginny was soon back to trading her skills and her eggs for stores.

A fortnight had come and gone when she heard the thunder of hooves and the rattle of a carriage coming up the path to her cottage. Manus was sitting on the edge of the well where she was drawing water, but he went invisible as soon as the first riders came into view. "Company," he said quietly. "Your reputation has traveled far."

She shushed him and set the bucket of water aside.

Three horsemen came first, wearing the livery of guards in the service to a Laird. They were followed by a carriage that drew to a halt just a short distance from where Ginny stood. Thistle charged out of the cottage with loud yaps, forcing her to snatch him back. One of the guards dismounted and stepped over to the carriage, opening the small door on the side.

The man who stepped out of the carriage held himself with great dignity. His fiery locks flowed about a bearded face that was fiercely handsome. He fixed Ginny with a strangely familiar gaze.

"Laird Gabhan MacArdagh?" she said softly and put Thistle down to offer a short curtsey. The moor terrier immediately launched himself at the carriage and began to mark each of the wheels in turn.

A smile spread across the Laird's face. "I see ye remember the names of yer hounds, my lady," he returned, flashing a warm expression. "It's all right, Fafne, my lad. You can come out now."

A slim-faced lad all decked in MacArdagh plaidie and wearing a shy grin slipped out of the carriage to stand beside his father. He looked so handsome in full human form.

"Fafne," Ginny said and reached out to take one of his hands. "You're looking well, lad."

"Thank you," he said. "When I heard Father was coming here, I had to come see you once more . . . to say thank you for all you have done."

"Oh, you're most welcome," Ginny said. "I'm just sorry we had to go through so much pain together."

"We all owe you a debt of gratitude, my lady," Laird Gabhan said. "Without your kindness and courage as well as that of your friends, I fear we would still be running about the moors, chasing hares, biting the fleas from our backs and howling at the moon."

"I thought that was normal for mortal men," Manus wind-whispered to Ginny, and she bit her tongue rather than scold him.

"Won't you come inside, my lord?" she said instead.

The Laird of Dun Ardagh shook his head. "Thank you, my lady, but we are on our way to attend to business. We only came by to give you our thanks and leave you with a gift."

"Oh, really, you don't have to . . ." Ginny stuttered.

But the carriage driver was already unloading a small sack from under his seat. He handed it to one of the mounted guards, who in turn gave it to the guard now on foot, and that man reverently placed the sack in the Laird of Dun Ardagh's hand. Ginny opened her mouth to protest again, but he merely waved a hand to stop her.

"I am aware of the fact that we cannot truly repay our debt to you, my lady," he said. "You saved our lives and took care of my son, and for that, I have arranged for you to receive a small pension of stores each month from the local innkeeper, who shall receive compensation for his time and effort at my expense. Oh, and Fafne thought you might have a use for these . . ."

He opened the small sack, spilling forth its contents. Bones clattered into a heap on the ground at Ginny's feet, all taken from slaughtered livestock. Her own eyes widened in uncertainty, but Thistle seemed to know exactly what to do.

The moor terrier dove at the pile, clamped jaws around the largest bone he was able to carry and bolted off to bury it in Tamhasg Wood.

About the Author

Laura J. Underwood is the author of several novels and numerous short stories in the fantasy field. Her books include *Ard Magister* (2002), *Chronicles of the Last War* (2004), *Dragon's Tongue* and *Wandering Lark* (forthcoming).

When not writing, Underwood is Supervisor of Periodicals for the Knox County Public Library System. In her spare time, she likes to hike, play harp, string beads, study folklore, draw, and play with swords. A former state fencing champion, Underwood now limits her swordplay to her writing, and to trading blade strokes and jibes as a member of the SFWA Musketeers. She is an Active Member of the Science Fiction & Fantasy Writers of America.